More Praise for

WHAT TO SAY NEXT

"A must-read about how we relate to each other and facing the truth about who we really are." —*PopSugar*

"All I want to do is read more. The story of Kit and David's unlikely friendship is so beautiful and relatable."
—ClassPass.com

"Buxbaum uses split first-person narration to give readers striking insight into both teens. . . . Readers will easily see David as a complex, brilliant individual. Discussion of Kit's family and heritage bring additional complexity and depth to this portrait of grief and recovery." —*PW*

"Teens who enjoy sweet, character-driven relationship stories will find their tribe with Kit and David." —*VOYA*

"There's a warmth and ease to [Kit and David's] relationship that the author captures effortlessly."
—*Kirkus Reviews*

"Julie Buxbaum has written my perfect love story—two brave, flawed characters ditching the idea of 'normal,' falling in love, and finding the unanswerable answers to life in each other. I adored it." —Cath Crowley, author of *Graffiti Moon* and *Words in Deep Blue*

ALSO BY JULIE BUXBAUM

Tell Me Three Things

WHAT TO SAY NEXT

Julie Buxbaum

EMBER

Text copyright © 2017 by Julie R. Buxbaum Inc.
Cover art copyright © 2017 by Thomas Slater

All rights reserved. Published in the United States by Ember, an imprint of
Random House Children's Books, a division of Penguin Random House LLC, New York.
Originally published in hardcover in the United States by Delacorte Press, an imprint of
Random House Children's Books, New York, in 2017.

Ember and the E colophon are registered trademarks of Penguin Random House LLC.

Visit us on the Web! GetUnderlined.com
Educators and librarians, for a variety of teaching tools,
visit us at RHTeachersLibrarians.com

The Library of Congress has cataloged the hardcover edition of this work as follows:
Names: Buxbaum, Julie, author.
Title: What to say next / Julie Buxbaum.
Description: New York : Delacorte Press, 2017. | Summary: When an unlikely friendship is
sparked between relatively popular Kit Lowell and socially isolated David Drucker, Kit asks
David for his help figuring out the how and why of her father's tragic car accident.
Identifiers: LCCN 2016018751 (print) | LCCN 2017000209 (ebook) |
ISBN 978-0-553-53568-6 (hardback) | ISBN 978-0-553-53569-3 (glb) |
ISBN 978-0-553-53570-9 (ebook)
Subjects: | CYAC: Friendship—Fiction. | Love—Fiction. | Grief—Fiction. |
High schools—Fiction. | Schools—Fiction.
Classification: LCC PZ7.1.B897 Wh 2017 (print) | LCC PZ7.1.B897 (ebook) |
DDC [Fic]—dc23

ISBN 978-0-553-53571-6 (tr. pbk.)

Printed in the United States of America
10 9 8 7 6 5 4 3
First Ember Edition 2018

Random House Children's Books supports the First Amendment
and celebrates the right to read.

For Josh, the president of my first tribe.
So happy you let me keep my lifetime membership.
I love you.
And for Indy, Elili, and Luca: my heart,
my reason, my home, my tribe, my life.

The book of love is long and boring.
No one can lift the damn thing.

—THE MAGNETIC FIELDS

CHAPTER 1

DAVID

An unprecedented event: Kit Lowell just sat down next to me in the cafeteria. I always sit alone, and when I say *always*, I don't mean that in the exaggerated vernacular favored by my classmates. In the 622 days I've attended this high school, not a single person has ever sat beside me at lunch, which is what justifies my calling her sitting there—so close that her elbow almost grazes mine—an "event." My first instinct is to reach for my notebook and look up her entry. Under *K* for *Kit*, not under *L* for *Lowell*, because though I'm good with facts and scholarly pursuits, I'm terrible with names. Partly this is because names are random words completely devoid of context, and partly this is because I believe names rarely fit the people they belong to, which, if you think about it, makes perfect sense. Parents name their child at a time when they have the absolute least amount of information they will ever have about the person they are naming. The whole practice is illogical.

Take Kit, for example, which is not actually her name, her name is Katherine, but I have never heard anyone call her Katherine, even in elementary school. Kit doesn't in any way look like a Kit, which is a name for someone who is boxy and stiff and easily understandable with step-by-step instructions. Instead the name of the girl sitting next to me should have a Z in it, because she's confusing and zigzagged and pops up in surprising places—like at my lunch table—and maybe the number eight, because she's hourglass-shaped, and the letter S too, because it's my favorite. I like Kit because she's never been mean to me, which is not something I can say about the vast majority of my classmates. It's a shame her parents got her name all wrong.

I'm a David, which also doesn't work, because there are lots of Davids in the world—at last check 3,786,417 of them in the United States alone—and so by virtue of my first name, one would assume I'd be like lots of other people. Or, at the very least, relatively neurotypical, which is a scientific, less offensive way of saying normal. That hasn't been the case. At school, no one calls me anything, except the occasional *homo* or *moron*, neither of which is in any way accurate—my IQ is 168 and I'm attracted to girls, not boys. Also, *homo* is a pejorative term for a gay person, and even if my classmates are mistaken about my sexual orientation, they should know better than to use that word. At home my mom calls me son—which I have no problem with because it's true—my dad calls me David, which feels like an itchy sweater with a too-tight neck, and my sister calls me Little D, which for some inexplicable reason fits just right, even though I'm not even a little bit little. I'm six foot two and 165 pounds. My sister is five foot three and 105 pounds. I should call her Little L, for Little Lauren, but I don't. I call her Miney, which is what I've been calling her since I was a baby, because she's always felt like the only thing in a confusing world that belongs to me.

Miney is away at college, and I miss her. She's my best friend—technically speaking, my only friend—but I feel like even if I had friends, she'd still be my best one. So far she's the only person I've ever known who has helped make being me a little less hard.

By now you've probably realized I'm different. It usually doesn't take people very long to figure that out. One doctor thought I might have a "borderline case of Asperger's," which is stupid, because you can't have a borderline case of Asperger's. Actually, you can't really have Asperger's at all anymore, because it was written out of the DSM-5 (the fifth edition of the *Diagnostic and Statistical Manual of Mental Disorders*) in 2013, and instead people with that group of characteristics are considered to have high-functioning autism (or HFA), which is also misleading. The autism spectrum is multidimensional, not linear. The doctor was obviously an idiot.

Out of curiosity, I've done my own reading in this area (I bought a used DSM-4 on eBay; the 5 was too pricey), and though I lack the necessary medical training required to make a full diagnostic assessment, I don't believe the label applies to me.

Yes, I can get myself into trouble in social situations; I like order and routine; when I'm interested in something, I can be hyperfocused to the exclusion of other activities; and, fine, I am clumsy. But when I have to, I can make eye contact. I don't flinch if you touch me. I tend to recognize most idioms, though I keep a running list in my notebook just in case. I like to think I'm empathetic, but I don't know if that's true.

I'm not sure it really matters if I have Asperger's, anyway, especially because it no longer exists. It's just another label. Take the word *jock*. If enough psychiatrists wanted to, they could add that to the *DSM* and diagnose all the guys on the Mapleview football team. Characteristics would include at least two of the following: (1) athleticism, especially while wearing spandex, (2) unnatural ease with the concept of strapping a hard cup around your penis, (3) being an asshole. It doesn't matter whether you call me an Aspie or a weirdo or even a moron. The fact remains that I very much wish I were more like everyone else. Not the jocks, necessarily. I don't want to be the kind of guy who gives kids like me a hard time. But if I got the chance to make some sort of cosmic upgrade—switch David 1.0 to a 2.0 version who understood what to say in day-to-day conversation—I'd do it in an instant.

Maybe when parents name their children they do it from the perspective of wishful thinking. Like when you go to a restaurant and ask for a rare steak, and even though there is no universally agreed definition of the word *rare,* you hope you get exactly what you want.

My mom and dad ordered a David. They got me instead.

In my notebook:

KIT LOWELL: Height: 5' 4". Weight: Approximately 125 lbs. Wavy brown hair, pulled into a ponytail on test days, rainy days, and most Mondays. Skin is brownish, because her dad—a dentist—is white and her mom is Indian (Southeast Asian, not Native American). Class ranking: 14. Activities: school newspaper, Spanish Club, Pep Club.

Notable Encounters

1. Third grade: Stopped Justin Cho from giving me a wedgie.
2. Sixth grade: Made me a valentine. (Note: KL made all the boys valentines, not just me. But still. It was nice. Except for the glitter. Because glitter is uncontainable and has sticky properties, and I generally don't like uncontainable and sticky things.)
3. Eighth grade: After math class, she asked what I got on my math test. I said: 100. She said: Wow, you must have studied hard. I said: No, quadratic equations are easy. She said: Um, okay. (Later, when I reenacted the conversation for Miney, she told me that I should have said that I had studied, even if that meant lying. I'm not a very good liar.)
4. Tenth grade: Kit smiled at me when only our two names were announced as National Merit semifinalists on the loudspeaker. I was going to say "Congratulations," but Justin Cho said "Damn, girl!" first and gave Kit a hug. And then she wasn't looking at me anymore.

Important Characteristics

1. On cold days, she stretches her sleeves to cover her whole hands instead of wearing gloves.
2. Her hair isn't curly, but it isn't straight either. It hangs in repetitive, alternating commas.
3. She's the prettiest girl in school.
4. She sits crisscross-applesauce on almost all chairs, even narrow ones.
5. She has a faint scar next to her left eyebrow that looks

almost like a Z. I once asked Miney if she thought I'd ever be able to touch that scar, because I'm curious what it feels like, and Miney said, "Sorry, Little D. But as the Magic 8 Ball says: My Sources Say No."

6. She drives a red Toyota Corolla, license plate XHD893.

<u>Friends</u>

Almost everyone, but mostly hangs out with Annie, Violet, and sometimes Dylan (the Girl Dylan, not the Boy Dylan). Common characteristics of friend group, with the exception of Kit, include flat-ironed hair, minor acne, and larger than average breasts. For five school days last year, Kit walked the halls holding hands with Gabriel, only occasionally stopping to make out, but now they don't do that anymore. I don't like Gabriel.

   Additional Notes: Nice. Miney puts her on the Trust List. I second.

Of course I don't open the notebook in front of her. Even I know better than that. But I do touch its spine, because having it nearby makes me feel less anxious. The notebook was Miney's idea. Back in middle school, after the Locker Room Incident, which is irrelevant to this discussion, Miney decided I was too trusting. Apparently, unlike me, when most people talk they aren't necessarily telling the truth. See for example the Test Lie suggested above. Why lie about whether I studied for a test? Ridiculous. Quadratic equations are easy. That's just a fact.

"So your dad is dead," I say, because it's the first thing that pops into my head when she sits down. This is new information that

I have not yet added to her notebook entry, only because I just found out. I'm usually the last to know things about my classmates, if I ever learn about them at all. But Annie and Violet were talking about Kit at Violet's locker this morning, which happens to be above mine. According to Annie, "Kit's been, like, a total mess since the whole thing with her dad, and I know it's been hard and whatever, but she's kind of being, I don't know, mean." I don't usually listen to the other kids at school—most of what they have to say is boring and feels like bad background music, something clanky and harsh, heavy metal, maybe—but for some reason this seeped through. Then they started talking about the funeral, how it was weird that they cried more than Kit, that it's not healthy for her to keep things bottled up inside, which is a ridiculous thing to say because feelings don't have mass, and also they are not doctors.

I would have liked to go to Kit's dad's funeral, if only because he was also on my Nice List, and I assume when someone on your Nice List dies, you should go to their funeral. Kit's dad, Dr. Lowell is—was—my dentist, and he never complained about my noise-canceling headphones getting in the way of his drill. He always gave me a red lollipop after a cleaning, which seems counterintuitive and yet was always appreciated.

I look at Kit. She doesn't look messy—in fact, she seems better groomed than usual and is wearing a man's white button-down shirt that looks recently ironed. Her cheeks are pink, and her eyes are a little wet, and I turn away because she is breathtakingly beautiful and therefore very hard to look at.

"I wish someone had told me, because I would have gone to his funeral. He used to give me lollipops," I say. Kit stares straight ahead, doesn't respond. I take this to mean I should keep talking.

"I don't believe in heaven. I'm with Richard Dawkins on that one. I think it's something people tell themselves to make the finality of death less scary. At the very least, it seems highly unlikely to me in the angels-and-white-cloud iteration you hear about. Do you believe in heaven?" I ask. Kit takes a bite of her sandwich, still doesn't turn her head. "I doubt it, because you are a highly intelligent person."

"No offense or anything, but would you mind if we didn't talk?" she asks. I'm pretty sure this is not a question she wants me to answer, but I do anyway. Miney has put the expression *no offense* on the Be Wary List. Apparently bad things usually follow.

"I'd prefer it, actually. But I'd like to say just one last thing: Your dad shouldn't have died. That's really unfair."

Kit nods, and the commas of her hair shake.

"Yup," she says. And then we eat the rest of our sandwiches—mine peanut butter and jelly since it's Monday—in silence.

But good silence.

I think.

CHAPTER 2

KIT

I don't really know why I decide not to sit with Annie and Violet at lunch. I can feel their eyes on me when I pass right by our usual table, which is at the front of the caf, the perfect table because you can see *everyone* from there. I always sit with them. Always. We are best friends—a three-person squad since middle school—and so I realize I'm making some sort of grand statement by not even waving hello. I just knew as soon as I came in and saw them huddled together talking and laughing and just being so normal, like nothing had changed at all—and yes, I realize that nothing *has* changed for them, that their families are no more or less screwed up than they were before my life imploded—that I couldn't do it. Couldn't sit down, take out my turkey sandwich, and act like I was the same old reliable Kit. The one who would make a self-deprecating joke about my shirt, which I'm wearing in some weird tribute to my dad, a silly attempt to feel closer to him even though it makes me feel like even more of an outcast and more confused about the whole thing than I was before I put it on. Just the kind of reminder I don't need. Like I could actually forget, for even a single minute.

I feel stupid. Could that be what grief does to you? It's like I'm walking around school with an astronaut's helmet on my head. A dome of dullness as impenetrable as glass. No one here understands what I'm going through. How could they? I don't even understand it.

It seemed safer somehow to sit over here, in the back, away from my friends, who have clearly already moved on to other important things, like whether Violet's thighs look fat in her new high-waisted jeans, and away from all the other people who have stopped me in the hall over the past couple of weeks with that faux-concerned look on their faces and said: "Kit, I'm like so, so, so sorry about your daaaad." Everyone seems to draw out the word *dad* like they are scared to get beyond that one sentence, to experience the conversational free fall of what to say next that inevitably follows. My mom claims that it's not our job to make other people feel comfortable—this is about us, not them, she told me just before the funeral—but her way, which is to weep and to throw her arms around sympathetic strangers, is not mine. I have not yet figured out my way.

Actually I'm starting to realize there is no way.

Certainly I'm not going to cry, which seems too easy, too dismissive. I've cried over bad grades and being grounded and once, embarrassingly, over a bad haircut. (In my defense, those bangs ended up taking three very long awkward years to grow out.) This? This is too big for woe-is-me silly girl tears. This is too big for everything.

Tears would be a privilege.

I figure sitting next to David Drucker is my best bet, since he's so quiet you forget he's even there. He's weird—he sits with his sketchbook and draws elaborate pictures of fish—and when he does talk, he stares at your mouth, like you might have something in your teeth. Don't get me wrong: I feel awkward and uncomfortable most of the time, but I've learned how to fake it. David, on the other hand, seems to have completely opted out of even trying to act like everyone else.

I've never seen him at a party or at a football game or even at one of the nerdy after-school activities he might enjoy, like Math Club or coding. For the record, I'm a huge fan of nerdy after-school activities since they'll be good for my college applications, though I tend toward the more literary and therefore ever-so-slightly cooler variety. The truth is I'm kind of a big nerd myself.

Who knows? Maybe he's on to something by tuning the rest of us out. Not a bad high school survival strategy. Showing up every day and doing his homework and rocking those giant noise-canceling headphones—and basically just waiting for high school to be over with.

I may be a little awkward, sometimes a bit too desperate to be liked—but until everything with my dad, I've never been quiet. It feels strange to sit at a table with just one other person, for the noise of the caf to be something that I want to block out. This is the opposite of my own previous survival strategy, which was to jump headfirst into the fray.

Oddly enough, David has an older sister, Lauren, who, until she graduated last year, was the most popular girl in school. His opposite in every way. President of her class and homecoming queen. (Somehow she managed to make something that clichéd seem cool again in her hipster ironic way.) Dated Peter Malvern, who every girl, including me, used to worship from afar because he played bass guitar and had the kind of facial hair that most guys our age are incapable of growing. Lauren Drucker is a living legend—smart and cool and beautiful—and if I could reincarnate as anyone else, just start this whole show over again and get to be someone different, I would choose to be her even though we've never actually met. No doubt she'd look awesome with bangs.

I'm pretty sure that if it hadn't been for Lauren, and the implicit threat that she would personally destroy anyone who made fun of her younger brother, David would have been eaten alive at Mapleview. Instead he's been left alone. And I mean that literally. He is *always* alone.

I hope I'm not rude when I tell him I don't feel like talking; fortunately he doesn't seem offended. He might be strange, but the world is shitty enough without people being shitty to each other, and he has a point about the whole heaven thing. Not that I have any desire to talk to David Drucker about what happened to my father—I can think of nothing I'd rather discuss less, except for maybe the size of Violet's thighs, because *who cares about her freaking jeans*—but I happen to agree. Heaven is like Santa Claus, a story to trick naive little kids. At the funeral, four different people had the nerve to tell me my father was in a *better place,* as if being buried six feet under is like taking a Caribbean vacation. Even worse were my dad's colleagues, who dared to say that *he was too good for this world.* Which, if you take even a second to think about it, doesn't even make sense. Are only bad people allowed to live, then? Is that why I'm still here?

My dad was the best person I knew, but no, he wasn't *too good* for this world. He isn't in *a better place.* And I sure as hell don't believe *everything happens for a reason,* that this is *God's plan,* that *it was just his time to go,* like he had an appointment that couldn't be missed.

Nope. I'm not buying any of it. We all know the truth. My dad got screwed.

Eventually David slips his headphones on and takes out a large hardcover book that has the words *Diagnostic and Statistical Manual of Mental Disorders IV* on the spine. We have almost all our classes together—we're both doing the junior-year AP overload thing—so I know this isn't school reading. If he wants to spend his free time studying "mental disorders," good for him, but I consider suggesting he get an iPad or something so no one else can see. Clearly his survival strategy should include Mapleview's number-one rule: Don't fly your freak flag too high here. Better to keep the freak buried, inconspicuous, maybe under a metaphorical astronaut's helmet if necessary. That may be the only way to get out alive.

I spend the rest of lunch mindlessly chewing my sad sandwich. My phone beeps every once in a while with text messages from my friends, but I try not to look over to their table.

Violet: Did we do something to hurt your feelings? Why are you sitting over there?

Annie: WTF!!?!?!?

Violet: At least write back. Tell us what's going on.

Annie: K! Earth to K!

Violet: Just tell me the truth: yay or nay on these jeans?

When you have two best friends, someone is always mad at someone else. Today, by not texting back, I'm basically volunteering to be the one on the outs. I just don't know how to explain that I can't sit with them today. That sitting at their table, right there in the front of the caf, and chatting about nonsense feels like a betrayal. I consider giving my verdict on Violet's pants, but my dad's dying has had the unfortunate side effect of taking away my filter. No need to tell her that though her thighs look fine, the high waist makes her look a little constipated.

My mom said no when I begged her to let me stay home from school today. I didn't want to have to walk back into this cafeteria, didn't want to go from class to class steeling myself for yet another succession of uncomfortable conversations. The truth is, people have been genuinely nice. Even borderline sincere, which almost never happens in this place. It's not their fault that everything—*high school*—suddenly feels incredibly stupid and pointless.

When I woke up this morning, I didn't have the blissful thirty-second amnesia that has carried me through lately, that beautiful half minute when my mind is blank, empty, and untortured. Instead I awoke feeling pure, full-throttled rage. It's been one whole month since the accident. Thirty impossible days. To be fair, I'm aware my friends can't win: If they had mentioned this to me, if they had said something sympathetic like "Kit, I know it's been a month since your dad died, and so today must be especially hard for you," I still would have been annoyed, because I probably would have fallen apart, and school is not where I want to be when that inevitably happens. On the other hand, I'm pretty sure Annie and Violet didn't mention it because they forgot altogether. They were all chatty, sipping their matching Starbucks lattes, talking about what guy they were hoping was going to ask them to junior prom, assuming I just had a bad case of the Mondays. I was expected to chime in.

I am somehow supposed to have bounced back.

I am not supposed to be moping around in my dad's old shirt.

One month ago today.

So strange that David Drucker of all people was the only one who said the exact right thing: *Your dad shouldn't have died. That's really unfair.*

"You've been back two weeks already," my mom said over breakfast, after I made one last plea to ditch. "The Band-Aid has already been ripped off." But I don't have a single Band-Aid. I'd rather have two black eyes, broken bones, internal bleeding, visible scarring. Maybe to not be here at all. Instead: Not a scratch on me. The worst kind of miracle.

"You're going to work?" I asked, because it seemed that if I was having trouble facing school, it should be hard for her to put back on her work clothes and heels and drive to the train. Of course my mom was aware of the significance of the date. In the beginning, once we got home from the hospital, she was in constant tears, while I was the one who was dry-eyed and numb. For the first few days, while she wept, I sat quietly with my knees drawn to my chest, my body racked with chills despite being bundled up in about a million layers. Still, a month later, I haven't managed to quite get warm.

My mom, however, seems to be pulling herself back together into someone I recognize. You wouldn't know it from looking at her on the weekends, when she wears yoga pants and sneakers and a ponytail, or from the way she looked right after the accident, shattered and gray and folded up, but in her working life my mom is a hard-core boss lady. She's CEO of an online-advertising agency called Disruptive Communications. Sometimes I overhear her yelling at her employees and using the kinds of words that would get me grounded. Occasionally her picture is on the cover of trade magazines with headlines like "The Diverse Future of Viral Media." She's the one who orchestrated that video with the singing dogs and cats that at last count had sixteen million hits, and that great breakfast cereal pop-up ad with the biracial gay dads. Before entering the throes of widowhood, she was pretty badass.

"Of course I'm going to work. Why wouldn't I?" my mom asked. And with that she picked up my cereal bowl, even though I wasn't yet finished, and dropped it into the sink so hard that it shattered.

She left, wearing her "work uniform"—a black cashmere sweater, a pencil skirt, and stilettos. I considered cleaning up the shards of glass in the sink. Maybe even accidentally-on-purpose letting one cut me. Just a little. I was curious whether I'd even feel it. But then I realized that despite my new post-Dad-dying-imbuing-every-single-tiny-thing-with-bigger-meaning stage, like wearing this men's work shirt to school, that was just way too metaphorical. Even for me. So I left the mess for my mom to clean up later.

CHAPTER 3

DAVID

After lunch with Kit Lowell, I take off my headphones. Usually I keep them on between classes so that when I walk through the halls the ambient noise is indistinct and muffled. That chatter and movement make me feel amped up and distracted and much more likely to trip. The shortest distance between two points is a straight line, and yet the boys in school dart from side to side full of random aggression. They jab their fists into each other's backs, tackle necks with smiles on their faces, high-five hard. Why do they want to constantly touch each other? Though the girls don't weave as much as the guys, they also stop and start, often out of nowhere, hugging every so often even though they just saw each other before last period.

I free-ear it because I am curious to hear if anyone is talking about Kit's dad. I Googled his name and pulled up this obituary, which was in the *Daily Courier,* section A16, three weeks and four days ago. Only three short sentences, which, though I appreciate its succinctness, left out some relevant details, like the lollipops and the whole "nice man" part.

Robert Lowell DDS passed away on Friday, January 15, in a car accident. He was born on September 21, 1971, in Princeton, New Jersey, and practiced dentistry in Mapleview for the past twelve years. He is survived by his wife, Mandip, and their daughter, Katherine.

Facts thus far learned from my quick search: (1) Kit's dad's name was Robert, which makes sense somehow, a familiar word and an even number of letters. I've always just thought of him as Dentist, which now that I think about it is way too limiting. (2) Kit's dad died in a car accident, which is a misnomer, because in the vast majority of car accidents where people end up dying, they don't actually die in the car but afterward, in the ambulance or at the hospital. I'll have to find out the specifics.

As I walk down the hall, I see Gabriel.

GABRIEL FORSYTH: Curly hair. Marble eyes. Clown mouth.

Notable Encounters

1. Seventh grade: Took my Oreos without asking. Snatched them from my insulated lunch bag and walked away.
2. Tenth grade: Held hands with Kit L. (That's not an encounter with me, but it's still notable.)
3. Eleventh grade: Sits next to me in physics, because our seats were assigned by the teacher on day one. When he saw how far he was from Justin Cho, he said, "Awww shit,

*really, Mr. Schmidt?" for which he got a first warning. I
did not point out that the seat was a relatively good one
in terms of acoustics and board perspective. Miney said it
was good that I kept that to myself.*

Friends

*The lacrosse team, the tennis team (which, of course
has considerable overlap due to the seasonal schedules).
Best friends with Justin Cho since second grade.*

*   Additional Notes: Miney puts him on the Do Not Trust
List.*

I do not look at him. Instead I keep my head down, concentrate on keeping up with the stops and starts in front of me.

"Yo, man, after practice. Pizza Palace," Gabriel says. Based on the sneakers and the context, I'm ninety-nine percent sure he is talking to Justin. I will not put Justin's notebook entry here, because I am tired of reading and rereading my notes about Justin and wondering why he hates me so much. An unsolvable equation. Our Notable Encounters list is five pages long. He is the president of the Do Not Trust Club.

The Pizza Palace is the second-best Italian restaurant in Mapleview, according to Yelp. Most people prefer Rocco's. If Gabriel were inviting me, which he is not, I would suggest we go to Pizza Pizza Pizza, which has two slices for the price of one from two to five p.m., and I believe the slight decrease in quality is more than made up for by the value. That said, I do get why they'd choose the Pizza Palace anyway, which is in no way a palace—just a small storefront on Main Street—because no matter how cheap the food is at Pizza Pizza Pizza, it feels funny to say the redundant name out loud.

That's what I'm doing, imagining that Gabriel said, "Yo, man, after practice, Pizza Pizza Pizza," and thinking how that would have been ridiculous, when I bump into a group of girls congregating around a locker. Jessica, Willow (who is notably the only Willow enrolled in our 397-student class and in our 1,579-student school), and Abby. Miney has labeled them in my notebook, in block letters and underlined with a Sharpie: THE POPULAR BITCHES.

When she first used this designation, Miney had to give me a long lecture about how this wasn't an oxymoron, how someone could be both popular, which I presumed meant that lots of people liked you, and at the same time also be a bitch, which I presumed would have the opposite outcome. Apparently popularity in the context of high school has a negative correlation with people actually liking you but a high correlation with people wanting to be your friend. After careful consideration, this makes sense, though in my case, I am both an outlier and a great example of the fact that correlation does not imply causation. I am nice to everyone but without any upside: People neither like me nor want to be my friend.

"Watch it," Jessica says, and rolls her eyes. Like I bumped into her on purpose. Haven't my classmates figured out that the feeling has become mutual? They want nothing to do with me? Fine. I want nothing to do with them either. Miney promises college will be better, though I highly doubt it. "And what's with all the talking to yourself?"

Have I been talking to myself? It's entirely possible and somewhat ironic that my entire thought process about Pizza Pizza Pizza and what a ridiculous name it is to say out loud actually occurred . . . out loud. Occasionally, I forget about the barrier between the inside of my head and the rest of the world.

"Sorry," I mutter to the floor, and pick up the book she dropped and hand it to her. She doesn't say thank you.

"Freak," Abby says, and laughs, like that's funny or original. I force myself to meet her eyes, to look straight at her, because Miney claims eye contact humanizes me. Again, I have no idea why I need to be humanized in the first place, why everyone assumes I am some exception to the universally acknowledged rule that we are all human beings with feelings. Still, I do it anyway. Such is the power of Miney. "What are you staring at?"

For a second I consider asking Abby, straight out, just saying it out loud, "What have I ever done to you?" I bumped into Jessica. Not her. We have had no Notable Encounters, positive or negative. But then the bell rings, and it's loud and uncomfortable, and everyone is rushing off to class, and I have physics. Which means I now have to spend the next forty-five minutes sitting next to Gabriel and trying to block out the fact that he smells like Axe Anarchy for Him body spray, and taps his pencil against his desk to an erratic beat, and clears his throat approximately every thirty-five seconds. No doubt, despite the acoustics and board perspective, I'd have been much better off sitting alone in the back.

Kit slips into class ten minutes into Mr. Schmidt's lecture on Newton's third law, which I've written down in Latin to keep it interesting.

"Lost track of time," Kit says, and takes her seat, which is two behind me and one to the right. Not the greatest excuse, considering the school uses a loud bell to remind us to get to class. Mr. Schmidt nods and doesn't yell at her or give her a first warning like he normally would. Once, when we had to make a shiva call to our next-door neighbor's, Miney told me that different rules apply to those who've just lost someone. I wonder how long that lasts, not the dead part, of course, but the special treatment part. Would Mr. Schmidt make allowances for me if my dad died?

Probably not. My dad is a medical researcher at Abbot Laboratories. I doubt he's on many people's Nice List, mostly because he's not the type of person to make it onto any lists other than science ones. If my mother died, on the other hand, people would notice. She and Miney are similar that way: Everyone loves them. My mom is always stopping to talk to other women in the checkout line at the supermarket or at the drugstore. She knows the names of all the kids in my class and their parents, and sometimes she'll even add information to my notebook. She's the one who told me that Justin and Jessica were dating—she saw them making out at the mall—and then later that they broke up. This was gleaned, somehow, while getting her nails done, because she shares a chatty manicurist with Jessica's mom.

Miney is the anti-me. She won numerous Senior Superlatives last year: Most Popular, Most Attractive, Most Likely to Succeed. I do not anticipate winning any. Though I guess Miney and I have one thing in common: Miney is also an example that correlation does not imply causation. She is popular but not a bitch. Unfortunately she has also led me to question the entire field of genetics, since we share fifty percent of our DNA.

My parents have been married for twenty-two years and they are still in love. This is statistically remarkable.

My mom says: "Opposites attract."

My dad says: "I just got seriously lucky."

Miney says: "Mom is a closet weirdo, and dad is a closet normal, and that's why they work."

I haven't put much thought into their marriage, but I like that my parents are still together. I wouldn't want to have to pack a bag every other weekend and sleep in some strange apartment and have to brush my teeth in a different sink. My mom claims my dad and I are a lot alike, which gives me cause for optimism. If he could get someone like my mother to love him—someone who is universally acknowledged to be all kinds of awesome—and not just love him but love him enough to spend the rest of her life with him, then maybe there is hope for me too.

Halfway through class, when Mr. Schmidt starts writing equations on the smart board, Kit stands up and walks out. No explanation. No asking for a bathroom pass. No excuses. She just leaves.

After the door closes behind her, the whispering starts.

Justin: That was badass.

Annie: She, like, needs to talk to us. She's totally shutting us out.

Violet: Her dad DIED, Annie. As in dead, dead forever. Cut her some slack.

Gabriel: I'm hungry.

Annie: I have a PowerBar.

Gabriel: You literally just saved my life.

This is how it goes. Conversation swirls around me, and the words all feel disconnected, like playing pinball blindfolded. What does Kit's dad dying have to do with Gabriel being hungry?

"Ladies and gentlemen, moving on," Mr. Schmidt says, and then claps three times—clap, clap, clap—for no discernible reason. Before I realize what I'm doing, my hand is in the air. "Yes, Mr. Drucker?"

"Can I be excused?" I ask.

"Excused? This is a classroom, not the dinner table. Let's get back to work."

"I meant can I go to the nurse? I have a migraine," I say, though this is a lie. Miney would be proud. She says I need to practice not telling the truth. That lying gets easier the more you do it. I consider making a moaning noise, as if I am in pain, but decide that would be overkill.

"Fine. Go," Mr. Schmidt says, and so I stand up and walk out the door, just like Kit did a few moments before. It's not like I'm going to miss anything here. I read the textbook last summer. The few questions it raised for me were answered with a couple of Google searches and expounded upon by a free online Stanford class.

Once I'm in the quiet hallway, my brain catches up with my body and I understand what I'm doing here. Although Mr. Schmidt's class is boring and a complete waste of my time, I usually obey instructions. I sit through my classes. Mostly keep my mouth shut. Unless I want to bypass high school and get a GED, I don't have much choice in the matter.

What I realize is: I want to find Kit. I need to know where she's going.

I jog down the hall and decide to head out the front door, ignoring Señora Rubenstein, the Spanish teacher, calling out to me in her heavy New Jersey accent: "*Adónde vas,* Señor Drucker?"

I scan the parking lot to my right, which is about six hundred feet northeast of the school's entrance. No Kit. But her red Corolla, which is parked like always in the second row, six cars back, space number forty-three of the upperclassmen's lot, is still here.

I walk around the school to the football field, which has

high bleachers and a decent view of Mapleview. Maybe she's sitting up there to get some fresh air. I don't like sporting events—too noisy and crowded—but I've always liked bleachers, things ordered vertically from high to low.

"Did Mr. Schmidt send you?" Kit asks. She's not in the bleachers, which is where I was looking, but in the concession hut. This is where kids from student government sell hot dogs and lemonade and candy at football games at inflated prices. The lights are off, and she's sitting on the dirty floor with her knees pulled into her chest. If she hadn't spoken, I don't know if I would have noticed her.

"No. I lied to him and said I had a migraine," I say, and force myself to make eye contact. It's easier than usual, since it's dark in there. Kit's cheeks are red from the cold. Her eyes are green. They've always been green, obviously, but today they are greener somehow. My new definition of green. Green used to equal Kermit the Frog. And sometimes spring. But no more. Now Kit's eyes equal green. An inextricable link. Like how when I think about the number three, I always, for no reason that I've been able to understand, also see the letter *R*.

"I wasn't trying to start a ditching trend," Kit says, and I smile, because if it's not exactly a joke, it is sort of related to one.

"In case you hadn't noticed, I don't usually follow trends," I say, and point to my pants, which are loose-fitting and khaki-colored and, according to Miney, a "crime against fashion." She's been begging to take me shopping for years, claims that I could look so much better if I put in just a tiny bit of effort. But I don't like shopping. Actually it's not the shopping I mind so much. I don't like the new clothes afterward. The feeling of an unfamiliar material against my skin.

Kit looks up at me, and then over my shoulder to the school.

"So are you following me? This isn't the nurse's office," she says. I can't make out her tone. Can't tell if she's annoyed. Her voice sounds scratchy and her face doesn't match any of the expression cards Miney once printed out for me.

"I just wanted to make sure you were okay." I hold up my hands, a signal to say *no harm,* like they do on cop shows.

"Everyone was talking about me when I left, right? I didn't mean to make a whole thing about it. I just couldn't sit there, suddenly," she says.

"Clearly," I say. "I mean, that you couldn't sit there. Not the making a whole thing about it." Now that I'm here, talking to Kit, twice in one day, when we haven't really spoken pretty much ever, except our few Notable Encounters, I realize how off schedule I find myself. None of this was part of today's plan.

Me following her outside.

Me electing myself the one to check on her.

Me suddenly redefining green.

CHAPTER 4

KIT

I'm in the concession hut and David Drucker is standing outside. The whole thing is so weird. Surely he knows that when I sat at his lunch table this afternoon I was just looking for a place to be alone. I don't want anything from him. Or for us to suddenly be besties or something. I don't mean that in a nasty way. I'm not usually like this. I don't abandon my friends in the cafeteria or walk out of class in the middle of the teacher's lecture or have any trouble lying and saying "Your ass looks awesome in those high-waisted jeans."

My dad's shirt is filthy.

This place reeks of rotting hot dogs and old gym sneakers.

Everything is wrong.

It's been one month.

I am still all wrong.

"I wasn't following you," David says, his eyes darting off the walls and then, finally, landing on mine. "I mean, I was. But just because someone needed to follow you. Does that make sense?"

"It's okay," I say, because he looks nervous and he makes me want to make things easier for him. "Here, help me up. I don't want to touch the floor."

David comes around to the side door. He puts out his hand, and I grab it and hike myself up to standing. "This place is gross," I say.

"The bleachers would have been the better choice."

"You know what? That's a great idea." I sprint toward the field and then up the stairs, taking two at a time, and the momentum feels good, air pumped directly to my cold, dead heart. When I get to the top, I take a seat.

I forgot how much I love being up here. I rarely miss a game, not because I care that much about football, but because I love being part of the crowd. Like there is nowhere else any of us is supposed to be except right here cheering on our team, perfect teenager clichés reporting for duty. I see David craning his neck to look up, probably deciding whether he should join me.

"Come on!" I call to him.

He takes the stairs more slowly than I did. Stares at the ground so as not to fall. David is one of those random people at school you don't think about at all, but now that I've invited him to sit next to me here, I scramble to remember everything I know about him. That will hopefully make things slightly less uncomfortable, because honestly I'd totally pick the stomach flu over awkward.

But the problem is, that's the first word I think of when I think of David: *awkward*. I don't know much else about him. I remember I used to go to his birthday parties, and when he turned five he had one that was space-themed. We all got these cool NASA badges (I still have mine, actually), and his parents rented a bouncy castle that looked like the moon. We were jumping and then bumping into each other, and out of nowhere he fell to the floor and started crying with his hands over his ears. We all went home early.

What else? I've seen him trip about a million times, and he has this bad habit of bumping into people. Maybe it's because he walks around with those huge headphones on and can't hear anything, or maybe it's because his mind is busy solving, like, global warming or something. And he's right. He's a terrible dresser. He looks like a missionary. Or like he has an after-school job at an electronics store at the mall.

Now that he's sitting up here, I quickly study his face and I realize he's not bad-looking. Actually a step up from Justin and Gabriel, who think they are hot shit despite their matching chin acne. If David got his hair cut and let people see his bottomless dark brown eyes, he'd be seriously cute. Probably the reason I invited him to sit next to me, if I'm honest with myself, is that my dad mentioned him out of the blue just a few months ago. At the dinner table one night, my dad announced that he thought I should get to know David Drucker.

"David Drucker was in my chair today, and I gotta tell you, that boy is interesting. He talked to me about quantum mechanics," my father said. And I'm sure I replied with something sarcastic, like "Sounds fascinating, Dad. I'll get right on that."

Do I want to go back in time and punch myself in the face? Yes, yes I do.

"The Arthur B. Pendlock Stadium can hold up to eight hundred and four people," David says, sitting next to me now but looking out at the field. You can make out the post office from here. The cupcake bakery. Sam's Bagels.

"That's what this place is called?" I ask. "The Arthur B. Pendlock Stadium?" David nods. "I never knew that. I think I would have guessed more than eight hundred and four people. It gets pretty packed at the games."

"I've never been," he says.

"To a game? Really? They're fun," I say, though I wonder if our definitions of the word *fun* are the same. He shrugs. I consider asking him about quantum mechanics, but I don't even know what quantum mechanics is. Or are? Is *quantum mechanics* plural?

"Not a sports fan, I take it?" I ask somewhat inanely. I'm not sure why I've always assumed that the responsibility of a conversation falls on me. Half the time, I'm better off just shutting up.

"Nope. I don't really understand the appeal. The suspense is inherently limited. Your team is either going to win or lose through some variation of throwing and catching balls. That said, I'd rather watch than play. Why would you let yourself be tackled to the ground and risk a potential head injury? It's confusing to me."

"I can see how that would be confusing," I say, and find myself smiling.

"I've considered whether some of the guys find it homoerotic, but most of them have girlfriends, so probably not."

I laugh.

"I'm only half joking," he says. He looks at me and then his eyes dart away again. "We can stop talking if you want. I assume you left class to get away from all that noise, though my assumptions usually have only a thirty percent accuracy rate."

"I did, actually," I say. I can see the grocery store parking lot from up here, where my dad taught me to drive not so long ago. We went there at odd hours on weekends and even some weeknights for the three months leading up to my birthday. He was patient with me, a good teacher, only getting annoyed in the beginning, when I got confused between the gas and the brake. I passed my test on the first try, and my parents and I celebrated with sparkling apple cider in fancy champagne glasses. My dad toasted to "all the roads Kit has yet to travel." He took a picture of me holding up my license, and then he teared up a little, because he said he was already starting to imagine what it was going to be like when I left for college, how his life would have a Kit-shaped hole.

My dad was supposed to miss me, not the other way around. That's how things were supposed to go.

I don't want to think about that.

After a while, quiet settles between David and me, and surprisingly it's not awkward at all. It's actually kind of nice to sit up here, away from school and the shitstorm that awaits at home, away from the terrifying concept of one whole month. It's nice to sit with someone and not have to think about what to say next.

I don't go back to class. Instead I go home and spend my time lying on the couch and watching Netflix. Though I've been here for hours, I did not study for tomorrow's physics quiz. I did not read fifty pages of *Heart of Darkness* and think about its thematic relevance to my own life (though that should have been an easy one) or start that essay for world history on migration. I also didn't write that article about the debate team for the school newspaper even though the deadline is tomorrow by three. We'll probably have to run a picture in its place. Clearly this is not the way to make editor in chief, which has been my goal for the past three years, but I can't seem to motivate.

"Egg rolls, scallion pancakes, General Tso's. All the bad stuff," my mom says, dropping a bulging bag of Chinese food onto the counter. She kicks off her shoes. "Does grief make your feet swell? Because these things are freaking killing me."

"I don't know." I get up and set the table for two, not the usual three. I need to stop noticing details like this.

"How was your day? As bad as you expected?" My mom kisses me on my head and then decides I need a hug too.

"Not really. I mean, it wasn't *good*." I don't tell her I skipped class. No need to freak her out. "But you were right. I needed to go. Yours?"

"I kicked ass, took names, even landed a new account. Not bad for a Monday."

"That's cool," I say, and we toast with our glasses.

"I need to up my game on the financial front." Wrinkles I haven't noticed before bracket her mouth. She shouldn't have to up her game. She already works too hard as it is. Bangs on her laptop after dinner and dashes off emails late into the night. When I was younger and brattier, I used to complain that she loved her work more than she loved me. Now that I'm older, I realize that's not true. My mother is just one of those people you miss, even when she's sitting right in front of you.

"I didn't think about the money thing," I say, and my stomach cramps with guilt. Soon there will be my college tuition, and what about when I leave? My mom will come home every day to this big empty house. A team of three knocked down to two, and then, finally, just one. Will she sell this place? I hope not.

"Don't worry. No one's going to starve. But you know what's

really stressing me out? How do I know when to change the oil in the car? Or what the name of our home insurance company is? And all our online passwords. I don't have any of them," my mom says. "Your name? Birthday? I feel completely in over my head. Work I can handle. It's the rest—it's real life—that's the problem."

I think about how my mom doesn't really have lots of people around to help other than me. My grandparents retired and moved back to Delhi like a million years ago. She and her parents have this complicated relationship anyway. When my mom was a kid, her parents did everything they could to make sure she assimilated into American culture—paid for her to go to a fancy-pants, mostly white private school they could barely afford, even packed PB&J in her lunch box because the other kids used to tease her that her Indian food was too stinky. The way she tells it, they raised her as an American and then were surprised and resentful when she didn't turn out to share their old-school values. I'm pretty sure "old-school values" in this case actually means "not cool with the fact she fell in love and married a white dude," because otherwise, she's totally on board with the rest of their beliefs—well, except for the fact that she's a straight-up, unapologetic carnivore and gets her hair cut and colored every six weeks. Still, we go to gurdwara in Glen Rock one Sunday a month, and my dad used to come with us sometimes, though less for a religious awakening and more for the home-made Indian food, which admittedly, now that I'm old enough to have a choice in the matter, is why I go too. At my grand-mother's request, my mom keeps in touch with all the relatives, even though they are in Delhi and Vancouver and London and distantly related and kind of a pain in the ass. And though I'm not quite fluent, my mom has taught me enough Punjabi that I can get by. My mother may be American-born, but she's never forgotten we're Indian too.

Everyone pretends things are okay with my impossible-to-please grandparents—we go to visit them in Delhi every other year, though my dad always stayed behind because "he had to work." We pretended this was true and that it had nothing to do with the fact that my grandparents didn't approve of him. Whenever my mom talks to Bibiji on the phone, she always puts on a voice I associate with her work, the advertising-executive voice. My mom's conversations with her parents have mostly consisted of a recitation of our small accomplishments—my grades, my mom's landing an account, my dad getting a local business award—as if these things are part of some campaign pitch that she made the right choices. And whenever I wear a lengha or a salwar kameez for some second cousin twice re-moved's birthday party, which requires three hours in the car to the middle of Pennsylvania, my mother makes sure to take a picture and email it to Bibiji immediately. *See,* she seems to want to say, *nothing's been lost here. I'm passing it all along.*

Here's the sad and horrifying part: The second I put on my Indian clothes, an alert goes out to her parents, yet when my dad died my mom didn't even call them until the day *after* the funeral. My mother explained to me that she knew they were traveling to a wedding that weekend and couldn't get back to the United States in time, so there was no point messing up their plans. Honestly I think my mom didn't want to know if they would come to pay their respects.

Of course I like to believe they would have. They may not have approved of my mom marrying my dad, but they're not monsters. They're just backwards. And, okay, a little bit racist.

Oddly enough, though they may not like the fact that I'm half white, they always compliment me on the color of my skin. *So fair,* Bibiji always says, like that's a wonderful, important thing, the fact that I'm a couple of shades lighter than my mother. *And I can see you enjoy your food.*

"I'll help you figure it all out," I say to my mother. "I'm sorry."

"Oh, honey, don't say that. It's going to be fine. *You* have nothing to be sorry for. I shouldn't have said anything."

I make myself busy dishing out the food, spoon out huge piles onto our plates. There are people who don't eat when they are sad, who lose their appetite and get crazy skinny. My mom and I are not those people.

"I love you, Mommy," I say. As soon as the words are out, I feel bad again, because it makes her eyes fill. I want her to know that I realize just how lucky I got in the mother department. That if I had to pick anyone in the whole world to go through this with, to have as a mom, it would be her. Only her. This is partially grief talking. Before all this, my mom often annoyed the crap out of me. She's master of the subtle criticism disguised as a suggestion: *Why don't you straighten your hair? Don't you think your nails would look so much better if you didn't bite them? That shirt is a little frumpy, no?* Now, though, I feel stupid for caring about that sort of thing. She could die tomorrow. "I didn't mean to make you cry."

"No. Good crying, I promise," she says, blotting under her eyes with a paper towel. It doesn't look like good crying. She looks on the verge of unraveling into a mess of tears and snot. Nothing like the woman she must have been at work today: fierce and tucked-in and totally under control. "I'm just so grateful that I have you, Kit."

I know she doesn't mean for her words to sting, but they do.

"I'm not going anywhere," I promise, and hold up my finger for a pinky swear.

"A whole month without him," she says, ignoring my out-stretched finger. "How is that even possible?"

"I don't know."

"Kit?" I wait for her to finally say it, to just go ahead and mention the accident outright, and then maybe murmur a few empty words that are supposed to be comforting. I brace myself to talk about all the things she's refused to talk about until now. "You have a little scallion in your teeth."

CHAPTER 5

DAVID

She sits at my table again. I didn't expect her to. Told myself it didn't matter. That I've sat alone 622 times, and that I like my ritual—the way I wait for Disher, the lunch lady, to be the one to serve me because she always wears gloves and, on good days, a hairnet; the way I spread my food out in front of me in the order I want to eat it, one bite from each plate, small to large and back again; the way I switch my music over the second I sit down, from Mozart, which is best for hall navigation, to the Beatles, which is social in the way the midday meal should be. That it would be okay too if we didn't ever talk again. I have two new Notable Encounters to add to my notebook now, one in which I made Kit Lowell laugh.

Out loud.

She even threw back her head.

"This okay?" she asks, though she's already sitting down.

She doesn't wait for my answer and instead reaches into her backpack and takes out an elaborate assortment of what appears to be leftover Chinese food. Probably from Szechuan Gardens, which is both the number-one Yelp-rated Chinese restaurant in Mapleview and also the only Chinese restaurant in Mapleview. I'm particularly fond of their hot and sour soup.

"You are always most welcome." From the look Kit gives me, I surmise this must be a weird thing to say. Usually the truth is. I can't think of many people I would actually welcome to my table—maybe José, who wears bifocals, or Stephanie L., whom I've never heard speak out loud. On second thought, maybe not. José would ask me to join the Academic League, which has happened twenty-six times in the past three years. Stephanie L., though on the plus side decidedly nonverbal, looks like someone who would be a loud chewer. I have misophonia and would prefer not to be enraged by her rabid mastication.

"Can I ask you a question?" Kit asks. I refrain from pointing out that she just asked me a question by asking me if she could ask me a question. When I noted the same thing to Miney recently, over our thrice-weekly prearranged FaceTime call, she said, "Little D, why are you so freakin' annoying?" Which is, of course, also a question, but a rhetorical one.

"Sure," I say now to Kit.

"Why do you always sit alone?"

I shrug, which is not something I often do, and it feels funny, that up-and-down shimmy of the shoulders. A little exaggerated. Like a confused person in a play.

"I'm not sitting alone right now."

"You know what I mean," Kit says. She is eating an egg roll and her lips are glossy with its grease. Only Kit Lowell could turn food into makeup.

"There aren't that many people at this school I'd like to sit and eat with," I say, proud of myself for not adding what Miney would call "too much information": *When I say there aren't that many people, I really mean only you, Kit.*

"We're not all terrible, you know," she says, and makes a hand gesture that I take to mean *there are a lot of people here to choose from,* though it's entirely possible she is just shooing away a gnat. I put the odds at eighty to twenty I'm right.

"Did you know we will spend one hundred eighty-five and a half hours in this cafeteria this school year alone? That seems like a lot of time to spend with people with whom I have nothing in common except for three insignificant coincidences. One: We, like millions of other people, were born in the same year. Two: We happened to be raised in the same small town. And three: Our parents chose to send us through the Mapleview public school system." While talking I count the numbers one, two, and three on my fingers, which my mother claims is obnoxious, and on reflection, I agree, but it's a hard habit to break. "On the parental level, I can see how this is enough to form a friendship, given all the shared choices—where to move, when to have kids, et cetera—but for me, particularly because I didn't choose any of this and wouldn't have chosen any of this if I were given any say in the matter, which I decidedly wasn't, it's not enough commonality. And a lot of these people you claim are not so terrible tend to be not so nice to me. So to answer your original, but not first, question—I think it might have been your third, actually—I have better things to do with my time than to waste it on . . ." After erring on the side that it was a gesture and not a swat, I copy Kit's wavy hand motion, which also feels a little theatrical, but appropriate and also very, very Kit. "These people."

"Nice speech," she says. "I feel that way too sometimes. Not the people-not-being-nice thing so much, but the nothing-in-common thing. Who knows? Maybe everyone feels like that. I didn't ask you what I really wanted to know, which is, I guess, my third or fourth question: Do you get lonely sitting here? Being by yourself all the time?"

I look up at her, meet her eyes. Green, green, green. Today she's not wearing a man's shirt. Instead she has on a sweater that looks soft, the kind that when I was a kid I would stop and pet whenever my mom forced me to go shopping. It's light yellow, the color of a baby chick. She wears a thin gold necklace with a big scripted *K* charm that she massages a lot with the rhythmic rubbing of forefinger and thumb, like it's a cross or rosary beads. Her jeans are ripped and her knees peek out of the holes. I wonder if they are cold.

The cafeteria is loud, so much louder without my headphones, which I took off when I first saw Kit head toward me and this table. I remember now why I like to wear them.

"You're up to five questions," I say. "And, yes, of course I get lonely. Just like everyone else."

"See, you have more in common with us than you thought," she says, and smiles, like what I said was something happy, not sad, which is weird, because I thought it was quite clearly the latter.

"My turn for a question," I say. A declarative statement, albeit a superfluous one. "What made you pick my table?"

"Honestly? I knew you'd leave me alone if I asked you to. I'm not dealing so well at the moment, if you hadn't noticed." I hadn't noticed, actually, but I don't say that. She looks fine to me. Much better than fine. Luminous, even. "And I just can't take everyone, you know, watching me all the time. Like if I were eating this in front of Vi and Annie, they'd be all judgy about me eating my feelings about, you know, everything, which of course I *know* I am. I really don't need them to hint that I don't want to get any fatter."

"That would imply you are already fat," I say. "And you're not fat. I mean, you're not skinny either. I'd say you are average weight for your height, maybe five pounds above average in your legs."

She laughs. This is the second time I've made her laugh, and it feels just as good as the first.

"Thank you for that," she says. "I guess straight-up honesty was one way to go."

"You're welcome. You shouldn't worry about your weight. You'd still look beautiful fat. You have plenty of room to grow." I try to make eye contact again, but this time she's the one looking away. Her cheeks are flushed.

"Are you warm?" I ask.

"It's freezing in here." It's approximately sixty-six degrees inside, but maybe it feels colder to her because of her bare knees.

"Do you have eczema?" I ask. Clearly her sympathetic nervous system has caused her blood vessels to dilate. The best way for me to figure out the cause is by process of elimination. I am not good with social niceties, but I know enough not to ask outright if I've embarrassed her.

"That's random. No. Why?"

"No reason." Ha! Another lie. I'm getting good at this. "I like that expression. *Eat your feelings.* I keep a list of idioms. I'll have to add that one."

"You're an idiom," she says, and at first my stomach drops—she is making fun of me—but then I look up and see she's wearing a friendly smile. *This is good teasing,* I think. This is banter, like in the old romantic comedies my mother likes to watch. I've never been much good at banter, which necessarily requires quick wit and an understanding of what to say next.

"Thank you very much for that," I say. And then it's my turn to blush. No need to go through a process of elimination. I know what caused it.

I watch a lot of movies, mostly as sociological research but also because I have a lot of time to fill, and what I've gleaned from them is that teenagers are supposed to actively dislike their parents. We should ask to be dropped a block away from school and on Saturday nights complain about our curfews. We should steal from our parents' liquor cabinets, get drunk in parking lots with our friends, and make stupid decisions that lead to avoidable car accidents. We should get particularly annoyed when our mother or father asks us questions about anything involving the future or planning.

One benefit to being different is that none of the above appeal to me. My parents did a terrible job of naming me, and my mom takes, on average, an extra thirteen minutes more than necessary to buy toothpaste. My father tends to give long lectures on topics I only have a marginal interest in, like traffic patterns and ornithology, and Miney left me behind to go to college, but I like my family. I actually look forward to our after-school discussions.

"How was your day?" my mom says today, as she does every day when I get home from school. She puts a lasagna in the oven. Today is Tuesday, which is a pasta day. Lasagna is broadening the category a bit, but my dad and I try to be flexible. Tuesday also means that I have a guitar lesson, which I love even more than I hate my teacher, Trey, which is to say a lot, and that later I will do sixty-three minutes of martial arts training.

"Kit sat at my lunch table again."

"No shit," my mom says. "Seriously?"

"Seriously," I say, and let her *no shit* pass without comment, even though she knows it's an expression I do not like. It makes me think of constipation, which makes me think about grunting, my least favorite noise, after squawking and chewing. I also have a list of favorite noises. It has one item on it: Kit's laugh.

"Did you talk? Did you take off your headphones?"

"Of course." My conversation with Kit is another Notable Encounter, a *positive* Notable Encounter, so pleasant that I don't want to put it in my notebook. I want to pretend, for just a moment, that this is not a rare occurrence, that this sort of thing happens to me all the time. That I'm not the sort of person who even requires a notebook in the first place. "I know she thinks I'm weird, but it's like she appreciates my weirdness. Like you guys, and Miney sometimes. Does that make sense?"

I ask this question a lot—*Does that make sense?*—usually to my family, because I appreciate clarity and assume others do as well. Much like ordering steak and naming children, language seems inherently and irrationally optimistic; we just assume other people understand what we are talking about. That we are, as the idiom goes, on the same wavelength. In my experience, we are not.

"Total sense. I can see you being friends with Kit, actually. She's always been a nice kid. She used to come to all your birthday parties when you were little. Did you know that?"

"No, though I'm not sure which birthday parties you attend

when you're little is a fair reflection of your future character." My mother doesn't sigh—she's good at suppressing the impulse—but if Miney were here that's exactly what she'd do. I've gotten better at hearing myself lately, I think. If she did sigh, I'd have deserved it. "I mean, you're right. She's nice."

"And freakishly smart, like you," my mom says.

"Not sure the word *freakish* applies in any way to Kit. She's exceedingly normal."

"And pretty," my mom says.

Pretty doesn't fit Kit.

It's too small a word. Like her name.

"Not pretty," I correct her. "Beautiful."

Trey's on time, like usual, since he knows I don't like when people are late. He's wearing what he always wears: a conch shell on a leather string around his neck that he got in "Bali, man," a ratty T-shirt with either a slogan (JUST DO IT!) or a platitude (YOLO!), and flip-flops, even though it's winter. He's a student at Princeton, but he looks nothing like the guys on the cover of the university brochure he once brought over for me. He does not wear khakis or belts or a blazer, and he's not white. I once asked him what he was, and, after he explained that was a rude question, he said a quarter Chinese, a quarter Indian (Southeast Asian, not Native American), and half African American. Kit's half Indian, but she looks nothing like Trey, which is just another example of why genetics is such a fascinating field.

"How's things, buddy?" Trey asks after we run through a few finger-warming exercises. I realize this is what people call small talk. I also realize the world would be a better place without it.

And why call me buddy? We are not friends. We are teacher and student.

"Fine," I say, and motion to the guitar to keep us on track. Maybe Trey has ADD. I should look up the diagnostic criteria in my *DSM*.

"So hear me out," he says, and I groan, because this is the thing about Trey, who, oddly enough, is the only person in my life who seems to have the exact right name: He's a kick-ass guitar teacher, but he doesn't stop at teaching me guitar, and I wish he'd learn to stick to his job. He likes to lecture about life and give me pointers for my notebook and "challenge" me to do things I'm not comfortable with. Like talk to someone new each week (which I did, finally, but I might keep that to myself because I don't want to give him the satisfaction). Or ask to borrow a pen from a classmate (which doesn't even make sense, since we all use laptops). Or join the Academic League (which seems to be a running theme in my life).

So hear me out is code for *I'm about to ask you to do something you don't want to do*. I'm not usually good at understanding subtext, but Trey keeps things pretty simple. "There's this showcase I'm doing."

"No," I say.

"You don't even know what I'm going to say."

"No," I say again. "Let's work on 'Stairway.'"

"I want you to perform."

"No."

"It's at a café. Totally low-pressure situation, and a bunch of my other students will also be there."

"Nope. Not going to happen."

"David, this will be good for you. And I think you'll like the others. They're all a lot like you."

"Like me . . . how?" I ask, because even though I don't know what he means, I still don't like where this is going.

He pauses. Strokes his chin, which is hairless. A total Trey gesture, which I've imitated a few times in the mirror. It did not suit me.

"They're all cool. And maybe a little shy. Not the type of people to feel comfortable doing a showcase."

"Logic dictates that we shouldn't do one, then," I say, and play a quick riff to let him know the conversation is over.

Later, when I practice my daily krav maga, instead of using my go-to fantasy that I've been jumped in the street by a gang of thugs who mistake me for a rival gang member—admittedly an unrealistic story, since I do not live in a place known for its drug wars—I let myself picture someone stealing Kit's purse on Main Street. In my mind, I chase down the culprit and neutralize him with a swift groin kick and then an uppercut elbow. True, in krav maga you are supposed to avoid confrontation and attack only in self-defense, but tonight I allow myself this exception. As I sweat and kick and punch, over and over again, I get to picture Kit's face, her cheeks pink, just like they were at lunch today. But instead of signaling embarrassment, this time she's signaling pride.

CHAPTER 6

KIT

Violet and Annie are waiting for me outside the computer lab after school, and they have that look on their faces that I've come to think of as faux pity: eyebrows scrunched up, concern dripping from their half smiles, like they're about to stage an intervention. Or like they are human emojis, premanufactured to send a particular message.

Or maybe it's real pity. I can't tell. Either way, I don't like the way it makes me feel.

Reminders everywhere.

"Hey," I say. I keep it casual. Pretend I haven't broken many of the unspoken rules of our friendship or that I don't know what's coming. I've ignored their calls and texts. I defected from our lunch table without explanation or reason. I never did give Violet my opinion on her high-waisted jeans. "What's up?"

"I think we should talk," Annie says, and though she's

trying to be nice, I get the sense that underneath she's pissed off but that she knows she's not allowed to be. My dad dying is the world's best and worst get-out-of-jail-free card. Violet puts an arm around my shoulder, and I try my best not to flinch. I don't want that kind of hug—a *buck up, camper* half hug—but I play along. I blink back the first sting of tears.

Violet's dressed in her usual über-preppy uniform: a button-down shirt with a collar, her blond hair kept off her face with a brain-squeezing headband and twisted into a complicated braid that rests on one shoulder. She looks like a J.Crew model. She's basically the whitest person I've ever met. Annie's white too—Mapleview is not a particularly diverse place; the default here is white—but she's less overtly white, if that makes sense. She's not at all preppy like Violet, and her parents don't golf at an exclusive country club or try to casually mention something about India or a random Indian person they know every time they talk to my mom. Annie's parents are liberal Jews who met while working for the Peace Corps in Kathmandu. They seem to understand that the world is a big, diverse place, and that different is not the same thing as scary. It's amazing to me how many people mistake the two.

If I hadn't known Violet since we were in the fourth grade, when her family first moved to Mapleview from Connecticut, I'd never have guessed that she and I would be best friends. The thing is, stiff collars and twee belts and subtly racist parents who have mastered the art of the micro-aggression notwithstanding, Violet's actually pretty gooey inside. She's the first to let me know if I have something caught in my teeth or stuck to my shoe. She writes long, inside-joke-filled messages in my yearbook in pink and purple ink. When Violet first heard about the accident, she drove straight over to my house and waited on my front stoop until my mom and I got home, and then she hugged me before I even had a chance to get out of the car. She's been doing everything right, been following the Best Friend Handbook to the letter. It's not her fault that I suddenly don't know how to talk to my friends. That I'd almost prefer it if they got pissed at me instead.

My friendship with Annie and Violet has always worked because we balance each other out. Annie's clashing prints and crazy jumpsuits, clothes perfectly aligned with her personality. Without her, I'm pretty sure we would spend every Saturday night in Violet's basement eating Oreos and vicariously party-going via Instagram. Annie makes us live bigger lives, which of course are still of Mapleview dimensions, which is to say very, very small. But, you know, still bigger than they would be otherwise.

"You guys, this whole lunch thing doesn't rise to the level of needing a 'talk.' I've just been a little MIA," I say, and use this opportunity to shift my backpack to the other shoulder, a way to dislodge Violet's arm without being rude. "I've just been busy."

Annie's been the source of my entire social life since elementary school. She's the reason we spend most afternoons at the Pizza Palace as satellites to planets Justin and Gabriel; she's the reason we have front-of-the-caf seating; she's the reason we get invited to actual parties. In my world, there's no such thing as busy without her.

"WTF?" Annie asks. She sometimes speaks in Text, a habit I just can't get behind.

In my head, I respond in kind: *OMG FML TTYL.*

"Annie, chill," Violet says.

"Sorry, I don't mean it that way," Annie says, giving me another one of those winces, as if she's doing something painful, like getting her eyebrows waxed. "I'm worried about you, Kit. You should talk to us. We're your best friends."

"I just need a little space," I say. "It's obviously not you guys, it's me."

"Why are you talking like you're breaking up with us? *It's not you, it's me. I need space.*" Annie laughs, trying to lighten the mood. As if she can turn my words into a joke, and we can giggle our way out of this one.

I almost say: *OTT.*

I almost say: *Laughs need to be earned now.*

I almost say: *Please just stop.*

I almost say: *I'm sorry.*

"It's so not a big deal. It's *lunch,*" I say.

"Kit means she's having a tough time. Because of everything," Violet says. I shake off my irrational annoyance at her euphemism. *Everything* is obviously my dad being dead. Why can't she just say that instead?

Even when the doctor came out of the emergency room to break the news to my mom and me, he used what my English teacher likes to call "purple prose." *We've lost him,* he said. *He's gone.* Like my dad was a credit card left behind at the supermarket or a puppy that slipped out the front door.

Yesterday, David just said the words right out loud. The unvarnished, ugly truth.

"Duh. That's why you have friends in the first place. So we can help you," Annie says. I look at her, wonder how she defines helping. Probably by trying to revive the old Kit. The pre-*everything* Kit. But that's impossible. The old Kit is as dead as my father.

We lost her, I think. *She's gone.*

50

"This isn't healthy. The way you're shutting us out," Annie says.

"Healthy," I repeat back in a flat tone, because suddenly I don't know what that word means. What does *healthy* have to do with how I'm feeling? The sort of unimaginable pain that makes it hard for me to get from one moment to the next? I know we've only been standing here for minutes, but it feels like hours or days. Time has turned interminable and impenetrable, something to be endured and passed through, however possible. Health isn't a factor. This can't be fixed with talking or green juice. Everything will not be fixed by a forty-eight-hour cleanse.

I wish I could say all this out loud, but I can't. I don't know how.

"Girls!" Mr. Galto, the newspaper adviser, calls to us from inside the classroom, sighing the sigh of teachers immemorial. As if we are difficult inmates instead of AP honors students. "If you want a chance at editor in chief, you better get yourselves in here."

Since I'm not gifted athletically or musically or anything -ically, I've been gunning for the EIC position for forever. Violet and Annie both want it too. It's how girls like us pad our college applications without having to sweat or join marching band. Today is the day we officially put ourselves up for nomination. I've missed a few deadlines lately, but I'm hoping my get-out-of-jail-free card extends to extracurriculars.

"Please," I say to Annie and Violet, which is the worst word I could have used, because that look is back. Real pity this time. I can see it through my grief haze.

"Please what?" Annie asks, her voice so gentle that it almost breaks me. Annie is not supposed to be gentle. Annie is supposed to be aggressive and sometimes a little mean because she's the only one of us who takes risks and gets shit done.

Annie is supposed to tell me to get over it and stop wallowing, and maybe we could have a fight about that—about how little she understands what's going on with me right now—since anything would be better than this.

My lower lip starts to quiver, and I realize that if I stand here for one more second I will burst into tears, right in the hallway. Just after the last bell. When there's maximum foot traffic.

Nope. Not going to cry here. Not going to happen.

"Last chance!" Mr. Galto calls from inside the room.

I do the only thing I can. I split. I throw away almost three whole years of work on the newspaper and my one shot at editor in chief.

I sprint down the hall.

When I finally get to my car, which I realize as soon as I get in is the last place in the world I want to be, I crank the windows wide open and blast the air conditioner. I turn up the radio. The tears don't come.

I'm too shaken to put the car into drive. Instead I sit and stare at the clock on the dashboard, marvel at how the numbers stay still.

"Please, please, please," I whisper again and again and again, an empty chant, because I still don't know what I'm begging for.

The landline—which has an actual spiral cord and is attached to the wall, like this is the eighteenth century or something—rings. Our *just in case of an emergency* phone that my dad insisted we install even though we each have our own cell. That's how he was. Every year, in celebration of *his* birthday, he'd change the batteries in our fire alarm and carbon monoxide detector. In the event of a Category 6 hurricane or a zombie apocalypse, we have a kit in our basement full of dried meats and canned foods and gallons of water. And on the fridge, there's a laminated card with the number for poison control, even though I'm sixteen and unlikely to accidentally swallow a dishwashing gel pack.

"You never know," he used to say. "You just never know. Unimaginably bad stuff happens."

My dad was orphaned in his early twenties. Both of my paternal grandparents died of cancer within a year of each other. Bone for my grandfather, breast for my grandmother Katherine, my namesake.

"Alliterative cancers," my dad would joke. "A freak thing."

It never occurred to me to think about what losing both of his parents must have been like. What it cost him to be forced to speak so casually about it to me, who was so stupid, who had never before weighed the magnitude of forever. Who laughed at the juxtaposition of the words *alliterative* and *cancer* like that was such a clever thing for him to say.

My mom told me that my father totally changed after his parents died. He stopped drinking beer with his buddies, put away his electric guitar, and cut his nineties-grunge hair. He started taking their relationship, which they'd both assumed was just a college fling, more seriously. He applied to dental school, despite having no particular passion for teeth or gums or the diagnosis of gingivitis. Practically overnight, he graduated to adulthood. He picked stability and practicality over passion.

Now I think about the box that my dad so carefully created for me—not just the one in the basement, but this safe town, this house with an alarm system, this family of three—and how it did nothing to protect us after all. Those were just things my dad did to make himself feel better. I realize we all walk around pretending we have some control over our fate, because to recognize the truth—that no matter what we do, the bottom will fall out when we least expect it—is just too unbearable to live with.

The phone rings again, and I jump, like I'm in a horror movie. I'm equally scared to answer and not answer.

"Kitty?" It's Uncle Jack, my dad's best friend and my godfather. He was my dad's freshman-year college roommate, the best man at my parents' wedding, and a frequent houseguest over the past year since his wife left him. Last month he added the job of executor of my father's estate.

"What's wrong?" I ask, because this is the *in case of emergency* phone. It is used to report *emergencies*.

"Nothing. Everything's fine. Well, not fine, but you know. Is your mom around, by any chance? I called her office and they said she wasn't in." My mom left for work as usual this morning, looking even better than yesterday.

"Sorry. Not home."

I've known Uncle Jack my entire life—the "uncle" being an Indian honorific we use out of respect even though he's not technically family (or Indian, for that matter). He used to pull pennies out from behind my ear, bend his thumb so it looked like it split in two. He came to my eighth-grade graduation ceremony just because he wanted to see me cross the stage. He has been saying the same thing in different ways for the past month, and I don't want to hear it again. *It was just a freak thing.*

I think about how the police told us about the malfunctioning traffic light (there was a work order to fix it later in the week), that when they administered a Breathalyzer about two hours after the accident the other driver was under the legal limit. That there was no crime here. Nothing to prosecute. I think of the way the other car plowed through the intersection into my dad. Literally. *Into* my dad. That's what killed him: the impact.

My mom doesn't know that the day after he died, when she was taking a Xanax nap, I took a cab to the junkyard to see for myself what was left of the car. I needed to make it feel real. To have evidence that my father was in fact dead. Not lost, like the doctor said, not just waiting somewhere else for us to find him.

There was nothing to see but Volvo origami. I took a picture, but it felt no more real than before. The accident was a blank. A story that was told to us about characters we did not know, lives we did not care about. But there was the car and my father was dead and I was not.

I was not.

I never got to meet my father's parents, my other grandparents, and if I ever have kids they will not get to know my dad. If I one day walk down an aisle, my dad will not be standing next to me. At graduation, it will be just my mom in the audience watching. Every happy moment from now on will have the lingering, bitter, heartbreaking aftertaste of loss.

"It was just a freak thing," Jack says, right on cue.

It's wrong that his words so precisely echo my father's. He uses the same empty refrain. For the first time I hear the lie implicit in them. Realize how the freakishness does nothing to lessen the reality. It's a misdirection. It's a verbal sleight of hand.

Not the truth. Not truth at all.

That night, my mom comes into my room to tuck me in, something she hasn't done in a long time, maybe years. These days we've been falling asleep mid-activity, stuffed with too much takeout. We just keep going until our bodies shut off.

"Sweetie?" My mom sits next to me on my bed, which makes the covers too tight across my neck. I don't ask her to shift over. I've taken four Advil to get rid of this unidentifiable feeling, a shaky emptiness, but Advil doesn't treat whatever this is. "I ran into Violet's mom today on the train."

"Yeah? She mention curry?" I ask, as if I have no idea what's coming next. Of course it was only a matter of time before one of my friends said something to their mom and their mom said something to my mom. Like how we used to play the game telephone as kids and whisper secrets from ear to ear.

My mom laughs at my nonjoke.

"Not this time. But she said that Violet told her you haven't been sitting with the girls at lunch." My mom smoothes down my hair, which is two shades lighter than hers. I've always wanted to color mine dark brown so we could match.

When I was little, I was convinced that my mom was actually a superhero. That Mandip Lowell was just a secret identity; that every night, after I went to sleep, she'd spend her evenings fighting crime, kicking bad guys with a loud *hi-yah!* Now I think she could totally play one of those too-pretty cops on a network television drama. The kind that sprint down dead-end alleys on a studio set. Prop gun raised and pointed: *Stop or I'll shoot.*

She's tough, my mother. And she can run in heels.

Though let's be honest. She's much more likely to be cast as a terrorist or a head-wagging taxi driver or a convenience store clerk. We don't often get to see people who look *and* sound like her on television.

"It's no big deal, Mom. I just needed a little space." She nods like she gets it. And maybe she does.

"I can't stand the thought of you sitting alone."

"I've been sitting with this guy, David Drucker? He's okay."

"David Drucker? Amy's son? He used to be an odd duck." She tugs at my hair with her finger and it springs right back into a wave. No doubt my mother is disappointed when she looks at me, her only child. Beautiful women are supposed to have beautiful daughters. At the very least, I bet she thought I'd turn out "exotic," an obnoxious word that every biracial person has heard like a million times. Though in my case, it's never really applied. My parents' features have come together to form someone easily forgettable. My skin is just brown enough that in this superwhite suburb, people sometimes are rude enough to ask me, "What are you?" They seem disappointed when I don't say Latina, which is everyone's first guess. Like figuring out my ethnicity is some sort of fun game.

"You used to go to David's birthday parties when you were little," my mom says.

"He's still totally weird, but it turns out he might be good-weird, you know?" I look at my mom and think about how there are no brown superheroes and about the fact that I'm probably too chubby to be on television. Maybe I should straighten my hair. Darken it too. Spend a little bit more time in the sun. That way my mom and I could look more alike. Without my father standing next to us, we don't make that much sense together.

I want to tell her David was Dad's patient, but I can't say that word out loud: *Dad*.

"Really? So you want to start playing with David again?" My mom raises her eyebrows.

"It's not like that."

"Is he still cute?"

I find myself smiling up at the ceiling in the dark. And I

57

almost laugh out loud, because of all the guys in my school, of all the guys in the whole wide world, I'm thinking about David Drucker. The oddest of ducks.

He is cute.

Sort of.

But he's still David Drucker.

"Any port in a storm, my love. Any port in a storm," my mom says, and laughs.

CHAPTER 7

DAVID

I cross my fingers. Childish, yes. And of course irrational. I am not superstitious. I don't believe in made-up things like fate. I believe in science. In what we can see and feel and calculate with well-calibrated instruments. Still, three days in a row of Kit sitting at my table seems like the probability equivalent of flipping a coin a hundred times and consistently getting heads. That sort of thing just doesn't happen.

No doubt I said something accidentally offensive yesterday, as I'm prone to do, and we will no longer be friends, if you can classify sitting together twice and talking in the bleachers as friendship. I do, of course, but I'm sure Kit has a higher tipping point. I recounted our conversation verbatim to Miney, and she said that under no circumstances should I ever talk about a girl's weight again, even if they bring it up first. She was so adamant about this that she made me put it in the Rules section of my notebook.

As a corollary, there is also only one correct answer when a girl poses the question *Do I look fat?*

That answer is no.

Which is why I cross my fingers, hoping against hope that I haven't ruined things already and that, despite all evidence to the contrary, wanting something can actually will it to happen. Five minutes into our lunch period, just as my optimism dissipates, there she is, Kit Lowell, walking directly toward my table. Maybe soon *our* table, though I don't know how many times we'll have to sit together for the plural possessive to be appropriate.

"I took notes for you in physics yesterday," I say as she takes out today's lunch, which is leftover Indian takeout. Hopefully from Star of Punjab, which is the second-highest-rated Indian place on Yelp in Mapleview. My dad and I both refuse to patronize the number-one-ranked Curryland, despite the statistical significance of the additional seven five-star reviews in their favor, because as a rule we avoid restaurants that rely on a theme, especially one as nonsensical as pretending that each customer is a tourist in a mythical place called Curryland.

"Thanks," she says, scooping both rice and a piece of naan onto her plate. A double serving of carbohydrates, which is a bad idea if she is, as she suggested yesterday, worried about gaining weight. I keep this observation to myself. *Thank you, Miney.*

"I don't usually take notes, and I bet your friends did it for you too, but I figured mine would be better," I say. She frowns at me, a common expression of displeasure, and I wonder where I've gone wrong. I've also made an outline for her for AP English Lit and AP World History, but Miney said not to offer these up unless she asks for them. I don't want to be "over the top," whatever that means.

60

"Holy crap, you don't kid around," Kit says as she looks at my notes, which include elaborate three-dimensional drawings for each step of our lab experiment with potassium permanganate, and just like that her face transforms. A smile. Which means I've made her happy. "These must have taken you forever. They're beautiful. For reals."

"Not forever. Approximately seventy-six minutes."

"These aren't physics notes. This is art. Seriously, you didn't have to do this."

"Seriously, I wanted to," I say.

"Well, thank you. Seriously," she says.

More *banter*, which may be my new favorite word.

"Star of Punjab?" I ask.

"Yup. I don't like Curryland. It's like Indian food for idiots," Kit says. I am grinning, but I can't help it. "Want some?"

I nod, even though I don't like to share food. Kit looks perfectly healthy, robust even, and anyhow she'd be worth getting sick for, presuming I don't catch something that lingers, like mononucleosis. At my house, my dad is the one who does most of the cooking, with the exception of Tuesday's pasta night, since my mother is Italian. I wonder if Dentist was interested in the culinary arts, which would explain Kit's family's recently acquired affinity for takeout. She used to eat only sandwiches, though I sat too far away from her old table to decipher what kind.

"You'd probably be surprised to learn that I'm a very good chef. I can make this," I say, pointing to the chicken tikka.

"Really? My mom keeps promising she'll teach me how to cook one day, but she never has the time. How'd you learn?" She leans forward, resting her chin on her hand. Her elbows are twenty centimeters from mine. Our knees are even closer. Better measured in millimeters. I wish I could take out my tape measure, because it would feel good to fix an exact number to the distance. A measurement that I could then write on a piece of paper and put in my pocket and take out on days when I needed the reassurance of a number.

"I like science. Gastronomy seemed a natural extension." I don't mention that I also cook to help out at home sometimes, especially with Miney away, because teen movies have made clear that it's not cool to help out your parents. Which makes little sense to me, as does everything else about the word *cool*.

"Please don't take this the wrong way, but you're so weird," she says. I look at her, or at least her chin, and discover that an offhand comment by Kit can disrupt my respiration. "But good-weird, you know?"

Good-weird.

Good-weird is what I've been telling myself I am for years, when being just plain weird was too much of a burden to carry. *Good-weird* is the only solution to the problem, when normal isn't a viable option. *Good-weird* may very well be the opposite of cool, but I've never aspired to cool. At least not the version of it I'm familiar with.

"Thank you."

"Speaking of weird, I have a random question for you. What can you tell me about quantum mechanics?" Kit asks, and a shiver makes its way from the bottom of my spine all the way to the top.

Miney suggested that I think up some small-talk ideas in case Kit came back to my table today.

Top of my list?

Quantum mechanics.

It's almost enough to make me reconsider the entire concept of fate.

Maybe it's because my brain is so saturated with Kit that I forget to keep my head down and my eyes trained on the floor. I have my headphones on, of course, but my volume is turned lower than usual, because unlike usual, I don't want to drown out my thoughts with sound. I want to dwell on lunch today, to replay Kit's *Well, thank you. Seriously,* over and over again. Her smile too. How our conversation went back and forth, specific and precise, leaving little room for misunderstanding.

"David! David!" José says, and waves his hands in my face so I have no choice but to stop and pause the music on my phone. This encounter will throw me off schedule, which means that there is little chance of Symphony no. 36 in C ending just as I slip into my seat in physics. Damn it.

JOSÉ GUTIERREZ: Glasses. Brown hair, center-parted. Unibrow. Second-smartest kid in school, after me.

Notable Encounters

Ninth grade: Wanted to borrow my notes after he was out sick with the flu. I gave them to him, and he said, "Thank you," and I said, "Well, I assume if I'm sick, I can borrow yours, though I don't really get sick," and he said, "Everyone gets sick. It's basic biology." And I said, "I mean, I really don't get sick often," and he said, "Okay."

Friends

Aaron C. because they run Physics Club together.

"David!" José says for a third time, though by now it's obvious he has gotten my attention.

"Please don't ask me to join the Academic League again. You've asked me twenty-six times already and I've said no twenty-six times." I volunteer this information.

"Twenty-seven times, actually. This will be twenty-eight," José says, and inexplicably remains standing in front of me, blocking my way. "Will you please join the team?"

"No," I say. Had it been twenty-seven times? It's unlike me to miscount. Math is not my chosen field—I'm more interested in the sciences—but I like accuracy.

"We need you. There's a big meet coming up against Ridgefield Tech, and they are really good. Name the mathematician who proved the infinitude of prime numbers."

"Duh. Euclid."

"See. You'd be perfect."

"Did you know Einstein said the definition of insanity is doing the same thing over and over again and expecting a different result?" I ask.

"I've heard the quote, but Einstein didn't say it. In fact, most of the quotes attributed to him in nonscientific contexts are misattributed."

"Really?"

"Yup. And I've thought about it, and realized that since each time I ask you it's one more time than the last time, it's not doing the exact same thing over and over again, and so there is, at least, a small possibility of a different result. Hence, I'm not insane. At least not because of this." José delivers his monologue to my left shoulder. "Also, do you believe in the multiverse?"

I blame Kit and her asking me about quantum mechanics and making me think anything can happen, because for a second I imagine it: me up on a stage and Kit in the audience, me answering question after question, saving Mapleview from

64

defeat at the hands of Ridgefield Tech. Kit impressed by my vast knowledge of thermodynamics and aroused by the size of the trophy I'll invariably take home. When talking trophies, size totally matters.

"Yes and yes," I say.

"Yes you'll join the team *and* yes you believe in the multiverse?"

"Yes," I say again, and then José smiles and I realize I have something new to add to his description in my notebook. How could I have not noticed until today that he wears braces with pink fluorescent rubber bands? I hope that distraction doesn't affect my performance.

Later, after school, I watch Kit walk to her red Corolla. Her hand shakes as she takes out her electronic key fob to open the lock. It's not that cold out, so I assume this tremor is most likely due to anxiety. We have two tests tomorrow, world history and English literature, and she missed yesterday's classes. I was relieved to see that she didn't flee campus again today. Things are better when she's at school, just across the room, no farther than fourteen feet away. I liked her being there even before she started talking to me.

I consider calling out. Breaking Miney's rule. My notes *would* be helpful, and certainly superior to whatever her friends have passed along. But no. Miney knows what she's talking about. Better to rely on the laws of comparative advantage and outsource my social decisions.

"Hey!" Kit calls out, and I look behind me to see who she's talking to. Probably Justin or Gabriel. "No, dummy. You!"

"Me?" I ask. I examine the context of our interaction. She's not being literal. *Dummy* may even qualify as a term of endearment here.

"Yeah. You need a ride home?"

My car, a 2009 Honda Civic hatchback with 93,875 miles, is parked, as it is every day, two rows over and six spaces behind hers. Spot number eighty-nine. I don't need Miney to know what the right call is here.

It's not even a real lie. People use the words *want* and *need* interchangeably all the time.

"Yes, please," I say. "I need a ride."

"Explain again the theory that consciousness survives death? Because that doesn't sound like science to me. That sounds a lot like religion," Kit says, checking that my seat belt is fastened before pulling out of the lot. She drives with her hands gripped at ten and two, and she flicks her attention to her rearview mirror every five seconds, as suggested by the guide handed out by the DMV. My mom, who taught both me and Miney to drive, would be impressed.

"Basically, the gist is that our brain is the repository of our feelings, thoughts, desires," I say, and blush. I wish I hadn't used that word: *desire*. "It's the in-box of our consciousness. And when we die and that physicality erodes, our consciousness may still live on."

Her eyebrows knit, and she leans forward farther over the wheel. I wonder how long I could watch her think without getting bored. I estimate at least thirty-nine minutes.

"The duality between body and mind mirrors that of the relationship between wave and particle, which leads modern quantum physicists to posit that the mind is ruled by the same quantum mechanic rules as particles, like it's a physical object," I say. I wonder for a moment if I'm right. I find this whole area fascinating, but it's a little slippery. One second it's clear in my brain—I can see it, the three-dimensionality of the theory laid out in front of me in pictures—and then a moment later, it's gone.

"My dad told me you talked to him about this stuff when you came in for an appointment. Is this what you guys discussed? Whether consciousness survives death?" she asks. If I had thought that what I said in Dentist's chair would get back to Kit, I would have been much more careful with my words. Maybe even strategic. Isn't there some sort of doctor-patient confidentiality? I know she thinks I'm weird. Good-weird, maybe, but still: weird. I don't need her to think I'm a dork too.

"Not really. We talked about a new quantum theory about the flow of time. I can tell you all about that too if you want."

"Nah, it's okay. My dad was always interested in random stuff. Like he had this collection of antique microscopes and magnifying glasses. And he loved art books, so our house is full of them. He was totally obsessed with meteorology and the Weather Channel and those tiny plants. Bonsais. That's what they're called. Anyhow, I'm rambling. My point is, he mentioned you to me and he liked you." I stare out the window as we drive down Main Street. Though still cold, it's sunny today, and people are out with strollers and dogs, their winter jackets on but unzipped.

There's too much to look at. Too many colors and people and shapes. Babies in fleece hats. Signs advertising one-day sales. An old-fashioned revolving barber pole. I turn my attention back to Kit and focus.

"The feeling was mutual." I picture Dentist, that bright light he wore on his forehead and how he always smelled like latex because of his rubber gloves. I'd have loved to discuss meteorology with him, as my own knowledge in that area is rudimentary at best. "Who knows? Maybe the physicists are right and he's not gone. I mean, of course your father's dead, but I think it's comforting to believe or at least hope that a small part of him, actually the most important part of him, his *consciousness,* may be out there somehow."

"Yeah, it is," she says.

"But it still sucks that you'll never ever be able to see him again. I mean, consciousness is not the same thing as him continuing to be your dad. Obviously that would have been the preferable outcome."

She snorts. I have no idea what that means. Whatever way it falls, a snort does not feel neutral.

"You sure tell it like it is. Not many people do that, you know."

"Yeah."

"Everyone tiptoes around me these days. Even my mom. Your brutal honesty is . . . bizarrely refreshing."

I tell her to turn right, that my house is up at the corner. She pulls into my driveway, and now there is nothing left to do but get out of the car.

"Thanks for the ride."

"Anytime," she says, and I want to ask what she means by that. If it's a real offer or just a courtesy. The English language, like all languages, is full of frustrating ambiguity. Well, except, of course, for Loglan, which was derived from mathematical principals of logic to avoid just this sort of confusion. Honestly, we'd all be better off if we spoke that instead.

Once inside the house, I watch from my front window as Kit's car retreats. The distance grows between us exponentially, and I wait there, hands on the glass, until I no longer have a sense of its measurement.

Ten minutes later, my mom drives me the five miles back to school to pick up my car.

She smiles the whole way there.

CHAPTER 8

KIT

To: Kit
From: Mom
Subject: The Five Stages of Everything Sucks

It's the middle of the night. Just stumbled across this attached article re the five stages of grief:

1. Denial
2. Anger
3. Bargaining
4. Depression
5. Acceptance

Of course BACON should totally be number one on this list. Also, I've decided I'm skipping over the first three steps and heading straight for DEPRESSION. You with me?

You should really text like a normal person. Who emails anymore? Things this list is missing: Chocolate. Netflix binges. Pajamas.

As for depression, already beat you to it. Sure am #livingmybestlife

....

"Hey!" Gabriel says when I walk in to the Pizza Palace. He is overly excited, as if I didn't just sit behind him in calc less than two hours ago. Like we are in the arrivals hall of a large international airport and I'm just back from a yearlong trip around the world. He lets go of Justin, who he has in a headlock, to envelop me in a big hug.

"Hey, guys," I say, and move my lips in the way I think approximates a smile. It requires complicated muscle coordination. More exhausting than that time Violet made me try Pilates.

I look over and Violet jumps out of the booth, runs over to me. Annie gives me a Brownie salute, which is one of our inside jokes, and I see I've won her over just by showing up. That makes me smile for real, and then the smiling makes me tear up, so I stop doing it.

"You came!" Violet says.

"I can't stay long." As soon as the words slip out, I realize they are true. After dropping David off, being alone in the car felt unbearable, and the Pizza Palace was closer than home. Since the accident, my mom has been making me drive at every opportunity. She claims she doesn't want me to develop a life-long phobia, and I guess her plan is mostly working. Still, when I'm alone in the car, I flinch at passing SUVs, and I'm way too aware of how fast all the other traffic is going, how thin the line is between us, how easily one mistake can kill us all.

Cars are terrible, powerful, destructive machines. Maybe sixteen-year-olds shouldn't be allowed to drive them. Maybe no one should.

Now, here with everyone, I feel no better than I did on the ride over. I'm sweaty around my friends lately, like socializing is a form of cardio but without the postexercise endorphins or smugness. I need to beg my body to push through this.

"Can't believe you ditched newspaper yesterday," Annie says. "After all that work, you're just going to throw away the chance at editor in chief?"

I shrug, and Gabriel uses that as an opportunity to start massaging my shoulders.

"You look tight," he says. For about five minutes last year, Gabriel and I were together. One of those stupid things that happen because you find yourselves in the corner of a room at a party where everyone is drunk. He kissed me suddenly, like a bird swooping to pick garbage from a can, and after I recovered from the surprise attack, I kissed him back. That Monday, he held my hand in the hallway at school, and then we made out again later in the 7-Eleven parking lot in between taking sips of our Slurpees. Two weeks later, he broke it off, said something about us being better off as friends, which was fine by me. I wasn't particularly into Gabriel, but it was fun having someone to kiss and hold hands with. Having, for just a little while, a pleasant distraction.

Now, though, I'd really like him to stop touching my shoulders. In fact, I wish there were a way to transfer his hands to Annie, who for the past few months has had a secret unexplainable crush on him. She's never said it out loud, but Violet and I know she's hoping he'll ask her to prom. There's nothing wrong with Gabriel on paper, but there isn't really much *there* there. Annie's not the type of girl who should have to settle for pleasant distractions. She's too cool for that.

Jessica, Willow, and Abby burst through the door in a loud explosion of giggles and then stop at the counter to get their Diet Cokes before heading to the back to join us. I don't really like these girls—I have never liked these girls—and yet somehow they are on the periphery of our friend group. Okay, fine, we are actually on the periphery of their friend group, since as a trio, Jessica, Willow, and Abby are by far the most popular girls in the junior class. I have no idea how they've managed to swing it—popularity is an undefinable thing at Mapleview, which as best I can tell involves a whole lot of unearned, effortless confidence and the ability to get other people to look at you for no reason at all.

Jessica is a blonde, Willow is a brunette, and Abby is a redhead, just like every teen friend group on television (except, in this case, sans a sassy black sidekick). Boom! Best friends for life. I assume there's more to their friendship than hair-color optics and an affinity for thong underwear. That taken individually there is the distant possibility they might actually be interesting people. I doubt I will ever know, though, since they travel as a pack.

The reason I don't like them is not because they're walking clichés and therefore like to dabble in being quintessential mean girls, but because their conversations are boring. We live in a small and privileged bubble in Mapleview, and I've never understood their desire to make it seem even smaller.

"Boys," Abby says by way of hello, and the way it rolls off her tongue makes it sound like she is both belittling them and flirting with them at the same time. I practice her intonation in my head, *boys,* file it away for use far, far in the future. Like college. No, that's just a year and a half away. Maybe it will come in handy if I go to graduate school. "And ladies."

The guys act differently when the three of them are around. More nervous, even louder. Gabriel mercifully stops his massage. Justin smiles goofily. He and Jessica used to hook up, but last I heard, she broke it off with him because she's been hanging out with a freshman from NYU. In the world of social climbing, college boy beats high school boy every time. Rumor has it that Justin is still devastated.

"So what's the deal with you and David Drucker?" Willow asks me, and for no good reason I feel my hands curl into fists. Guess I am moving through the five stages of grief after all. Making my designated pit stop at number two: anger.

"Nothing's up. We're friends," I say.

"Come on, you're not *really* friends with David Drucker," Abby says, and sighs dramatically. Like everything I have to say is frustrating. "Sitting at someone's lunch table doesn't make you besties."

"What do you care?" I ask. I'm a little too eager to engage and take them down. Which is stupid. They are my friends, sort of. This is not what I do.

"Of course we don't care," Jessica says, and laughs. And it's true. I'm sure she doesn't care.

"He got in your car today, though," Willow says. "I saw

him." I decide suddenly that I hate Willow the most. She was born with more than her fair share of the same magic Lauren Drucker has, but without the warmth.

"Like I said: We're friends. He's pretty interesting, actually."

"Interesting?" Gabriel asks, though it's in no way a question. Leave it to Gabriel to always go for the easiest response: reflexive, empty sarcasm.

My anger deflates. It's not real anyway. It's just a stupid stage in a stupid article. That's how desperate my mom and I are. We look for guidance from Oprah.com. Too bad there's another step they forgot to list: the sudden onset of not-giving-a-crap-about-anything-ness. What I now think of as astronaut helmet syndrome.

Suddenly I look around and see everyone talking and laughing, no less than two feet in front of me, and they feel miles away. We are all strangers to each other in the end.

Turns out grief not only morphs time, but space too. Somehow increases the distance between you and other people. I should ask David if there's any science behind that idea.

"Whatever. Let's talk about much more important things," Jessica says.

"Right. One word," Willow says.

"Prom," Abby finishes.

Annie quickly glances at Gabriel, but if he notices her looking at him, he doesn't show it.

"Gross," my mom says as she shovels the Weight Watchers version of fettuccine Alfredo into her mouth. Lately, during dinner, we talk in single-word sentences, a shorthand we've adopted because we're too tired for anything more. When I close my eyes at night, the projector in my brain flips on and there it is, right on the ceiling: a repeat loop of a bird's-eye view of the crash. Like it's fun for me watching this imaginary horror film. To stand by and watch the other car—a navy-blue Ford Explorer—plow into my father, on repeat, again and then again. I smell rubber and smoke. Metallic blood, so sharp and recognizable it can't be anything other than what it is. A taste and a smell in one.

Life and its opposite.

I attempt to figure out at what point a foot would have needed to touch the brake for there never to have been a crash at all. As if high-school-level math could, just this once, come in handy.

When I finally do fall asleep, I have a dream about Newton's third law: For every action, there is an equal and opposing reaction. Force against force. The car crushed and disposed of like an empty potato chip bag. Snap, crackle, pop.

Here now, though, it's just my mom and me and the sad sounds of us chewing. And then, inexplicably, there's a key in the lock.

Could the doctor have been right and my dad was just lost? Momentarily misplaced? He will waltz in the door and ruffle my hair and call me Kitty Cat.

Of course that doesn't happen. My dad has not risen from the dead. Even David's ridiculous theory of consciousness doesn't allow for that.

It's just Uncle Jack, the only other *living* person who has a key to our home. Right. Much more logical.

"What are you doing here?" my mom asks. Her tone is sharp and betrays her disappointment.

It's okay, I want to say. *I thought it was going to be Dad too.*

Normally my mom would be happy to see Jack. When he first got divorced, it was my mother's idea to invite him to stay over at our house on the weekends his boys were with Aunt Katie. He was sad then too, and my mom cooked him hearty, comforting breakfasts. Pancakes and eggs and bacon and the good coffee.

"The cure for a broken heart," she'd say. She would serve the food on our good platters, and then the three of them, my mom, Dad, and Jack, would sit at the dining table passing around sections of *The New York Times* while I played with my phone.

"This right here is my definition of heaven," my dad used to say. "My best friend and my two girls and the paper of record."

"You're not answering your cell and I was . . . worried," Jack says, and looks at my mother, but she stares at her gelatinous noodles. Jack's tall and bald and lanky. He wears glasses, big plastic ones that are both dorky and cool at the same time, and swanky suits that look imported from England. He's not good-looking—his nose is too big for his face, his eyes are a little squinty behind his frames, he's a little pasty—but there's something familiar and comforting about him.

"Want some dinner?" I ask, and jump up to check the freezer. "We have a Lean Cuisine."

"You do realize that's not real food, right?" He keeps his tone light, so much lighter than the feeling in the room.

"How about a glass of wine?" my mom asks, suddenly unfreezing, as if her play button has been pushed, and she busies herself getting a bottle out, opening it up, and pouring herself a large glass. She gulps it down. Only then does she pour out two more: another for her and one for Jack.

"Ice cream too," I say, tossing him the pint of mint chocolate chip I find in the freezer. He grabs a spoon from the drawer and digs right in to the container. Uncle Jack hasn't bothered to shave, and his almost-beard is dotted with gray hairs. He looks about as depressed as my mother and I feel.

"How's Evan?" I ask, just to make some conversation. Evan is one of Jack's sons; he's fourteen and also goes to Mapleview. We used to hang out when we were younger, when our families would vacation together before his parents got divorced. Evan and I and his younger brother, Alex, would make sand castles and tackle each other in the ocean, and I used to complain to Auntie Katie that they should have made at least one girl for me to play with. Those trips don't feel real anymore. Like a memory of something I once saw on television.

"Going to junior prom, apparently," Jack says, and smiles.

"That's a big deal for a freshman," I say.

"How about you?"

"Nah, not going." I avoid looking at my mother. I have a feeling my skipping prom falls under the same category as my not sitting with my friends at lunch. It will inspire, at the very least, a discussion.

"Your dad would have wanted you to go. He'd want you to have fun," Jack says. "Not mope around with us old folks."

"Let's not talk about what Robert would have wanted," my mom cuts in, her voice icy and sharp.

"I didn't mean to step on any toes," Jack says softly.

"Then don't."

"Mandi, you can't avoid me forever."

"I can try."

"I'm just doing my job as executor. There's estate stuff we need to take care of. I don't have the authority to—"

"Wow, it's getting late and I actually have a lot of work to do." My mom jumps out of her chair, and just like that she walks out of the room, taking her glass of wine with her.

"I'll help," I say to Jack, after what feels like a long time in which we've both sat here staring at the empty space my mother left behind. "Just tell me what you need and I'll do it."

My voice sounds empty. I'm as useless as I feel. Uncle Jack hands me the pint of ice cream, and the two of us pass it back and forth until it's finished.

CHAPTER 9

DAVID

"Little D!" Miney says, and there she is, at the dinner table, sitting in her seat, which we leave open in her absence out of protocol. Her hair is a little longer, but at least at first glance, she looks pretty much the same. Like my sister. "I'm home!"

Yes, this is obvious, though I refrain from telling her that. From past experience I've learned this is rude. What is not immediately obvious is why she is here. She's not supposed to be home for another forty-nine days, her spring break, which does not in any way overlap with mine. We have already scheduled around this inconvenience. I will skip school on that Tuesday with my parents' permission—they have already agreed to write a note in which they will claim I have an important doctor's appointment—and Miney and I will re-create what we have mutually agreed was the Perfect Day of All the Days Ever. It will involve lunch from Sayonara Sushi, ice cream from Straw, forty-seven minutes at our favorite bookstore, and then a trip down the shore to the aquarium.

"Why are you here?" I ask.

"Some things never change. Always straight to the point," Miney says, and makes a sound that is similar to Kit's snort. A laugh that is not really a laugh but is something wholly unidentifiable by me. Someone should make a YouTube video that identifies the range of female noises, not unlike the ones they have for avid birders. "I just needed a break from school. And I missed you guys."

Though I think it highly unlikely that Miney missed me—I've estimated that I irritate her about eighty percent of the time we spend together—I'm thrilled that she's here. Kit at my lunch table and Miney home on the same day feel like something more than coincidence. A cosmic alignment.

"When are you leaving?" I ask. Departures are easier for me if I have some lead time to prepare and plan, to imagine the befores and afters of the scenario.

"You'll be the first to know when I figure it out. Now, get over here," she says, and stands up and opens her arms for a hug. I'm generally not a fan of displays of affection, but I make an exception for my parents and Miney. Well, really just for my mom and Miney. My dad is more of a thumbs-up kind of guy.

Her arms wrap around me, and I immediately start to look for sneaky changes. Miney's perfume is no longer citrus. Instead it's something sandalwood-based, borderline musty, and her clothes don't smell recently laundered. A chunk of her hair is now purple, and she's added a piercing to the top part of her ear. Her eyes are bloodshot.

She better not have gotten a tattoo. I couldn't handle that.

Miney was perfect the way she was when she left in

September. I don't like that each time she comes home, I need to readjust to a new iteration. I find I have trouble with the purple stripe. It looks like noise.

"Mom says Kit drove you home from school today," she says, which isn't a question, but she somehow makes it sound like one.

"Yup," I say. "We talked all about quantum mechanics."

"Oh my God, D. Have I taught you nothing?" she says.

"You've taught me lots of things. I didn't mention her weight, if that's what you're worried about."

"What are we going to do with you?" she asks, and my stomach clenches. Freshman year, when I would find myself in trouble at school on a biweekly basis, Principal Hoch would pose this question, which is both idiomatic and rhetorical. *What are we going to do with you?* Like I was a group project.

Just once I'd like the answer to be: *nothing.*

Just once I'd like the answer to be: *You are just fine as is.*

Just once I'd like the question not to be asked in the first place.

"Get your notebook," Miney demands, and I pull it out of my bag. I smooth the familiar blue cover, a tic left over from when I needed to look through it hourly. Lately, though, the notebook stays in my bag for longer periods. I can almost imagine a time I won't need it at all. "An opportunity like Kit comes around once in a lifetime, if that."

"Kit is a girl. Though statistically speaking, it is unlikely that she is actually the best girl in the world, it feels that way. No doubt she's the best girl in Mapleview. What Kit is not is an opportunity," I say.

"I'm just saying we have some serious work to do. I'm not letting you blow this."

"That's what she said," I joke. I've been waiting weeks for the chance to use a variation of the "that's what he/she said" thing since I've learned how it's done, and so I can't help but grin when Miney cracks up. Her face looks lighter and softer when she laughs. Her purple hair feels quieter too. The sum of her parts now equals the familiar.

I just wish Miney's eyes weren't bloodshot.

"I was wrong. Maybe some things do change," she says, and ruffles my hair, like I'm a small boy. And though I don't quite understand the reason behind her gesture, I find myself leaning into her hands.

Today, the fourth time Kit sits at my lunch table, she eats a sandwich and an apple. On close inspection, it appears to be hummus and turkey on whole wheat. Her black nail polish is chipped, and her shirt hangs off of her right shoulder, just like one of Miney's, which makes me think this must be a sartorial choice and not a mistake of sizing. She has a bunch of freckles near the center of her clavicle that form a small circle. It's a soft detail, like how her bottom lip pushes out just a millimeter from her top lip, or how when she pushes her hands through her hair, the commas fall forward, as if taking a bow.

Usually people are too bright, too loud, too overpowering. Jessica's blond hair hurts my eyes. Willow's elbows and knees look sharp; when she passes me in the hall, I imagine them cutting me like tiny knives. And Abby, the third girl in their triumvirate and the one who called me a freak the other day, wears so much sickly sweet perfume, I can smell her even before she enters a classroom. But Kit is entirely quiet. She never offends my senses.

"I always thought it was strange that your dad gave out lol-lipops to his patients," I say, and once the words are out I realize I would prefer not to have to talk about Dentist in the past tense. And yet that's what happens with the dead. They get to take no part in the present or the future.

"He only gave them to kids," she says.

"I've never left his office without one," I say, which sounds like a cool line, I think. I don't add that his hygienist, Barbara, always slipped me an extra. That would be bragging. She liked me. Adults generally do. It's fellow teenagers I have a problem with.

"They were sugar-free." *Of course,* I think. I'm embarrassed that this—a dentist giving out lollipops—has confused me for years. What a silly thing to fixate on. And yet I do that. Find a tiny nugget—an inaccuracy or a contradiction—and it niggles at the back of my brain. I don't like open loops. "So you drive yourself to school every day? I saw you in the parking lot this morning."

I don't tell her that we've been in the parking lot at the same time almost every morning since the beginning of the school year. I always arrive at 7:57, which is exactly the amount of time one needs to stop at one's locker, pick up a book or two, and be on time to a first-period class in the north wing. I shouldn't be surprised that she's never noticed me out there before. I seem to fall into one of two extremes for people. To the Justin Chos of the world, I stick out. I'm the equivalent of one of Willow's elbows. Unpleasant and somehow disruptive, even when I don't say a word. For everyone else, I'm mostly invisible. When Kit first sat down at my lunch table, I assumed she didn't notice me there. I'm terrified of the inevitable day when someone acciden-tally sits on my lap.

"Yeah. Why?" I ask.

"Well, I drove you home yesterday." My cheeks warm, and my palms sweat. Damn. It didn't even occur to me that she'd find out I didn't need a ride.

"Right." I scramble for a reasonable explanation. In other words, my nemesis: a good lie. I come up empty. I opt for uncomfortable silence. I look at her clavicle freckle cluster. It is suitably distracting. I think about the ratio of the circumference to its diameter, which of course leads me to pi. Who doesn't love the endless, rhythmic beauty of pi?

"So you left your car here last night? You know they tow, right?" she asks.

I nod. I know this.

"My mom brought me back just after you dropped me off." I hear the words I have just said out loud and realize I am a ridiculous person. I will always be a ridiculous person. How could I have been worried yesterday that Kit would think I was a dork? Of course she already does. I am fooling no one.

What are we going to do with you?

I decide to stick with what I do best. The truth.

"I just like talking to you. So though I didn't technically *need* a ride, I wanted one."

"Okay," she says, and looks up, and for a quick second our eyes meet. I break contact first. "I kinda like talking to you too."

Later, at the end of the school day, I see Kit as she walks to her car. Even though we have five classes together, with the wonderful lunch exception it seems we have tacitly agreed not to talk to each other during the day while *in* school. This is fine by me, since I like my routine. I have a playlist and my headphones for all classroom transitions. But now that we are outside, I wave with my keys in my hands. I think of this as the equivalent of laughing at myself, which my family often reminds me I need to do more often. She smiles.

"Yeah, so I'm not going to offer you a ride home again," she says. "It wouldn't be fair to your mom."

"That's too bad. You're a very good driver." Kit's face closes. I am not sure exactly what I mean—she has not moved a single muscle, but she's suddenly like a computer that's been powered down. I prefer her face when it's open.

"See you later," she says, and slips into her red Toyota Corolla, a car that suits her in a way her name does not. I wave once more, a silly gesture that I instantly regret when I notice what must have made Kit close her face. Gabriel and Justin are watching us.

"Wait, she said those words: *I kinda like talking to you too.* Seriously?" Miney asks when I get home from school. She's lying on the couch in a way that makes it seem like she has been there all day. Her hair is tangled and she's wearing her favorite pajamas: the ones I bought for her for Christmas two years ago that say ODD next to a picture of a duck wearing a tiara. She forgot them when she left for college, and though I offered to FedEx them, she told me it was too much of a hassle. When I said I didn't mind, she said she liked knowing they were home safe, where they couldn't get lost or stolen. That's how I know they are her favorite.

"Yes. Those exact words. And then we chatted about how much we both liked old eighties movies. She's a John Hughes fan too. I told her that he died at the age of fifty-nine. Just dropped dead of a heart attack. Here one day, gone the next. Just like her dad. I mean, Kit's dad died in a car accident, but same concept. Blink here. Blink gone."

"Little D." Miney sits up and shakes her head. "You can't. I mean, you got to be careful about the dead dad stuff."

"Kit says she likes that I tell the truth. She called it 'brutal honesty,' but I think it's the same thing."

Miney stays still for a minute. She's wearing her thinking face.

"I think you need to ask Kit out."

"What?"

"Not like on a date or anything. Not yet. Something super-casual. Maybe to study. Or to work on a school project together. You need to up your time together in a way that feels like a natural extension of lunch." Miney pulls her hair back from her face and ties it in a ponytail. The purple gets mostly hidden, and I feel the tightness in my chest lighten. Her eyes are still blood-shot, and there are triangles of blue below them. I will pick up some zinc lozenges from the drugstore later in case she's getting sick. "I wish I remembered Kit from when I went to Mapleview. I looked up her Twitter and Instagram and stuff, but it didn't tell me much. She seems surprisingly normal."

"Why is that surprising? I told you she was perfect. Also, she's the prettiest girl in school."

"Eh, she's cute enough." I have no idea what she's cute enough for, but I don't ask. Whatever Kit is, I like it.

"Why would we study together? I'm way ahead in all my subjects. It would be inefficient." I stare at the right side of Miney's face. That way I can't see the new piercing. Like the purple stripe, it screams at me. No, there's a slight octave shift. It feels like it's demanding something, but I don't know what.

"Missing the point. But before we get to any of that, if you want any shot here, we need to clean you up. The time has come, Little D."

Miney smiles in that way she does when she's about to force me to do something scary. She's like Trey that way. Always pushing me out of what she calls "my comfort zone," which I'll never understand. Why would you purposely make yourself uncomfortable?

Since Miney is number one on the Trust List, I try hard to do whatever she asks. That's not always possible.

"The time has come for what?" I think of Kit's clavicle. The perfect little circle of freckles. Pi. It relaxes me, like counting backward.

"Shopping, Little D. Time to get over your fear of the big bad mall." Yup, I was right. Horrifying.

CHAPTER 10

KIT

David Drucker is officially everywhere. In the parking lot before and after school. In almost all my classes. And, of course, at lunch, since I continue to choose his table as a refuge. Presumably he has always been in all these places, but until now I've never noticed him. You would think someone who is that bizarre wouldn't be able to camouflage, but he is so entirely self-contained on his strange headphone island that he moves silently through school. He causes almost no ripple.

Still, after what is shaping up to be the Week of David, it's just plain weird when I run into him at the drugstore. And I mean that literally. We are both looking down when our shoulders crash. Ouch.

"Are you following me?" I ask in a jokey tone. I'm borderline flirting with him in front of the maxi pads with wings. I drop my jumbo pack of super-absorbent Tampax and kick it behind me so he doesn't see.

"No, of course not," David says, and he sounds offended, like I've accused him of something.

"I didn't mean . . . Never mind. It's just funny to see you here."

"Just picking up some stuff for Miney," he says, and it occurs to me that actually I've been the one seeking him out lately, with the notable exception of the football snack shack. I chose his lunch table after all. I offered him a ride home yesterday. Maybe I'm annoying him?

"Miney?"

"My sister."

"You have two sisters?" I wonder if Miney is as effortlessly cool as Lauren. I decide not. Not only does she have a weird name—who would name their kid *Miney*?—but no one is as effortlessly cool as Lauren Drucker. I glance at his basket: a bunch of different cold medicines.

"Just the one. Miney's a nickname. Lauren graduated last year."

"I know."

"You know Miney?" he asks.

"I mean, I know who she is. Everyone at school does." I wish I could somehow move us out of the feminine hygiene aisle, but condoms and lubricants are next.

"Really?"

"Of course. President of her class. Homecoming queen. She's, like, Mapleview royalty." If I were talking to Justin, I probably wouldn't have admitted knowing all this info about his family. I don't bother playing it cool with David. Not sure he'd notice.

"You don't have any siblings, right?" he asks, and for the first time I see that he looks a lot like his sister. Different demeanor and mannerisms and voice, but the same face. Dark eyes and long eyelashes and full lips. If it weren't for his jaw, which is square and strong and always has a dusting of five-o'clock shadow, he'd be almost pretty.

"Just me. All by my lonesome." He nods, as if confirming that which he already knew.

"You seem like an only child."

"I can't decide if that's an insult or a compliment."

"Neither. It's an observation. I've always thought it would be even lonelier not having a sister."

"Are you saying I seem lonely?" This is what it is like to talk to David Drucker. Dive straight into the center. No matter that we are in a drugstore, surrounded by tampons and Monistat. We make good conversational partners, I think: I've forgotten the art of small, inconsequential talk, and he's never learned it.

"No, not really. But there's a stillness to you. Like if you were a radio wave, you'd have your very own frequency. Which is isolating because I don't think everyone can hear you." He delivers his speech to my feet but then suddenly looks up and stares into my eyes. The eye contact feels raw and intimate, and I shiver. I blink first. "I mean, you have lots of other waves too, all those commonly shared frequencies, the ones I most certainly lack, but the most important waves, the *core you ones,* those are harder for other people to decipher. That's my theory, anyway."

I don't know what to say to this. David Drucker has a theory about my metaphorical radio waves.

★ ★ ★

Once we are outside in the bitter cold, standing with our hands stuffed into our winter jacket pockets, I suggest we get something to eat. I don't want to get back into the car. I don't want to go home. Both of these involve feeling feelings, which I prefer to avoid. Distraction is what I need. Distraction keeps time from being in slo-mo.

"Pizza Palace?" David asks. It's just a few doors down. I picture my friends all huddled in a booth in the back. No need to combine David with my real life.

"Nah."

"I figured you wouldn't want to go there. Pizza Pizza Pizza is so much better and has that great two-for-one deal. I just didn't want to suggest it," David says.

"Why?"

"The name. It's not like they have three times more pizza than other places. Ridiculous."

"How about we not get pizza at all?"

"I thought you might say that too, since you had such a hearty, well-balanced lunch." He pauses. Clears his throat. Stares at the single car making its way down Main Street. "That's going to be one of those things I said out loud and then will regret later, isn't it?"

I laugh and it feels good. He looks sweet when he realizes he's said the wrong thing. His eyes go big and wide. To rescue him, I link my arm with his and start us walking down the street.

"Just so you know, if asked, I would have no idea how to describe your frequency," I say.

"Honestly, sometimes I think only dogs can hear me," he says.

"For what it's worth, I can hear you just fine."

"It's worth a lot," David says, and I blush, and I'm pretty sure he does too.

We end up at the counter at Straw and we order double cones of vanilla and chocolate brownie ice cream, despite the fact that it's cold out. It's easier this way, sitting at the counter facing forward, so we don't have to look at each other while we talk. It's crazy but I don't feel self-conscious around David like I do with pretty much everyone else, but still, staring at the old-fashioned mini jukebox instead of his face helps me to forget myself.

"Do you believe in the butterfly effect?" David asks out of nowhere.

"English, please."

"In chaos theory there's this concept that one small change can have increasingly bigger effects. So, like, a butterfly flaps its wings here in New Jersey and it disturbs the atmosphere, and somehow that eventually leads to, like, a hurricane in the Galápagos Islands." I nod and think about how exactly thirty-four days ago, a man called George Wilson, a name for a portly next-door neighbor in a sitcom, not a real person, decided to meet a friend for a drink. I think about how exactly thirty-five days ago, a work order to fix a traffic light was sent up the chain for approval, and how it got stuck in bureaucratic traffic along the way. I think about a foot not fast enough on the brake.

Seemingly small, inconsequential things.

I think about a butterfly flapping its wings and now my father is dead.

"I do. But I wish I didn't, because it makes me realize just how much of our lives are out of our control," I say.

"Like your dad dying." He says it like the words have no power at all. I feel winded, like David punched me right in the gut. And also a little high because he read my mind and said it out loud. Straight out. With the exception of last night, my mom barely even says my father's name, not to mention the whole him-being-dead part.

So many available words: Expired. Killed. Departed. Liquidated. Gone.

All have been banned from my house.

"Sort of," I say. "That was a car accident, though. A bunch of things added up, but there were *two* drivers. Human mistakes were made. That's different from an atmospheric disturbance, right?"

"Maybe. But take each one of those human mistakes in isolation and you'd have a totally different outcome. Your dad could have walked away without a scratch."

I lick my ice cream, which is suddenly sickly sweet. I should have gotten it like David did: asked for the chocolate brownie on the bottom. Worked down to the decadence.

"I was thinking about the butterfly effect and about how a series of events brought you to sit at my lunch table, and you sitting there has led us to sit here. A week ago we wouldn't have had ice cream together."

"Probably not."

"And then I may say the wrong thing, and that will lead us to never eating ice cream together again." I look at the side of David's face. He's not as impervious to the world around him as he seems.

"You can't get rid of me that easily," I say. "I'm like a rash."

"What?"

"Nothing," I say, embarrassed. Did I just compare myself to a skin condition? Yes, yes I did. "Nothing at all."

A little while later, we're still sitting here in the empty ice cream store, legs dangling from stools. David has a bit of chocolate on his chin, but I don't tell him. It's kind of adorable.

"If you could be anyone else, who would you want to be?" I ask, because I've decided that I admire how David doesn't self-censor. I should try it too.

I think about this all the time. Waking up in the morning, looking in the mirror, and seeing someone wholly different staring back. These days I'd give anything to be the old me, the pre-accident me, who could sit at my old lunch table and chat about nothing. The pre-accident me who aspired to be more like Lauren Drucker, former benevolent ruler and social chair of Mapleview. I really wouldn't mind being entirely full of shit, so long as I didn't notice.

"There's this guy Trey who teaches me guitar," David says. "He kind of pisses me off, actually, but he's just the type of guy everyone likes. He always knows exactly what to say. Like has annoyingly pitch-perfect radio waves. So I guess him?"

"I used to want my metaphorical radio waves to play music that was, like, quirky but also perfectly curated, you know? Something cool. But now I feel like I've become traffic on the hour."

"You are so not traffic on the hour," he says, and to my dismay dabs at his chin with a napkin. "Though I wouldn't mind even being that. Reliable, informative, albeit repetitive. At least people actually listen to it."

"I think your signal is in Morse code," I say with a smile.

"When I was eight, I taught myself Morse code. The clicks are highly irritating."

I lean over and for no reason I can think of—maybe because I have nothing smart to say, maybe because with David I feel like someone else entirely, I *want* to be someone else entirely—I take a lick of his ice cream. The vanilla part. He stares at my lips, as shocked as I am.

"Sorry," I say. "I liked your order better."

"The cold medicine is not for me. Just to be clear," he says.

"Wasn't worried."

I wonder what would happen if I looked into a mirror right now. Who would be staring back at me? Did time just leap forward with that single lick?

Later, when I'm home in my room working on a problem set, though it's long past time to go to sleep, I receive my very first text from David.

David: I am usually anti-text, but I thought I'd make an exception.

Me: I'm honored. Why the staunch anti-text stance?

David: I have trouble conceptualizing the idea of words traveling like this. And I worry that how they sound to me might sound different to you. I'm not good with tone.

Me: I should know to expect a real answer from you. But still. It's surprising.

David: When you ask a question, you get an answer.

I take my phone and snap a quick selfie. Me in my pajamas, hair in a bun on top of my head, giving him a thumbs-up. Far from a pretty picture, but I think it would offend David if I put a filter on it. I press send.

Me: Is it easier for you if we communicate in pictures?

There's a long pause, and I wonder what's happening on the

other end of the phone. Did his mom just come into his room asking why he hasn't yet gone to bed? Is he looking at my picture, disgusted by the messy, pudgy girl who keeps overstepping his boundaries? I keep thinking about how I leaned over and licked his ice cream cone, and hate that person, the me of just a couple of hours ago. Presumptuous and flirtatious, when I had no intention to be either with David. I didn't realize I could like myself even less than I did this morning.

I wait another interminable minute.

David: :)

David: That was my very first emoticon. Or emoji. Must Google to learn the difference.

Me: Finally something I know and you don't!

David: There are lots of things you know and I don't. You obviously have a very high social IQ, for example.

Me: Thanks, I guess. You obviously have a very high IQ IQ.

David: 168 at last check.

Me: Sometimes I can't tell if you are joking or being serious. Why aren't you sleeping? It's late.

David: Something else I'm not so good at.

Me: Me neither. Especially lately.

David: What do you do when you can't sleep?

I pause. Realize if I were texting with, say, Gabriel during those two weeks we went out last year, I'd respond with something casual. A nonanswer. Maybe an emoji of a lamb to show counting sheep. Or a funny GIF. There would be no reason at all to stop and think about the truth.

Me: Right now, homework. But usually I think about the accident and what happened to my dad.

David: Why would you do that?

I stop writing again. Look at my fingertips. Wonder what

they have to say. I seem to act on impulse around David. Nothing premeditated. Who licks someone else's ice cream cone? Honesty is not the best policy.

Me: Ever press a bruise?

David: Of course.

Me: Well, it's partially that.

I put down my phone and then pick it up again.

Me: But it's also like a puzzle. I want to understand when it could have been stopped . . . if it could have been stopped. What was the very last second someone should have put their foot on the brake? It doesn't matter, really.

David: Of course it matters. It's an open loop. I hate open loops.

Me: Me too.

David: I could help you figure it out. If you really want to know.

Me: You could?

David: Of course I could. It's not rocket science. It's just physics.

I pull up the picture of the crushed Volvo on my phone. I force myself to look at it, and my whole body shudders. And then I close my eyes and hit send.

CHAPTER 11

DAVID

At breakfast, Miney is again wearing her odd-duck pajamas. She's sulking because my mom woke her up this morning, even though she is legally an adult and has nowhere she needs to be. The cold medicine I bought is still unopened on the countertop. Something is wrong with Miney, but I'm starting to think it's not congestion.

"Be careful with the texting. You could put yourself in the friend zone," she says.

"I don't know what that means."

"She licked your ice cream cone. That's called flirting." Miney freaked out last night when I told her about that. She kept repeating, *No way, no way,* over and over again and clapping her hands. To which I had to say, *Yes way, yes way,* until she believed me. It was her idea to start texting Kit in the first place, and I have to admit now that I've started doing it I'm not sure why I was ever opposed to the idea. I no longer have to suffer through that thick silence while I translate what people are saying into what they mean and then wait again while I process the appropriate thing to say next. Leave it to modern technology to find a brilliant work-around to my social problems. With the obvious exceptions of my parents, Miney, Kit, and Siri, whose hands-free capabilities are helpful when driving, if I could I would text all the time and never speak out loud again. "You want to kiss her, right?"

"What?" I have lost track of our conversation. I was thinking about how if Kit called me her friend, then I would have multiplied my number of them by a factor of two. And then I considered the word *flirting,* how it sounds like *fluttering,* which is what butterflies do. Which of course looped me back to chaos theory and my realization that I'd like to have more information to provide Kit on the topic.

"Do. You. Want. To. Kiss. Her?" Miney asks again.

"Yes, of course I do. Who wouldn't want to kiss Kit?"

"I don't want to kiss Kit," Miney says, doing that thing where she imitates me and how I answer rhetorical questions. Though her intention is to mock rather than to educate, it's actually been a rather informative technique to demonstrate my tendency toward taking people too literally. "Mom doesn't want to kiss Kit. I don't know about Dad, but I doubt it."

My father doesn't look up. His face is buried in a book about the mating patterns of migratory birds. It's too bad our scholarly interests have never overlapped. Breakfast would be so much more interesting if we could discuss our work.

"So if you want to kiss Kit, that means you want her to see you like a *real guy,*" Miney says, and points at me with her cup of coffee. She's drinking it black. Maybe there's nothing wrong with Miney. Maybe she's just tired.

"I am a *real guy.*" How come even my own sister sees me as something not quite human? Something other. "I have a penis."

"And just when I think we've made progress you go and mention your penis."

"What? Fact: I have a penis. That makes me a guy. Though technically there are some trans people who have penises but self-identify as girls."

"Please stop saying that word."

"What word? *Penis?*"

"Yes."

"Do you prefer member? Shlong? Wang? Johnson?" I ask. "Dongle, perhaps?"

"I would prefer we not discuss your man parts at all."

"Wait, should I text Kit immediately and clarify that I do in fact have man parts?" I pick up my phone and start typing. "Dear Kit. Just to be clear. I have a penis."

"Oh my God. Do not text her. Seriously, stop." Miney puts her coffee down hard. She'll climb over the table and tackle me if she has to.

"Ha! Totally got you!" I smile, as proud as I was the other day for my *that's what she said* joke.

"Who are you?" Miney asks, but she's grinning too. I'll admit it takes a second—something about the disconnect between her confused tone and her happy face—and I almost, almost say out loud: *Duh, I'm Little D.* Instead I let her rhetorical question hang, just like I'm supposed to.

★   ★   ★

Day five and Kit is again at my table. Which means she has sat here, with me, for an entire week. Five consecutive days. This makes me elated, a feeling that is as good as it is unfamiliar, especially at school.

"So I just want to say something to you and it's kind of embarrassing, but I think I just need to get it off my chest," Kit says, and I can't help it, I look right at her chest, which is small and round and perfectly proportional. I have imagined what she'd look like without her shirt on, what is hiding there under her bra, which I guesstimate is a size 34B, and it takes effort for me not to think about that right now.

Of course, it's disrespectful to think about her breasts when she is sitting directly across from me and trying to tell me something. I'll think about them later, when there's no chance of her knowing about it.

"I'm sorry about licking your ice cream cone yesterday. That was sort of, I don't know, inappropriate," she says.

"You don't have to be sorry," I say, wondering if this is the equivalent of her taking back her flirting, and a tiny, immature part of me wants to scream out: *No backsies!* "I'm happy to share my ice cream with you anytime."

I look at the food in front of me—my chicken sandwich, a bag of chips, a banana—and wonder if I should offer up something as a gesture. I like sharing food with Kit. It makes me feel like we are in cahoots, an expression that had little meaning to me until recently.

"Okay, then," she says.

"Okay," I say, though I have no idea what it is, exactly, we have just agreed on.

"You'll be proud of my lunch. It's exceptionally well

102

balanced." Kit takes a paper bag from her backpack and presents me with one small cup of Greek yogurt.

"That's it?" I ask, suddenly worried that she is not taking proper care of herself. I preferred it when she was overeating. "No leftovers today?"

"Nah. We had cereal for dinner last night. It's like my mom has forgotten how to cook or something. Not that she cooked all that much before, you know, *before,* but now it's like feast or famine in my house. Excessive amounts of takeout or nothing at all."

"Do you know how they make Greek yogurt?" I ask her.

"No, and I don't want to know," she says, and the smile still on my face gets a little bit bigger. I like that Kit tells me what she does and doesn't want to talk about. It keeps me from going on about stuff she's not interested in, which according to my mom and Miney is one of my biggest problems: I don't always notice when other people do not share my fascinations.

"Okay, then," I say, a callback to her earlier use, since that technique is often used in movie banter. "We could discuss string theory instead."

"Nope. Not that either."

"We could start on the Accident Project," I say, because I am eager to help Kit understand what happened to her dad. I've read all about the five stages of grief and I assume this endeavor means she's already moved passed denial.

"Not here. Not at school."

"Okay."

"So that history quiz? If you tell me it was easy I will smack you." I think about Kit hitting me, and it doesn't sound altogether unpleasant, because it would mean her hand would have to touch my face. We have only touched twice. On Monday, when I helped her stand up in the concession hut, and yesterday, when she linked her arm with mine on Main Street.

"It wasn't hard," I say. And then she does it. She really does it. Kit leans across the table and playfully taps my face with the palm of her hand.

One early summer morning, when I was four, my mom took me to the Y to go swimming. Before then I had refused to get into the pool: too many kids screaming, and splashing, and throwing around fluorescent polyethylene foam cylinders—Miney called them "noodles," but they were neither edible nor harmless. That day the pool was deserted and I was wearing Wonder Wings, which disappointingly bestowed neither the gift of wonder nor of flight and were tight and unfamiliar. I complained, already imagining the red ridges they would leave behind on my arms, but then my mom held my hand and we stepped into the water, and I felt that first cold gasp. I somehow got the courage to put my face right into the pool, all the way past my ears, and the world went blue and dimmed and muffled and finally, finally quiet.

This is my home, I remember thinking. This. Here. Where there is room to breathe but no air. This is my home.

And that's exactly how it feels when Kit's palm touches my face. Like swimming for the very first time. Like discovering the magic that is water. Like coming home.

CHAPTER 12

KIT

It turns out clichés are clichés for a reason—they are true. And this one is most definitely true: *You never know what you've got till it's gone.*

Jack and I are in my dad's den, which is half office, half man cave, and it smells like *before* in here. We are looking for papers. A life insurance policy, information about our mortgage (though I don't even really know what a mortgage is), bank account passwords. All important stuff Jack claims will likely be found in a single file. My mother, who has clearly reverted back to stage one, *denial*, or maybe pre–stage one, *bacon*, has taken to her bed, stuffed with an array of pig products. She's left us alone to this masochists' exercise.

Too many memories in here. On my dad's desk, there's a photo of me at the age of eight proudly holding up a rainbow lollipop the size of my head at Disney World. One of my dad and me all dressed up at my elementary school's father-daughter dance, which I turned around as soon as we walked in so I didn't have to look at it. Another of just him and my mom, on their honeymoon, looking ridiculously young and in love, my mom's arms, still elaborately hennaed from the wedding, thrown around my dad's shoulders on top of a mountain. And last, my favorite picture of my family taken at my mother's fortieth-birthday party, which is now face down: My dad is holding me on his hip, even though I'm ten and way too big to be carried, and we're all laughing at a joke he just cracked about my mom getting too old for him. We look happier than anyone deserves to be.

Jack and I shouldn't be in here violating this sacred space, but my mom needs our help. When I was little, I used to beg to play in this office, right here on the beige carpet by my dad's feet. I'd promise—*cross my fingers, hope to die*—not to make any noise and to let my father do whatever mysterious things he came in here to do. Of course, I never kept my mouth shut. I'd ask inane questions—did he know that octopus blood is blue? that male sea horses carry their babies?—just because I wanted to hear my dad's voice, I guess.

I loved the sound of his voice: deep and gravelly. The sound of home.

"Sea horses can carry up to two thousand babies at a time, though it's usually closer to fifteen hundred. And octopus blood is blue because it has a special protein to make them able to live in extreme temperatures. Now out, Kitty Cat. This is a no-kids zone," my dad would say, ushering me through the door.

I tell myself that it's okay to be in here. That I'm not a kid. Not anymore.

And my father's blood, it turns out, was neither blue nor red. It was a coppery brown. The color of dirty pennies.

Jack and I work in silence. We have three bags: keep, donate, trash. Occasionally one of us will pick something up, like the random silver rabbit my dad used as a paperweight, and ask the other with a wordless shrug where it should go. *Keep*, I point, more times than I should. It's not lost on me that I have no problem staying quiet in here now. The room seems to demand it.

I tear up when I find a file marked *Kit*. Inside, there are ten years' worth of my report cards kept chronologically, pictures of my mom and me, the certificate declaring me a National Merit semifinalist, the project I did for Culture Day in kindergarten, where I drew my family holding hands and colored my dad in with a peach crayon, my mother with a brown one, and me half and half, divided straight down the middle. On my forehead, I drew a Christmas tree bindi. The picture became a running joke that my left side is Indian and Sikh and my right is American and Episcopalian.

"Get your left side ready," my dad would joke. "Mom is taking you to temple tomorrow morning."

This file is proof of that which I already knew: Our lives were good. Maybe even perfect.

And then, in a simple folder, I see a five-page, single-spaced legal document. I read it. There must be some mistake. This cannot be what I think it is. Jack sees my face and comes to read over my shoulder.

"Oh crap," he says. "You shouldn't. I mean, I didn't know he even . . . Kitty Cat, don't read that—"

"My name is not Kitty Cat!" I yell, though this is not Jack's fault. It's my dad's.

On the top of the page are written the words *Petition for Divorce from the Bonds of Marriage*. I may not officially be a grown-up, may not be able to accurately define the word *mortgage*, but I am not stupid. I know what it means. And I know what this word means too, found under a section entitled "Grounds" in underline and bold: **adultery.**

I run up the stairs two at a time and bang on my mother's door.

"Mom!" I scream, and run into her room before she even says to come in. The tears are flowing down my face, and I hate myself for it. I've kept it together for five weeks, have not let a single person see me cry, and it's this that finally makes me break. Half of my friends have been here. Annie's parents got divorced. Jack is divorced from Katie.

Marriages fall apart all the time, but I never thought it would happen to my parents. They seemed above that somehow.

And then it hits me that ironically there are no real consequences. My dad is dead. I don't have to deal with two homes and complicated weekend arrangements and awkward Thanksgiving negotiations. This changes nothing about my future.

Still, it changes everything I believed about my past. How I feel about the person I've lost.

"What the hell? Dad cheated on you and you were getting a divorce? How could I not have known? How could you guys have kept this from me?" I wipe my nose on my sleeve. I need to stop crying, but I can't seem to stop the flow of water or the heaving of my shoulders. I shove the papers at her, but she refuses to take them.

"Kit, it's not what you think. We weren't getting a divorce.

We were still talking about things. Your dad and I were going to see someone. A couples therapist," she says, and pats the bed next to her as if she thinks I could sit at a time like this. She is neither surprised nor crying. In fact, she looks almost serene.

"When? When did you guys go to a therapist?"

"On Tuesday nights. We didn't really take up bridge." I used to tease my parents about their weekly card game. Told them that they should have chosen to play something cool, like poker. And they had humored me. Smiled, kissed me on my forehead, said, "Don't stay up too late," on their way out the door. They were actually going to talk to a doctor about my dad sleeping with another woman. Get an expert opinion on whether they could save their marriage.

So many lies.

Last week I suggested that my mother start playing bridge again. I thought it would be good for her to see her friends. She shook her head mournfully and said, "I just couldn't without your father."

Bullshit. All bullshit.

"I didn't know he kept the papers," my mother says. "I don't know what would have happened if he hadn't . . ." My mom trails off and I want to scream it out loud—*Died, if he hadn't died, Mom*—but I don't.

"But he cheated on you. How could he . . . ?" My voice breaks and I start over. "How could he do that to us?"

"Wait, Kit. He didn't. Dad didn't cheat on me."

"I'm not stupid, Mom. It says so right here." I point again to the sheet of paper, which now lies on the floor. I should have listened to the rules and not gone into my dad's den: a *no-kids zone*. With the snot and the tears and my childish temper tantrum, it's clear to me that I did not—do not—belong in there. Even now. Even after everything.

"He didn't cheat on me," she repeats.

"But, Mom!"

She sighs.

"I cheated on him." Her tone reminds me of David's. Flat. Neutral. Matter-of-fact. Like she's Siri telling me tomorrow's weather. She's not crying, and I think back over the past month, to all her tears and wails and the million used tissues she left littered in messy balls around the house. Was that all a show for my benefit?

"I like to think I was going to tell you. At some point. When you were older, maybe," she says, and shakes her head. "Or not. Some mistakes are better kept secret."

"What? *You* cheated? When? With who?" I ask, and despite myself, I hear her correction in my head: *With whom*. This is, of course, not what I really want to know. What I want to know is *Why?* and *How could you?* and *What do I do now?* That last one in particular.

She doesn't answer. Uncle Jack comes up the stairs, two at a time, and stands in the doorway behind me.

"Kit," he says, using the same lion-tamer voice he used on my mother just a few nights ago. I see why she stormed out. It's infuriating.

"This is none of your business, Uncle Jack," I say, and turn back to my mother. I wonder how long I need to wait till she tells me the truth. I will probably have to stand here forever. But it turns out my mom's not even looking at me. She's looking right over my shoulder at Jack, who shakes his head at her, just once, so fast I almost miss it.

Oh no, I think. *No, no, no.*

Because now I understand everything. My mom doesn't have to say a single word out loud.

Just when I assume things can't get any worse, they do. They always do.

It was Jack.

My mother had an affair with Uncle Jack.

CHAPTER 13

DAVID

I am no longer invisible. Eighty-three percent of the people I have walked by this morning stopped and stared and then whispered to their friends. The other seventeen percent did actual double takes, the kind I've heretofore only seen in cartoons where necks are bendable. I look different. My hair is short and choppy instead of hanging long and in my face. My clothes look more like what the popular guys in school wear.

I try not to think about the random fold by my left shin or that the denim feels tight and bends in all the wrong places. With each step, I miss my old khakis, of which I have three identical pairs that I've rotated on a daily basis for the past two years. I can smell my new hair putty, which is coconut-y and not altogether unpleasant, so long as I don't dwell on its sticky texture. Miney applied it this morning, using a dose the volume of two quarters, and I filmed the process so I will be able to do it the exact same way once she goes back to school.

"Holy crap, Little D. I can't believe you didn't let me do this sooner," Miney said this morning over breakfast, after I came downstairs and, at my mother's insistence, stood still so they could get a look at the new me.

"You're going to have the girls eating out of your hand," my mom added.

As I walk down the hallway now, I think of all those montage scenes in teen movies where the main character, invariably a girl, tries on a plethora of outrageous dresses and hats, closes and opens dressing room doors in keeping with the music's beat, and then finally emerges supposedly transformed by something as mundane as a new hairdo and a skimpy dress. What I've never understood is why the boys are always shocked when they get their first glance of their newly made-up date, as if the girls weren't already beautiful despite their penchant for androgynous clothing. Do screenwriters think teenage boys lack all power of imagination? At least for me, the opposite is true. I'm pretty confident I already know what Kit looks like naked.

Despite Miney's best efforts, I do not feel transformed. I cannot imagine Kit at the bottom of a staircase looking up at me with a slack jaw. And certainly, the thought of anyone eating from my hand like a goat at a petting zoo grosses me out. Is that really a thing?

"Wow, smokin', Señor Drucker," Abby says as I walk into AP Spanish. My headphones are on, but my music is off in case I see Kit, who wasn't in the parking lot at 7:57 as I had hoped and has so far missed our morning classes. This is the second time in my entire high school career that Abby has spoken to me, the first being four days ago when I bumped into Jessica and she called me a freak. I don't understand if she's making fun of me, so I just ignore her. Also, I cannot communicate with anyone who wears that much perfume.

"He looks like a different person," Willow says. Does she think I can't hear her because of my headphones, or does she just not care? "I mean, *dude.*"

I practice her inflection in my head, the way she emphasizes the *dude,* to run it by Miney later so she can translate. I mean, *dude.*

"Lo siento," Kit says to Señora Rubenstein when she finally slips into class thirteen minutes after the bell. "Car *problemos.*"

Today, Kit's again wearing that big white button-down shirt, and her hair is pulled up in its Monday messiness, though it's looped into a bagel-shaped bun instead of its usual ponytail. Her face looks puffy, like she woke up only moments ago. I'm four seats behind her, so I study the back of her neck. She has a small round mole at the base of her nape, and it sits right there, primly, like it's the perfect ending to an exquisite sentence. I don't trust myself to remember its exact dimensions later, so I reach for my notebook and start drawing.

"I see you've gotten a haircut, Señor Drucker," Señora Rubenstein says in Spanish, apropos of nothing I can decipher, and at first I don't bother looking up. I've just sketched the two swerves of Kit's collar, and I want to get them right. "Señor Drucker. *Presta atención,* Señor Drucker."

"Sí," I say, and lift my head to find the entire class staring

at me. I ignore Señora Rubenstein and her tapping foot and all those curious faces and look to Kit to attempt the impossible and read her expression. She raises her right eyebrow approximately one millimeter, keeps her lips in a straight, grim line, and then turns back to face the front of the room. Her eyes are bloodshot like Miney's. Maybe conjunctivitis is going around.

"Sí, tengo un corte de cabello."

Señora Rubenstein somehow uses my haircut to transition to her unit on Spanish customs and culture, a clunky and illogical connection, but no one else seems bothered. Kit faces forward, her neck straight, and she doesn't turn around for the rest of class.

Clearly she hates my new hair.

Maybe she hates me.

I keep drawing. That way at least I'll have some small part of her to save for later.

After class I end up walking beside José, and before I can slip on my headphones, he starts peppering me with questions.

"What are you wearing?" he asks. I guess since we're now teammates he assumes we must adhere to social niceties, like chitchat. I wish I could politely dispel him of this myth.

"Clothes."

"Where did you get them?"

"The mall."

"Could you be more specific?"

"Why?"

"Because I think I should get some. Girls are actually talking about you."

"My sister picked them out."

"Your sister is hot."

"Not sure how that's relevant."

"Well, could she pick some clothes out for me?"

"She could, but I don't think she will."

"Don't forget we have the decathlon meeting tomorrow after school."

"I don't forget things."

"Me neither. Well, obviously, I don't remember everything, but almost everything. My earliest memory is from when I was two years and five months old. What's your earliest memory?"

"I have to think about it."

"Were they expensive?"

"What?"

"The clothes."

"Define expensive," I say, and then José surprises me. Because he does. He defines the word *expensive* with impressive specificity.

I told myself I could secretly start calling the lunch table ours if we made it to a second week of sharing and here we are: week two, day one.

"*Muy guapo,*" Kit says, and points to her own head. I force myself to make eye contact, but there's too much going on in her pupils. Attempting to unravel it and at the same time hold still makes my processing speed slow down.

"Huh?"

"Your haircut. *Muy guapo.*"

I don't need Miney to translate this one. *Muy guapo,* is of course, Spanish for "very handsome." I'm so glad I didn't take

116

Latin, which I had considered, since it would be helpful if I decided one day to go to medical school.

"Thank you. I mean, *gracias*." Her pupils seem to be pushing and pulling at once, like a resistance exercise. I give up and look at her clavicle instead. The circular constellation of freckles.

"How does it feel?" she asks.

"How does what feel?"

She doesn't answer but motions from the top of her head down to her toes.

"I mean, it feels weird having so much less hair, and I miss my old clothes. These are a little stiff. But Miney says it was about time and that change is good. I'm not sure if I agree with her on that latter point."

"You look so . . . different," Kit says.

"Really?" I ask, which is stupid, since I already know I look different. What I want to ask is: *Do you like it?*

"I almost didn't recognize you. You look like a totally different person. Not that you looked bad before. I didn't mean that."

"I didn't take it that way," I say.

"It's just you look . . . good. Really good. Like, totally different. Never mind. I'll stop talking now."

I look up at her again and our eyes catch, and this time I decide to push through the discomfort and hold on. She smiles, but I'm pretty sure it's a sad smile, because I want her to stop doing it. Her face is all closed up again.

"Are you okay?" I ask.

"Honestly, I don't know," she says. "Also, I forgot to pack my lunch."

I push forward two of my small plates—a cookie and an apple—before it hits me. This is the opportunity Miney has been talking about. I should ask Kit to grab some food after school. That would "keep up the momentum," which Miney claims is necessary if I ever want Kit to press her lips against mine. Which I do want. Very much.

"Do you care to—?" I don't get to finish my question—I don't get to say, *Do you care to go to the diner with me after school?*—because Justin hurls himself across the cafeteria and lands in the chair beside Kit. His arrival is like an alien invasion. No, worse. A nuclear bomb.

"Holy crap, you scared me!" Kit says. I don't say anything, because I don't like to talk around Justin. Past experience has demonstrated that nothing good can come from that. Not a second later, Gabriel is here too, because the two of them have some strange symbiotic relationship. A sea anemone to a hermit crab. One cannot function without the other.

"Nice haircut," Gabriel says, and reaches out his hands toward my head. I flinch and bend away. "For a second there, I thought you were your sister."

I'm about to say thank you, because my sister is universally acknowledged as an attractive person, but then I catch myself. Of course he's not complimenting me. I hear Miney in my head: *Remember who you are talking to. Always stop and examine the context.*

"Leave him alone," Kit says, and leans over and grabs my apple. She takes a big bite, as if she is proving some point. Maybe that she and I share food sometimes.

"What is this, *Extreme Makeover: Retard Edition?*" Justin asks, and then gets an overly enthusiastic high five from Gabriel.

"You guys are idiots," Kit says, and I don't like how this is going. I don't want her to think of me as the kind of person who needs defending. I am not.

After the Locker Room Incident, again irrelevant to present

circumstances, my father hung a leather punching bag in our basement and taught me how to box. He said that it was obvious that I was like him, that school would be hard for me, that at some point I was going to be forced to defend myself. Since that day, I've dedicated fourteen hours a week to physical exercise and self-defense training and have dabbled in various martial arts. I know if I had to, I could easily kick both of their asses. I mean that both literally and figuratively. When I studied kung fu, I learned how to do a swivel kick and pin my opponent to the ground, face down.

"Would you please excuse us? We were having a conversation," I say, turning my attention back to Kit, hoping that what my mother used to tell me when I was little would finally hold true: *If you ignore them, they will go away.*

Nope, nothing has changed. Didn't work then. Doesn't work now.

"Would you please excuse us?" Justin says, imitating me but in a fake British accent, which makes no sense. I'm obviously not British. We've gone to school together since kindergarten. In *New Jersey.*

"Go away, guys," Kit says. "I really can't deal with your crap today."

"Relax. We just wanted to say hey. We miss you, girl," Gabriel says, all smiles. Like he and Kit are best friends. Which I don't believe they are, despite the fact that they held hands on at least eight separate occasions for two weeks last year.

I've thought about how Kit's hand would feel in mine. I have concluded it would feel like the exact opposite of that fold in my new jeans.

A few more words are exchanged—Justin says something to Kit and she says something back—but I'm not listening. I study the back of my water bottle. Demote them to background noise. I think back to middle school, all those times I did whatever Justin asked. Snapped a teacher's bra. Pulled down my own pants. Other things I won't mention. In seventh grade I was flattered by his attention, by the fact that when I was with him, we could make people laugh. I thought we were best friends.

I thought a lot of things that weren't true then.

I reach for my notebook and put it next to my plate. Rub my hands over the cover. I will not open it here, but having Miney's rules set out and nearby helps. Justin and Gabriel are at the top of the Do Not Trust list. That's all I need to remember.

Rule #1: *Do not engage with people on the DNT list.*
Rule #2: *Do not engage with people on the DNT list.*
Rule #3: *Do not engage with people on the DNT list.*

Miney put it in there three times, rendering it even more important than her latest edict not to talk to a girl about her weight.

Finally, Justin pops up as if he is ready to leave our table. I feel something release in my chest. But I should know better. My Notable Encounters list will tell you that I've never left a conversation with Justin unscathed. He leans down to whisper in my ear, his hand firmly planted on my head.

"You may have gotten a haircut, but you're still weird as hell," he says, his tongue so close to my ear I can feel his wet, disgusting breath. I clench my fists. I want to turn around and punch him right in the face.

He has no right to touch me.

I know that if I hit him, there will be consequences, as there always are with Justin. Suspension or detention, notes on my permanent record. The kind of stuff that could hurt my chances of getting into a good college. Before Kit joined my lunch table, that's all I could think about. That one day I would get to leave Mapleview and hopefully go to a school where I could start over. Where no one knew about my mistakes.

And also there is this: If I were to hit Justin, there's a good chance I'd break his nose, and if I broke his nose, I'd get his blood and skin cells and DNA all over my knuckles. I do not want to have to wash Justin off. Disgusting.

I focus instead on Kit. Ignore my instincts and stare directly into her eyes.

I talk to her without talking: *Please tell me you know I'm better than them. Pick me. Pick me.*

She stares right back, though I have no idea what she's saying. I never know what anyone is saying.

It is only later, during AP Physics, that I realize exactly what that eye contact cost me. While I was busy staring at Kit, Justin swiped my notebook.

CHAPTER 14

KIT

So now everyone knows: David Drucker is hot. Once you look at him, like really look at him, which I did that first time in the bleachers, it's so obvious, you are amazed you haven't noticed it before. Like one of those weird optical illusions that my mom likes to show me on Facebook.

"Is that why you've been sitting with him? You knew there was, like, this freakin' hot guy underneath all that hair?" Annie asks. She and Violet are so excited by the revelation that is David, they are practically vibrating. We are between periods, standing in our usual spot by my locker. Throngs of kids squeeze past us in the halls. I shake my head. "I guess we shouldn't be so surprised, because Lauren Drucker is so stunning it's unfair. But still. David?"

To be honest, I'm not sure what I think about David's

transformation. He now feels somehow less mine. As if he has exposed what was once small and private, a secret we shared, to the rest of school. A haircut and now Gabriel and Justin are bothering us at lunch.

All I want is for everyone to leave us alone.

"I just think he's interesting," I say. I chose David's table for his silence and for his refuge. I keep going back because it turns out I like being around him, even though I'm not sure exactly why.

I guess I'm not being fair about his new look. Good for him that other girls will notice him now. That his world will grow bigger. It's not his fault that I'm desperate to keep mine so small.

"Interesting like the Hemsworth brothers are interesting," Violet says.

"Whatever, he's still weird, though," Annie says.

"Good-weird," I say, and they both look at me like I've lost my mind. And maybe I have, though not about David Drucker. I consider explaining everything to my friends. Finally coming clean. Telling the whole story of this nightmare from beginning to end. But I can't. There are some words we are not allowed to say out loud. I don't know how to explain that I spent the weekend in my bedroom because my mother and I are no longer on speaking terms. That my mother betrayed my father, had an *affair*—a word I hate because it sounds so harmless, like she threw a cocktail party, not like she screwed my dad's best friend. I don't know how any of the past five weeks actually happened.

It still doesn't feel real. I keep repeating it in my mind, as if it will eventually make sense. My mother had sex, probably repeatedly, with Jack. When my father found out, he was devastated and was planning to leave her, or us. I don't know. Now he is dead. The first two facts are in no way related to the third, and yet they are commingled forever in my brain and playing continually on repeat.

A triple whammy.

Maybe I should just say these words out loud: *I no longer have two parents.*

That's the shorthand version.

Until recently I thought I was the exception: I had a happy family. I don't understand what I have left now.

I get that I'm being melodramatic. After all, I'm pretty sure Annie's father cheated on her mom, and Annie didn't have a mental breakdown. Her dad moved in with his assistant the same week he left their house, and though Annie's still pissed off about the whole thing, she lets him buy her guilt presents and stays at his new place on alternating weekends. She says the whole arrangement isn't so bad.

Is it different when it's the mom who does the cheating? It shouldn't be. And yet I don't know. I'm so angry at my mother that I found myself punching the wall last night. My knuckles are bruised and red. They don't hurt as much as I wish they would. That seems to be the paradox of grief: There is so much pain and yet sometimes, when I need to feel it, not nearly enough.

"Has he asked you to prom yet?" Annie asks, but I'm too lost in thought to answer. I'm imagining my dad finding out about my mom and Jack. How had that terrible scene played out? And were their tears at the funeral real? Was it grief or guilt?

My mother knocked on my door a bunch of times over the weekend, and again this morning, when I didn't get up on time for school. I ignored her. She texted too. Variations of: *Let me explain. Can we talk? I'm sorry.* I wonder if she sent these same texts to my dad before he died.

I'm sorry. I'm sorry. I'm sorry.

I'd check his phone, but it's gone along with everything else. Pulverized.

Or maybe I have the story all wrong. Maybe my mother was psyched to divorce my dad and start a whole new life. No doubt I've learned in the past five weeks that my mom has a complicated relationship with the truth. No lie is too big. She'll lie about *anything*.

"What? Who?"

"Hello? David Drucker? Prom?" Annie repeats.

"Oh. No, course not. I'm not going." Violet shoots me a concerned look. I ignore her. She is waiting for me to get with our regularly scheduled program. To return to the Land of Normal. I don't know how to tell her I'm never coming back.

"First you're just, like, bailing on editor in chief, and now you're not even going to the prom?" Violet asks.

I don't answer, because it doesn't feel like a question.

"I know it's been hard and whatever, but you've got to at least try to start having some fun again," Violet says.

I shrug, because prom doesn't sound like fun to me. It sounds like torture.

"I want Gabe to ask me," Annie says in a confiding tone, and Violet and I pretend like we didn't know this already. That it hasn't been obvious for months. This is what good friends do.

Or maybe not. Maybe I should take a page out of David's book and just say it like it is: Gabriel is a jerk. Annie, you can do better. So much better. Gabriel is the human equivalent of *insert generic, almost-but-not-quite-popular high school boy here*. There is nothing particularly interesting or appealing about him. Even when he's rude, like he was to David today, he's boring and unoriginal. He gets all his dimension by standing next to Justin, who, albeit also a jerk, is at least a clever one.

"Why don't you ask him?" I decide this sounds like a good alternative. A way to put control back into her hands. If he says no, screw him. Life is short and cruel and we shouldn't waste a single second of it worrying about stupid things like school dances. Of course, yes, Annie should ask Gabriel to the prom. And I should . . . I should what? Move out? Never speak to my mother again? Kiss David Drucker? Kill myself?

I am not brave enough for any of it. I am only brave enough to sit at a quiet lunch table, to hide in my bedroom, to pretend to my friends for only ten minutes at a time that everything is— that I am—okay.

"I don't just want to go with him, I want him to ask me. Duh," Annie says, and peers into my locker. As if its dark, woefully underdecorated depths will tell her something. "It doesn't matter. I bet he's going to ask Willow."

"I'm getting a little tired of those girls," Violet says.

"I'm so over them," Annie says. "Kit, they show up at Pizza Palace every day now, and they act like we're not even there. Like Justin and Gabriel are only their friends." As she speaks, she somehow conjures them up, and Willow, Jessica, and Abby walk by. They don't say hello, just pick up their hands in a silent simultaneous wave. Like they choreographed it. Annie, Violet, and I used to be in sync like that, I think. But not anymore. Another thing that's my fault.

"I overheard them talking about David Drucker," Violet says, interrupting my thoughts.

"Everyone is talking about D.D. That's what they're calling him now. D.D.," Annie says. I don't ask who *they* are. Again she works her magic, because suddenly David appears. He walks by, his headphones covering his ears, his eyes fixed straight ahead, and he doesn't see us. He's obviously off in his own world, so I can get a good look at him without getting caught. His hoodie pulls across his broad shoulders and he's muscly under there. He smells good too. David's lemony. Fresh. Sweet.

"Is that an outline of a six-pack?" I ask.

"Never noticed that before," Violet says.

"Yum," Annie adds after he passes, her eyes now fixed on his butt, which is showcased in perfect jeans. "I mean. Just. Yum."

My phone buzzes in physics and I sneak it out of my bag and glance at it under the desk.

David: Busy after school?

I glance back at him. For a moment I forgot how different he looks, and I'm startled all over again. My stomach clenches. Annie's not wrong. He's delicious.

Me: Nope. What'd you have in mind?

David: First we need to feed you.

Me: K.

David: Then we start the Accident Project like we talked about.

Right, the Accident Project. David's idea to help me figure things out. Is there such a thing as Masochists Anonymous? Because clearly I need to go there pronto.

I look at Mr. Schmidt. I don't want to listen to him drone on about Newton's third law and stare in suspense as I wait for that little flake of tuna fish stuck to his mustache to fall. I'd much rather be out of class, eating with David and even, yes, undertaking the Accident Project, as sick as that may be.

Me: Let's go now.

David: Now? But . . . physics.

My hand raises in the air, an impulsive move, and I talk without waiting for Mr. Schmidt to call on me.

"I'm going to the nurse," I say assertively, like I'm not asking for permission. I pack up my books and my computer and walk out the door, my brain still a few steps behind my legs. Better make good use of my one short life.

I leave it up to David whether he wants to follow me.

CHAPTER 15

DAVID

If I hadn't gotten Miney's makeover, I could have just walked right out. Slipped through the door without a single person noticing. Now, because of new clothes and three fewer inches of hair, I need to come up with an excuse, a *lie*, because I have shed my cloak of invisibility. Of course I'm following her. That's not even up for debate. There's just no way I could stay here and finish out the remaining forty-two minutes of this period staring mournfully at her empty chair. Also, Gabriel is sitting next to me in all his olfactory glory and I can't bring myself to ask about my missing notebook. It's gone. Stolen. I feel it nearby, though, like a phantom limb. I've decided not to worry. Surely they'll read the first page, realize it's not full of history or physics notes, and then give it right back. No harm, no foul.

"Mr. Schmidt? I need to . . ." I make a mental note that next time I will think of my excuse before I raise my hand. He's looking at me. No, not just Mr. Schmidt. The entire class. Again. "I need to empty my bowels."

I say it loudly and with confidence, which Miney claims is the key to a good lie. Sounding like you believe it yourself. There is laughter, but it holds a different quality than usual. It doesn't sound like breaking glass. It sounds collaborative. Could the change be a result of my haircut and new clothes? Nah. I may not like my classmates, but they can't be so stupid that their opinion of me could be swayed by something as inconsequential as my appearance.

"TMI," Mr. Schmidt says, which I know from Urban Dictionary means *too much information,* an expression that makes little sense to me, because my defining ethos is that there is never enough information. That's how one gets smarter. "Go, Mr. Drucker."

He points to the door, and though it doesn't fit my cover story—I'm a terrible liar—I throw my backpack over my shoulder and run.

I find Kit in the school parking lot, standing in the middle of the road with her head back and her arms outstretched.

"It's snowing," she says. "Can you believe it?"

I nod because I can believe it. Last night, when I checked my NOAA Radar Pro weather app, it said there was a seventy-two percent chance of precipitation today between the hours of one and five p.m. It's twenty-six degrees.

"Sorry to make you skip. I just thought—" She doesn't finish her sentence, just lets the words trail off into the air. Sublimated into another form, like snow to fog. I reach over and catch a flake just before it lands on her cheek.

"Did you know that it's not mathematically impossible for two snowflakes to be identical? They're made up of a quintillion molecules that can form in various geometries, so it's just highly improbable."

"A quintillion?"

"Picture a one and then add eighteen zeros." She shrugs and I don't think she pictures it. Which is too bad because the image of a quintillion looks just like a line of poetry. "The point is it's totally possible. Unlikely, of course. The chances are like one in a gazillion. Which is not an actual number but an exaggerative placeholder, but you get my point. It's *possible*."

I look at the falling snow. Wonder if any of these flakes have a twin somewhere, if they have somehow defied the odds. Here's the thing about making a friend that I didn't understand before I started talking to Kit: They grow your world. Allow for previously inconceivable possibilities.

Before Kit, I never used the word *lonely*, though that's exactly what I was. My mind felt too tight, too populated by a single voice. I don't like excessive noise or light or smell, which are the inevitable by-products of human interaction, and yet my consciousness—that which will hopefully survive my inevitable death—still longs for personal connection. Just like everyone else's.

It's basic physics, really. We all need an equal and opposing force.

Kit stares at me, and I stare back. Eye contact usually feels like an ice headache. Just too much, too fast. Sharp and unpleasant. With Kit it feels like the first few seconds on a roller coaster, all gravitational force, no escape, pure thrill.

I am nervous. I keep talking.

"There's something comforting about the thought, isn't

there? That even something crazy like that—two identical snowflakes—can actually happen? I think about that sometimes when I'm upset." She flashes her perfect smile at me, which isn't perfect, not really. Her third tooth from the left is slightly chipped. But it's literally breathtaking, and so I stop talking because I don't want to activate my asthma.

"Everything is so unbelievably shitty right now," she says, even though she's still smiling. "I can't even begin to tell you how shitty."

I nod. I don't know what to say to this. I want her words to match her face or, maybe to a lesser degree, vice versa. A tear escapes out of the corner of her eye, and she wipes it away, fast.

"But I'm going to take that as good news. The snowflake thingy," Kit says. "So thank you for that."

"Should we walk?" I ask, because I suddenly don't want to climb into a car. I want to stay outside, in this light, quiet snow. I want to stand next to Kit, watch her brace herself against the wind, hear the tiny whoosh of snow as it falls onto her jacket.

"Yes, please," she says, and then, like it's the most natural thing in the world, like we do it all the time, she interlaces her fingers with mine.

We hold hands for two minutes and twenty-nine seconds, but when we turn the corner onto Clancy Boulevard, we stop, and I wish I knew who initiated the release. Did I get distracted by the counting and accidentally reduce my pressure, thus signaling a desire to let go? I don't know. There's a ninety-two percent chance it was Kit. I liked the feeling of her hand in mine. Her fingers were longer than I would have guessed, the collective weight of a dog's paw. I think about what it would be like to kiss her, to touch my fingertip to her clavicle cluster, to not worry about our physical boundaries. I imagine it would be like splitting an atom, a distillation into component parts. Everything small enough to be countable. Everything as perfect and forever as pi.

"You're quiet today," Kit says. We haven't spoken in two minutes and twenty-nine seconds. Too hard to talk and hold hands at the same time. That would be system overload.

"Was just thinking," I say.

"Me too. I wish I could do it less."

"What?"

"Thinking." I look over and see that Kit's face is wet. From the snow? From tears? Has she been crying since we left school?

"You're sad," I say, and it occurs to me that it is entirely possible, likely even, that I've been having the best two minutes and twenty-nine seconds of my life while Kit has been crying.

No, I was wrong: There will never be two identical snowflakes and I will forever be out of synch with the rest of the world.

I look at the mini mall across the street because I don't want to see Kit's face. The mini mall is an emotion-free zone. A bagel place, a dry cleaner, the Liquor Mart, and a knickknack store that sells an assortment of useless items like miniature figurines and napkin holders. Why do they wrap everything up in clear cellophane and twirled ribbon? Little Moments, that's what that store is called. *Little Moments.* I hate that place almost as much as I hate Justin.

"My mom cheated on my dad. I just found out," Kit says, and uses both of her hands to wipe her face. "How screwed up is that?"

I don't say anything, because I'm pretty sure her question is rhetorical. And if it's not, I wouldn't even know how to begin to measure the precise dimensions of how screwed up something is. So I stay quiet and wait for her to say more. This technique seems to work with Kit.

"I don't even know what to do, you know? Like what the hell am I supposed to do with that information?" she asks, and this time I think she is seriously asking, but before I can answer she goes on. "It's all irrelevant now anyway. I mean, he's dead. *D-E-A-D*. Dead. Adios, amigo. Hasta la vista, baby. Why should it matter?"

"I'm sorry." I picture a Venn diagram and three circles overlapping for this catchall phrase, *I'm sorry,* best used (1) when someone is sad, (2) when someone dies, and (3) when you have no idea what else to say. In this case, all three apply. In my mind I scribble the word *Kit* in the overlap. "It probably doesn't matter, but I get upset all the time about things that don't matter. Like open loops, for instance."

We cross at the light, and I let Kit lead the way. I have thirty-three dollars and fifteen cents on me, more than enough cash to pay for a meal for both of us in most of Mapleview's under-two-dollar-sign Yelp-rated restaurants. I doubt Kit would pick three dollar signs.

"I don't know why I'm telling you all this," she adds. "I haven't even told Vi or Annie."

"We're friends." I say it like it's no big deal, like it's the truth and has always been the truth, and also like I'm not suddenly terrified that just by uttering the words out loud I've put myself in the "I will never get the opportunity to kiss Kit Lowell" zone. "Anyhow, I wish there were a way to fix this for you. I would undo it if I could."

"You're sweet," she says, and that smile is back, the one that

I'm starting to realize is not a smile at all. It just resembles one in form. The snow is starting to fall harder now, in bigger geometrical formations, rendering the possibility of two matching ones infinitely more remote.

"You know what we need? To rip a major hole in the space-time continuum. And then we could go back in time and fix everything for you." I realize with a pang that time travel would do nothing to fix me. I'm different at the genetic molecular level. We'd have to alter my dad's sperm or my mother's egg, which would, in effect, undo my very existence. I don't want that. "Have you asked your mom why?"

"Why she cheated on my dad?"

"Yeah."

"No."

"Maybe you should. Could help close the loop."

"You are obsessed with this loop concept."

"Think about the infinity sign," I say, and I wait for her to do it. To imagine it. She stops walking and so I assume that's what's happening. She's letting me paint pictures in her mind. *Picture me kissing you*, I want to say. *Picture that.* "You see how it just flows into itself. Or even the concept of pi. It has an order and a rhythm and doesn't end. Ever. Continuous flow. That's how everything should be. Closed loops. Just ask your mom why."

"I like your new haircut," she answers, apropos of nothing, and then reaches up—to touch my head, I think, but then she jams her hands back into her jacket pockets. "Your outsides match your insides better now."

"I don't know what that means," I reply.

She doesn't answer me, though. Kit just stares up at the sky and lets the snow bathe her face with its infinite variation.

CHAPTER 16

I pull out my phone. Text my mother. One word and a question mark: Why?

She writes back immediately.

Mom: Let's do this in person.

Me: No. Just tell me. Simple question.

Mom: It's complicated.

Me: Try me.

Mom: You won't understand.

Me: Never mind.

Mom: I was lonely. And stupid. But mostly lonely.

"I texted and asked and my mom says she was lonely," I say to David, ignoring the absurdity of the whole situation. Me sharing the intimate details of my family life with him of all people. That we are sitting here in McCormick's, eating hamburgers in a purple vinyl booth, like an almost-date. That he looks like an ad from a magazine for boxer briefs and I'm dressed again in my dad's shirt, making the same mistake twice. That I've listened to David in the first place and broken my silence with my mother and texted at his casual suggestion. That we keep talking about this concept of open loops, like everything can be fixed if we just put our collective brain power into it.

He smiles, like this is good news.

"That makes sense," he says.

"No, it doesn't," I say. "Nothing makes sense."

"It's sad to think about, though," he says, as though he didn't hear me. "Being married and still being lonely."

"She's just making excuses for herself."

"Have you ever heard of twin prime numbers?" David asks. I see him revving up to a new topic, and I can't decide if I want to go down this road with him. My mind feels mushy and overused. Maybe this wasn't a good idea. Skipping class, taking this long walk in the snow. I liked holding David's hand, though. That part—the snow dampening my face, letting my tears mix without anyone seeing, his fingers snug in mine—that was nice. His hand was heavier than I would have guessed. More solid. Like he could keep me from flying away.

"Nope," I say. I take a bite of hamburger, think about Annie's obsession with the concept of mindfulness. She's always telling me it's important to be in the here and now. To taste your food. To feel your breathing. To notice when you go from sitting to standing. Since her parents' divorce, her mother has gone total hippie. She takes Annie on meditation and yoga retreats and burns incense in the house to get rid of bad energy, and whenever I go over there, she tells me all about her *adrenal fatigue,* as if those are words I understand put together.

Of course that stuff has trickled down to Annie and then out to me and Violet. And so I decide to be here, in the now, whatever that means. I taste my burger; I really taste it. It's over-ketchuped and too pickle-y. The here and now is overrated.

I let David fill our table up with conversation, his words like cartoon bubbles taking up the space I can't seem to fill. Which is a long way of saying if he wants to talk prime numbers, so be it.

"Twin primes are prime numbers that differ from each other by two. Like three and five. Or forty-one and forty-three. But what's cool about them is that they still exist even as you go higher and higher. Even though, as everyone knows, the gap between primes grows the higher the numbers."

"Of course *everyone* knows that," I say.

"Right, so it's this strange, wonderful phenomenon."

What does that mean, *I was lonely and stupid*? My mother is the smartest person I know. And I say that while I'm sitting across the table from David Drucker, who scored the highest on his PSATs of anyone in the tri-state area. Though my mother rarely lets her nerd flag fly, when she does, her brain is a phenomenal thing. I wonder if that's why Jack liked her. Wait, was it like? Or was it love? Did Jack love her? *Does* he love her? Are they going to get married and Evan and Alex will become my stepbrothers, and we'll go on family vacations all together again, and we'll pretend that it's not weird we've found ourselves in this new, previously unfathomable combination? Will we pretend that my dad never existed in the first place?

"I'm not sure what prime numbers have to do with anything," I say in a gentle voice.

"Prime numbers have to do with *everything*. But to clarify, that's what I imagine falling in love is like and then staying married. You start out as low twin primes and as time goes on, if you manage to defy the statistical odds and not get divorced, you become like those rarer twin primes, still only separated by two. That's an amazing feat."

"How romantic," I say sarcastically, because to me the idea of falling in love, admittedly something I've never had the pleasure of experiencing, has nothing to do with prime numbers or mathematics or even quantum mechanics. It's more like music or art or poetry. Something awe-inspiring and beautiful. Maybe even surprising, like how I used to see my parents' relationship.

"It actually is. Super-romantic." David looks down and fiddles with his straw. I think he's blushing, which makes me blush, even though I have no idea what he's talking about. Of course, when a good-looking guy uses the word *romantic* in all seriousness and blushes, whatever the context, even if you are talking about *prime numbers,* you're going to blush too. It's reflexive. It doesn't mean anything. "I just thought, like, maybe your parents were, um, prime numbers that were drifting apart, and that's why your mom felt lonely. Because her twin was too far away."

"Maybe," I say, not able to share his sympathetic views. I don't think my mother was lonely. She was just selfish. Or even worse: horny. Ew. I am seriously feeling ill.

"Is that why you were crying? Because of your mom and dad?" David asks. I haven't quite gotten used to this about him. As if the only way to go is straight through.

And, of course, there's the flip side to David's directness. I don't really want to talk about my crying.

"It's just . . . a lot of things."

"You look beautiful even when you cry. I mean, not that you don't look beautiful when you're happy. Of course you're beautiful all the time. But out there in the snow, you were stunning." My stomach tightens and I let out a little laugh. No, more like a gasp. What are you supposed to say when a guy says you are beautiful? This has never once come up. My body warms and buzzes with his words.

My mind is racing. McCormick's is a good place. They sell milk shakes and have a little sign discouraging you from talking on your cell phone. I like sitting here with David, basking in his undeserved compliments.

"Thanks," I say finally, after what feels like a long time in which I've been trying to think of what to say next. "Thanks for that."

"You're welcome." He jumps up, reaches out for my hand, and I let him take it. "Now let's go check out the place your dad died and close that loop."

Over the course of the three-block walk, I think of and abandon at least five different excuses to turn around. I never really meant it seriously, I tell myself. I never had any intention of embarking on what David has named the Accident Project. For David, obviously, this is nothing more than some sort of equation, or a puzzle to be solved. Another one of his open loops to

140

close. He can't tell that I'm sweating, even though it's freezing out, or that I feel dizzy with fear.

And then I see the intersection of Plum and First. This corner is on the way to the grocery store, to the ballet classes I took until third grade, to Violet's house, to Star of Punjab, to a million other landmarks of my childhood. The playground where Kenny Kibelwitz kissed me on the lips as part of a dare when we were ten. The park where, on many Sunday mornings when I was little, my dad and I would set up a picnic blanket and have a tea party with my teddy bears while my mom slept in and caught up on her "beauty rest." Here it is, this intersection, looking as innocuous as always. No shattered glass. No flowers to mark the spot.

My phone dings, a text message, and I assume it's from my mother. I don't want to think about her, because thinking about her leads me to this inescapable fact: My dad did not die peaceful or happy with his place in the world. My dad died betrayed. Minutes away from a freaking divorce filing.

Right over there, right over there, right over there.

X marks the spot with a circle and a dot.

I pull my phone out of my pocket with the hand not holding David's. A text will buy me some time. Thinking about my mom having sex with Jack is preferable to thinking about the fact that my dad was mutilated by a navy-blue Ford Explorer. Pain, it turns out, has a hierarchy.

Not my mother after all. It's a text from Violet instead, in all caps, three exclamation points. Weird. Annie's the text screamer among us. The one who deploys excessive punctuation for no reason. I'M HUNGRY!!!! she'll write. Or MY SHOES ARE KILLING ME!!!!!! AHHHHH! Violet prefers all lowercase, her texts as dainty as her clothes.

141

Violet: omg, kit!!! have you seen this?!?!

There's a link to someone's Tumblr: "The Retard's Guide to Mapleview." Whatever. I don't need to read another one of my classmate's dumb offensive blogs. Last year someone anonymously posted a "How to Get the Ladies to Sex You" guide, which was as disgusting as it sounds. I decide not to click. Whatever.

"The snow makes this more complicated," David says, and drops my hand to reach into his backpack. He pulls out measuring tape. There's something about the gesture—the fact that he brought *measuring tape* to school—that brings more tears to my eyes. I wonder what else is hiding in his bag. I picture a compass and maybe a scientific calculator. I imagine he's fully prepared for the zombie apocalypse, just like my dad. "I don't think it's falling that fast, so we can just measure its density once, and take that into account."

I have no idea what it is we're actually doing. What are we measuring? I think about the word *density* and suddenly don't remember what it means.

"The report said your dad died at six-fifty-two p.m. Do you know if he died on impact? Because if he did, that can be the time we work back from." David's voice is flat, dimensionless.

"I'm not sure this a good idea." I say it out loud, that which has been repeating in my head. *Not a good idea. Not a good idea. Not a good idea.* And also this: *Run, run. run.* "Let's not do this."

David turns and looks me up and down. I'm trembling from head to toe.

"This is hard for you," he says matter-of-factly. As if it is just occurring to him.

"Yes," I say.

"It's just a place. If you want, I can pull up our coordinates.

That way it's not even a place," he says, and then he does it. He gives me our location based on latitudinal and longitudinal measurements. If my ears weren't whooshing, if my stomach wasn't pulled tight into my throat, I'd laugh. "If you don't want to do this, we don't have to. But I don't like that you aren't sleeping. We need sleep for our bodies to function efficiently."

"He died afterward. Not in the car. At the hospital," I answer, and match his tone. Clinical detachment. Maybe I can do this and not shatter like the Volvo's windshield. And if I don't break, I like to think I have a chance of getting better. Or at least closing my eyes at night and not opening them again until morning. Maybe there is a good reason we are doing this. Answers. I could use some answers.

"Let's not work by time, then. Let's figure out where the car had to have stopped before there would have been a collision. Would that be okay with you?"

I don't answer. We are now at the corner, staring at the middle of the intersection. There are no cars around. If I wanted to, I could walk right into the center of the road.

There's nothing here. Just some trash dancing in the wind.

"We're missing a bunch of variables, but I think we can make reasonable estimations."

I am going to throw up. Because it's replaying right in front of me, as if I were watching it live. The screeching of tires. An explosion of blue. Everything turning black. The smell. Oh God, the smell.

"I'm sorry, I can't," I say, and turn around and put my hand over my mouth. I bite back the bile. No, I do not want to throw up in front of David. I will not display my digested burger on the pristine snow. Still, the trembling is getting worse, and the nausea curdles into vertigo. The world starts to spin and the ground begins to undulate, like I've stepped into a three-dimensional fun house mirror. I need to get out of here. Now.

"If you want I can do the math without you," he says, but to my back, because I'm already running, slipping on the wet ground, hurling myself as fast as I can to get away.

CHAPTER 17

DAVID

After Kit ran away from me, I spent another fifty-five minutes outside in the snow by myself, measuring velocity and rate of acceleration and doing calculations in my head and on my phone, since I didn't have my notebook to write them down.

Now that I'm home, I need to readjust after all that time alone, after all those words and numbers tumbled and boomeranged in my brain. After watching Kit's departing back, and wondering why she left me there without so much as a goodbye. I know that if I were someone else, I'd get that elusive subtext that everyone else seems to come preprogrammed with and understand why she suddenly, without warning, found me so *disgusting*. That's the only word I can use to describe the look on her face: *disgust*. Did she know I wanted to kiss her?

I'm not ready for Miney, who greets me at the door as if she is going to hug me. The purple stripe in her hair is blaring. Like a trumpet. No, like car brakes screeching to a halt.

"It's everywhere," Miney says, and I notice she's still in her odd-duck pajamas. Again, she hasn't left the house. Her eyes are red-rimmed but not crusty. Not pink eye, then. If she had an infection, there would be secretions.

"What's everywhere?" I ask, but I don't really care. All I am thinking about is Kit's hand in mine, how she makes me brave. How did she know I wanted to kiss her? I already know I'm a terrible liar, but it's not like she asked me outright: *Do you want to kiss me?*

"Your notebook."

I have no idea what Miney's talking about. What does that mean, *my notebook is everywhere*? A notebook is a fixed object. The laws of physics don't allow it to be in more than one place at a time. Unless we are talking about the multiverse, but Miney doesn't understand the concept. I've tried explaining it lots of times.

"Someone put it on the Internet," Miney says, and hands me her phone. Tumblr. The title: "The Retard's Guide to Mapleview." My body shakes, just once, as if absorbing a single blow.

"Oh," I say.

"Oh? That's it?"

"I thought they stole it for my physics notes. That they would give it right back when they realized it wasn't going to be helpful. Why would they do this?" I'm not sure why I even bother to ask, because I should know by now I will never understand the answer. Why anyone ever does anything. "My notebook was supposed to be private."

"Who did this?" she asks.

I don't answer. It doesn't matter. My notebook is no longer a tangible thing. It's like a dead person's consciousness. There but not there. Everywhere at once.

"Little D, *who*?" Miney grabs me by the shoulders, forces me to look her in the eye.

"Justin Cho and Gabriel Forsyth."

"I'll kill them," Miney says, which is a nice offer, but I don't want her to go to jail. Then I wouldn't be able to talk to her whenever I wanted. We'd have to sit across from each other in a dirty vestibule, converse through bulletproof glass. Miney is a picky eater. She'd hate prison food.

"Maybe people will stop reading as soon as they realize that it's private," I say, hopeful. Still stupidly hopeful. I never learn.

"Not likely. Six of my friends sent it to me in the past few minutes." I picture the word *viral*, a soiled word, and imagine my book as a pathogen. Multiplying exponentially. Replicating itself like a cancer cell.

I nod. I get it now. As usual, it just takes me a few extra beats. My body reacts first: My hands flap side to side, and my legs shake up and down. I look like a bird readying for flight. I haven't flapped like this since the sixth grade, when Miney filmed me on her phone and explained that if I ever wanted to have any friends, I needed to stop. And to my amazement, next time I caught myself doing it, I was able to quit; I replaced the motion with silent counting, though by then the damage had already been done. Apparently no one wants to be friends with the kid who *used to* flap.

"How bad is it, Miney? Tell me. How bad?" I am hoping there's something I'm missing here. Maybe it's not so strange. Maybe other people do this same thing. Keep a notebook about their classmates. Or maybe it will be helpful, after all, just like my physics notes would have been.

Nope. Justin and Gabriel titled the page "The Retard's Guide to Mapleview." Don't they realize you aren't supposed to use that word? That it's offensive even to those who actually *have* Down syndrome? Unless they meant the adjective form of the word, i.e., *retarded,* as in slow or limited, rather than the noun they've used. Not sure if that's a fair or politically correct usage, but this sort of thing—this abject humiliation—doesn't seem to happen to the neurotypical.

I picture Kit running away from me. Not even slowing down as she slipped on the snow. I picture Kit reading my notebook. Relieved she got away from me just in time.

"This is bad. Like very, very, very bad," Miney says. "I'm sorry."

"I'm going to go see the principal. She'll make those animals take it down," my mother says as she comes running into our living room from the kitchen, her car keys already in her hand. She's heading toward the front door. "We could take legal action. That violates your constitutional right to privacy!"

"You saw it too?" I ask. My eyes are closed now. The darkness helps. Too many sounds. Too many thoughts. Too much of everything. I need darkness and quiet.

"We'll fix this," my mom says. Her voice breaks, like a thirteen-year-old boy's. I'm glad I can't see her face. I don't want to know what I'd see there. I consider sticking my fingers in my ears, but that would be going too far, even for me. "I promise."

"Mom. You can't go to school," Miney says. "You'll just make it worse."

"They can't get away with this. They just can't. . . ."

Miney and my mother go on like this for a few minutes,

arguing about what they should do next. Just from their tone, I can tell this is so much worse than the Locker Room Incident, when Justin stuffed me in a locker in seventh grade right after convincing me to join him in a bathroom stall because he said he had something cool to show me. That was a lie. Instead, he grabbed my neck and gave me a swirly in a dirty toilet. And that was bad. I know because my mom cried when she came to pick me up from school that time and spent the whole next day in bed. I know because my dad's self-defense training started soon thereafter. I know because the next week my sister bought me a notebook and started making me write down rules and telling me who I could and could not trust. I know because I couldn't shake the smell for weeks. I know because some of the kids still call me *shithead*.

I know because later, when I really allowed myself to think about it and what I had allowed to happen to me, that day cracked me wide open.

I stop listening. No, this isn't fixable. I see that now. Reading my notebook is like opening up my brain and exposing to the uncaring world all the parts that don't make sense. The parts that make me a freak or a moron or a loser or whatever words people like to throw at me.

The parts to them that make me other.

The parts to me that make me me.

Miney is right. This is very, very, very bad.

Your outsides match your insides better now, Kit said earlier, but she was wrong. No, now my real insides are all on the outside for everyone to pick apart and laugh at. I'm like roadkill. I'll be looked at, examined, but I won't even be eaten. I'm not worth that much.

Kit was right about one thing: I am *disgusting*.

I don't say anything to Miney or my mother. I don't really care what they decide to do. Doesn't matter at all.

Notebook or not, I'll still be me.

Someone who disgusts.

So instead I go up to my bedroom and close the door.

CHAPTER 18

KIT

"The Retard's Guide to Mapleview"—which is horribly offensive—reads like a compilation of strange online dating profiles. I've made it back to school and to my car and even through the terrible drive home without throwing up. I open the link because I need distraction.

I'm tired of the constant hole in my stomach, that slow burn of loss. I will never see my father again. Nothing I will ever do can change that. I wonder if one day soon I will forget the sound of his voice. I can't imagine a world where I can't conjure up its deep bass. Where I can't conjure up the planes of his face or the feeling of his hand on my forehead. That's not a world I want to live in.

At first glance, the guide just looks like a bunch of scanned pages from a handwritten notebook. Alphabetical entries about different people in our class. A list of rules, the first three of which say, "Do not engage with anyone on the DNT list." What does DNT mean? Annie, who speaks acronym, would probably know.

There's a long list of people's names with random descriptions and observations that are equal parts poetic and bizarre. Violet is described as "cinched" because of her predilection for pointed collars and belts; Jessica's blond hair is called "offensively fluorescent," Abby's perfume "the olfactory equivalent of dying of asphyxiation by an old lady's farts," which is, come to think of it, remarkably accurate. A list of Notable Encounters for almost every person in our class and elaborate charts about different friend groups.

What the hell is this?

My phone dings.

Violet: KIT DID YOU GET THE LINK I SENT!?!?

Annie: READ IT NOW!!! HOLY CRAP!!!

Something about their texts makes me look away from the screen for a second. I try to think of other things. David's hand in mine. That was nice. Innocent, friendly hand-holding. I think of his tape measure. And his haircut. I think about what it might be like to kiss him. Not that I really think of him that way—like a *boyfriend* or even just a hookup—but still, I imagine kissing him would feel good.

A true thing. A real thing. I imagine he tastes like honesty.

And then I see it, while I'm absentmindedly flipping through the pages on my phone. A lovely sketch of the back of a girl's neck. A drawing of a circle of freckles on a clavicle.

They look oddly familiar.

That's my neck. That's my clavicle.

And then it hits me—this is David's notebook.

Oh. Shit.

CHAPTER 19

DAVID

3.141592653589793238462643383279502884197169399375105820
9749445923078164062862089986280348253421170679821480865
3282306647093844609550582231725359408128481117450284102701
19385211055596446229489549303819644288109756659334461284
564823378678316527120190914564856692346034861045432664821
339360726024914127372458700660631558817488152092096282925
409171536436789259036001133053054882046652138414695194151
160943305727036575959195309218611738193261179310511854807
462379962749567351885752724891227938183011949129833673362
440656643086021394946395224737190702179860943702770539211
717629317675238467481846766940513200056812714526356082778
5771342757789609173637178721468440901224953430146549585377
105079227968925892354201995611212902196086403441815981362
977477130996051870721134999999983729780499510597317328160
631859502445945534690830264252230825334468503526193118817

101000313783875288658753320838142061717766914730359825349042875546873115956286388235378759375195778185778053217122680661300192787661119590921642019893809525720106548586327886593615338182796823030195203530185296899577362259941389124972177528347

Again: 3.141592653589793238462643383279502884197169399375105820974944592307816406286208998628034825342117067982148086513282306647093844609550582231725359408128481117450284102701938521105559644622948954930381964428810975665933446128475648233786783165271201909145648566923460348610454326648213393607260249141273724587006606315588174881520920962829254091715364367892590360011330530548820466521384146951941511609433057270365759591953092186117381932611793105118548074462379962749567351885752724891227938183011949129833673362440656643086021394946395224737190702179860943702770539217176293176752384674818467669405132000568127145263560827785771342757789609173637178721468440901224953430146549585371050792279689258923542019956112129021960864034418159813629774771309960518707211349999998372978049951059731732816096318595024459455346908302642522308253344685035261931188171010003137838752886587533208381420617177766914730359825349042875546873115956286388235378759375195778185778053217122680661300192787661119590921642019893809525720106548586327886593615338182796823030195203530185296899577362259941389124972177528347

Stop. No. It's too much. The noise and the light and the vibrations and the thoughts in my head, looping tighter and tighter, like they're fingers choking my neck, and the sun stabbing my eyes and an unknown hand squeezing my balls, all at once.

I burrow under my heavy blankets. One last time. I need to

escape this feeling one last time: 3.14159265358979323846264338

3279502884197169399375105820974944592307816406286208998 62

8034825342117067982148086513282306647093844609550582231 7

2535940812848111745028410270193852110555964462294895493 03

8196442881097566593344612847564823378678316527120190914 56

4856692346034861045432664821339360726024914127372458700 6

6063155881748815209209628292540917153643678925903600113 30

5305488204665213841469519415116094330572703657595919530 92

1861173819326117931051185480744623799627495673518857527 248

9122793818301194912983367336244065664308602139494639522 47

3719070217986094370277053921717629317675238467481846766 94

0513200056812714526356082778577134275778960917363717872 14

6844090122495343014654958537105079227968925892354201995 61

1212902196086403441815981362977477130996051870721134999 9

9983729780499510597317328160963185950244594553469083026 42

5223082533446850352619311881710100031378387528865875332 08

3814206171776691473035982534904287554687311595628638823 53

7875937519577818577805321712268066130019278766111959092 16

4201989380952572010654858632788659361533818279682303019 52

0353018529689957736225994138912497217752834 7

CHAPTER 20

KIT

"Listen, I'm not saying you're ugly or anything, you're totally cute enough, but you're so not the prettiest girl in school," Willow says, by way of greeting, when I march into the Pizza Palace, and as expected they are all gathered around a laptop reading from David's notebook. No one seems to care that this is his private journal or diary or whatever. Justin and Gabriel and Jessica-Willow-Abby are here. Annie and Violet too, though they are sitting in a separate booth.

"Shut your piehole. Kit's beautiful," Annie says, and I want to high-five her for defending me, for still being on my team, despite the fact that I suck lately. Not that I disagree with Willow. Despite David's delusions, I am in no way one of the more attractive girls at school. I don't know who David sees when he looks at me—if he has fun-house-mirror eyes—but it's certainly not the same me everyone else sees. He's right about the other stuff, though, and it's sweet of him to have noticed: I do sit cross-legged on most chairs, and I have a nervous habit of covering my fingers with my sweatshirt sleeves, which annoys my mom because I always stretch them out.

His writing down my license plate number? All right, fine. That's borderline creepy.

"I think you're the one who needs to do that," Willow says to Annie. "Did you read what David Drucker said about your jeans being too tight?"

"Obvi you're going to stop being friends with him, right?" Jessica asks, and I try to remember what notes David made about her, but the only thing I can come up with is her hair. It *is* too bright. Hair color should not be viewable from space.

I'm still not sure why he described each member of our class, but the entries read like the shorthand I sometimes use when I'm programming the number of someone whose name I'm not likely to remember into my phone: *Eyebrow-piercing boy from Model UN. Redheaded girl from PSAT class.* Maybe David has a problem with names?

"Why would I do that?" I ask, but then realize I'm getting distracted. I'm not here to deal with these girls. I don't want to dip my toes into their smallness. Why do they care what David has to say about them, anyway? They've all said so much worse about him over the years.

No, I'm here to see Gabriel and Justin, who have both opened their arms out wide to me for a hug. *The cheap feels,* Violet calls it, when the boys try to touch us for no good reason. Arms over shoulders. A squeeze of our sides. Even sometimes a yank of a ponytail like we are kindergartners. It's not sexual. It's more like how people grab a handful of free mints from a bowl as they're leaving a restaurant. Greedy.

David doesn't do any of that. Just holds my hand like it's something delicate.

"Did you do it?" I ask Justin, trying to look tough. Which is silly, since I have never looked tough, am just too goddamn normal to look tough. David's list of Notable Encounters with Justin was five pages long, going all the way back to elementary school.

Justin's plans to humiliate David were ambitious. I'll give him that. And perfectly tailored to his adversary's weaknesses. Why would someone want to so utterly destroy someone else? Is Justin a sociopath? And how come we were all so willing to stand next to him and laugh? I had forgotten about the time in middle school he tortured David in the bathroom. What did I say when I heard? Did I laugh too? I hope not, but I can't be sure. It was a long time ago.

I know I didn't call him *shithead* like lots of people did afterward. Not just then too. But for years.

At least I didn't do that.

Still, small solace.

The truth is David wasn't a real person to me until he was.

"What are you talking about?" Justin pats the seat next to him, with two fingers, like I'm a puppy who takes directions via pointing. Like Jessica's hair, how have I never before noticed his cruel streak? How did I ever find him amusing? I've been overly impressed by the fact that he's smart and athletic and occasionally witty, stupid distractions that somehow kept me from realizing he's actually a big asshole.

"The . . . The 'Guide to Mapleview.' You guys posted it, right?" I hate that I pose it as a question. Give them room to say, *No, sorry, didn't do it.*

"Nope," Justin says, right on cue, though the corners of his mouth lift and betray him. He's proud of himself. "Wasn't us."

"Dude, your boyfriend's weird," Gabriel says, and my first instinct is to say, *He's not my boyfriend.* But I don't. Not because David *is* my boyfriend, but because it feels disloyal. Like I'm embarrassed to be associated with him now. I really don't care what they think; I'm disgusted by these people, which is perhaps the only upside I can think of to what has happened to me in the past month. My life will be better without Justin and Gabriel and afternoons like this one.

Sure, David is even more awkward than I realized. Okay, not just awkward, but deeply different. So unaware of social norms that he has to keep a notebook to learn them, like an exchange student from Mars.

Who cares?

If someone published the pages of my journal—which I will burn the second I get home, come to think of it—there'd be some weirdo stuff in there too. I think about my dad's favorite expression: *People in glass houses shouldn't throw stones.*

What is my house made of?

Paper, I decide. Like in a pop-up book. Easily collapsible.

"You guys really are such douches," I say. "I bet you're enjoying this."

"It's kind of funny," Gabriel says.

"Whatever, it's, like, so rude that he said all that stuff about us," Willow says, pouting, though she doesn't actually look upset. More like she's posing for a selfie. Do any of them have real human emotions? Why do I suddenly feel like I'm surrounded by actors cast as teenagers? Like I'm the only one with a real and messy life. I realize that can't be true. I've heard that

Abby goes to an outpatient eating-disorder clinic, and that Jessica has experimented with cutting, which suggests that despite their shiny exteriors, they're also fighting their own demons. Willow, I'm not so sure. It's entirely possible she truly believes she's starring in her own reality show. "I mean, he's clearly so not a nice person."

"I *like* your elbows," Jessica says.

"And I *like* your hair," Willow says.

"You ladies are all beautiful in my book," Gabriel says, though he is only looking at Willow, and I wonder if he has always been this patronizing. When did we decide that these people would be our friends? What if we took the time to get to know some of the kids in the other cliques, like the artsy types or the theater dorks? What if we all jumped out of our boxes and chewed up our stupid labels? Who would we discover?

Gabriel's not going to ask Annie to the prom, I realize with a sick feeling, even though she is ten times cooler than Willow and the rest of them. He'll be afraid she'll wear something outrageous. That she'll be too Annie.

I try a different tactic. I sit down next to Justin. Close. Put a hand on his arm.

"Please. Pretty please. Tell me," I say. "I just want to know."

My tone reminds me of the kind of girl I've never been: needling, faux cutesy, hyperflirty. I came here for one reason and one reason only, and I will not leave until I've fixed this for David. I feel like I owe him one, maybe because I abandoned him in the snow with his tape measure. Or maybe because I understand just how much this whole thing will suck for him. I know what it's like to walk down halls with your back the target of a million eyeballs. Hearing the ripple of echoes you leave in your wake: *Did you hear? Her dad died her dad died her dad died.*

"Darling, we don't know what you're talking about," Justin says, and Jessica laughs, maybe at his condescending *darling*. I want to smack them both across the face. Hard.

"Come on. I know you guys stole his notebook." My tone shifts again. Back to anger. I consider standing up one more time.

"Seriously, chillax, Kit," Abby says. "It's so not a big deal. We're not saying you're not pretty."

"I'm going to Principal Hoch." I barely even register Abby and her hybrid word and yet another unsolicited comment on my appearance. For a while there, when Justin and Jessica were hooking up, everyone called them *Justica* and I would think, every single time, *I can't wait to go to college*. "I'll tell her I saw you take it."

I look to Violet and Annie for backup here, though I'm not sure if I'll get it. They are not exactly on #teamdavid.

"Why would you do that?" Justin asks me. "We're your friends." He sounds both surprised and hurt. Like he'd never expect me to turn on him like that. I think back to what David said, about how the coincidence of landing in the same school at the same time wasn't enough for him to fit in here. Did Justin used to be my friend? I mean, for real? He came to my father's funeral, told me he was sorry afterward, just like everyone else, and then he and Gabriel hung around the parking lot for a little bit, doing their headlock-and-tripping-each-other thing. I have sat with them more times than I can count in this very booth, gossiping and watching YouTube videos on each other's phones. But do we know each other at all? Have we ever had a real conversation? I don't think so.

No one except David has asked me what I think about God, or an afterlife, whether I place my trust in science or religion.

No one except David knows about the accident playing each night on my ceiling. I trusted him enough to tell him about my mother's betrayal. It would never occur to me to be honest with Gabriel and Justin, to lift that muzzle of self-consciousness and share. To let them see me cry.

No, we are not friends. We are placeholders. But I was not as strong as David. I couldn't go it alone. I probably still can't.

"Because it's cruel. Because he *is* a good person. Because," I say.

"I wouldn't risk it, guys. If you get caught that could really hurt your college applications," Violet says, and stands up, as if to join me in my protest. I notice she's untucked her shirt, which makes me ache.

"Kit's right. Take it down, and if you don't, I'm going to tell on you guys too," Annie says, and I see she's wearing a fitted denim jumpsuit over a tie-dyed peasant blouse and big seventies disco ball earrings. She looks ridiculous and so much like herself that I want to hug her. Now we are three strong. "That was his private journal, or whatever. Posting it wasn't cool."

"It was just a joke," Justin says.

"Now," I demand, and point to the computer.

"Seriously? It can't wait till I get home? It's not like taking it down does anything. Everyone's seen it already."

"Now," I say again, and for once I actually sound tough. Maybe it's because I know Violet and Annie have my back. That my squad hasn't totally dissolved. Justin moves his fingers over the keyboard and *poof,* just like that, the link is disabled. Too bad he's right. It doesn't really matter. The harm has already been done, and no doubt there are a zillion screenshots everywhere. Nothing ever really gets deleted from the Internet. "And give me the notebook."

Again, to my surprise, he does. It has a plain blue cover and a spiral edge and the name *David Drucker* written in small block print at the bottom. Charmingly retro, like something a fourth grader would carry. I'm tempted to flick it open and look at his drawings.

I love how he made my neck look like something worth looking at.

"Honestly, Kit, I can't believe you'd pick *shithead* over us," Justin says, leaning over for a high five from Gabriel.

"Oh man, that was classic," Gabriel says. "Classic."

A few minutes later, I'm standing outside with Violet and Annie.

"Thanks for defending me back there," I say, staring at my feet. "You guys are the best."

"Yeah, well, Gabe asked Willow to the prom. So screw him," Annie says, and though she makes it sound like no big deal, I know it is.

"I'm sorry. That sucks." I wish I were more surprised by this information. I wish we could all see each other more clearly.

"David's right: He really does have a clown mouth," Violet says, bumping her elbow against Annie's. "You don't really want to go to the prom with a guy who looks like the Joker."

Annie doesn't laugh. Just blinks a few times to suck back the water in her eyes.

"You don't want to go to prom with a jerk," I say. "What he and Justin did was really wrong."

"Yeah, maybe. Still, there's some weird shit in that notebook," Annie says, fiddling with her giant earrings. "Be careful around that guy, Kit."

"Come on, out of context everyone's journal is weird," I say, not sure why I feel the need to defend David, even to Violet and Annie. He's not mine to defend. "But I didn't read the whole thing. Just enough to get the gist."

"Really?" Violet asks, her eyebrow cocked in surprise.

"It just didn't seem right."

"You should," Annie says. I shrug. Before everything with my dad, I didn't really understand the need for privacy, for the desire to be free of other people's questions. Now I do.

"What's the Accident Project?" Violet asks, in a voice that's soft, tentative. Almost a lullaby. Like she's asking something easy. Like what's my favorite food or television show or if she can borrow my Spanish notes. "Is that why you keep skipping classes and didn't go to the newspaper meeting? Because you are working on that?"

"What?"

"The Accident Project. What. Is. It?" Annie asks, with none of Violet's gentleness. "We have almost all the same classes, so I know it's not for school. What are you doing with David?"

"That's . . . that's, um, in there?" I ask, wondering how much David has written down. Did he expose me to all of Mapleview? I try to remember how I've even framed the question for him. I want to know the exact last second my dad's accident could have been avoided. When the brakes needed to have been pressed. If the whole thing could have been stopped in the first place. I want to make mathematical sense out of the inexplicable. Now it just sounds insane.

"Like I said, you should read it. See who you're ditching us for," Annie says. "So you're not going to tell us? About the Accident Project."

"It's nothing. Really. And I'm not ditching—" Annie shakes her head at me, gives me the palm of her hand, and before I can finish speaking she's already halfway toward her car. I turn to Violet. "I'm not ditching you guys. It's not like that."

"She's just, you know, pissed about Gabe," Violet says. "And we miss you."

"I'm sorry," I say. *This hurts,* I want to say. *Even just standing here talking to you. It all hurts more than you could possibly imagine.* I want to show her my watch, how time barely moves forward. How I don't much care for this version of me either. I stay quiet.

"Do you really like him? David, I mean," Violet asks, and her voice is hopeful, as if my liking him will excuse everything else, like the fact that I no longer want to hang out with her and Annie. I don't deserve her forgiveness or her understanding. If things were the other way around, if Violet suddenly ditched me for some random guy without much of an explanation, I'd have no sympathy.

"I don't know. He's really easy to talk to," I say. "I like being around him."

What I don't say: I can tell him things that I can't tell anyone else. Like about my dad and my mom. Maybe one day about me. He weighs information honestly.

What I don't say: He moves time forward.

Violet nods, but she looks sad.

"You used to like being around us too."

It's bad enough that I get a guilt trip from Violet and Annie, but then a few minutes later, as I sit in my car and garner up the courage to put the keys in the ignition and head home, I get a text from my mom. Awesome.

Mom: I know I'm not your favorite person right now, and my

timing isn't great, but I really don't think you should hang out with David Drucker anymore.

Me: ARE YOU KIDDING ME?

Mom: Saw that "Guide to Mapleview" link. Annie's mom sent it to me.

Me: How dare you. THAT WAS HIS PRIVATE JOURNAL.

Mom: I'm just worried about you. That's all.

Me: Leave me alone.

Mom: Sweetheart, what's "the Accident Project"?

Me: Screw you.

CHAPTER 21

DAVID

Pi doesn't work. Neither does the periodic table. I try simple counting, and I make it all the way to three hundred thousand, but I cannot let any of it go. My notebook is in the public domain. Kit must have read the whole thing by now. Even positing the assumptions that (1) she didn't see the link until after four p.m., which allots thirty-five minutes for a pit stop on her way home from our meeting and 2) that she reads at a painstakingly slow rate, a page every five minutes, which I realize makes no sense given her high PSAT scores, she would have made it all the way to the end at least an hour ago. Which means that it's all over: us sitting together at lunch, the Accident Project, me being in any zone. The Venn diagram of our relationship has un-Venned.

I consider texting her, but I am too scared to turn on my phone. As soon as I got home it started buzzing from numbers I don't recognize.

u little shithead. I'm gonna kill u.

How dare u say my gf looks like a miss piggy? Next time I c u, u r fn dead.

die retard.

weirdo turd. ur the pizzaface.

wtf is WRONG WITH YOU?

do us all a favor and DIE.

That's a recurring motif in the texts and also in the online comments. My classmates' desire for me to die. Which seems disproportional to the crime, as it is obvious that I was not the one who published my diary. How can people be angry for things I never expected or wanted them to see? It's illogical. Like prosecuting someone for a thought crime.

And they want me *dead*. For real. Like, for my heart to stop beating, for my mother to lose a son and Miney to lose a brother, for me to no longer exist, at least in my current form. All that just because I filled a notebook with simple observations to help me remember people's names and who to trust and how to survive in this confusing world called high school. Joe Mangino, the captain of the football team, looks nothing like a Joe, but he does look a lot like a ferret and used to squeeze my nipples when he passed me in the hallways at school. Was it so wrong of me to write that down? To make a note to myself that when I saw a rodentlike meathead, I should get out of the way? Purple nurples hurt.

I'm assuming that the threats to kill me are not literal. Miney used to threaten me all the time when we were little and I don't believe she ever meant it. But I see no other way to interpret the desire for me to be dead. Maybe they do not want to do it by their own hands and actually *murder* me, which could risk them getting caught and going to jail, not to mention force them to cross certain universally agreed-upon moral boundaries, but certainly they want the same end result. For me to no longer be living.

do us all a favor and DIE.

Kill urself u piece of shit.

No, it gets even more specific. They don't just want me dead, they want me to commit suicide. Apparently the best way I can contribute to this world is by leaving it.

My hands are flapping again. Tears are running down my face. I am losing control. Slipping into a vertiginous vortex. I used to think loneliness was being stuck with only the one voice in your head. I was wrong. Loneliness is hearing everyone else's voices too, except they are stuck on repeat: *Die, die, die.*

A knock on my door. Then it opens. I don't bother looking up. Not sure I could even if I wanted to. I know it's Miney by the one-knuckled sound and the smell that follows. Her new sandalwood perfume and dirty hair.

"It's down," she says. "The link. It's down. I thought you'd want to know."

I don't say anything. Continue to rock, head to knees, my hands tucked in, so the flapping makes me swing forward and back. My mom must have gone to Principal Hoch after all. Too bad it's too late. Everyone who matters has seen it, and I'm sure it's cached on at least a hundred hard drives.

Kit will never talk to me again.

Miney asks if she can rub my back. I shake my head no. Once. Hard. I can't quite make out words yet. Orange. The world is orange, like the blazing center of a cartoon sun. Or a volcano.

No touching. Just oblivion. Give the people what they want, as the expression goes.

"Okay. I love you, you know. This will be okay. I promise, Little D," she says, but it comes out all garbled. Instead there is orange, and a sound like roaring. Not soothing like the ocean, but loud. Deafening. Annihilating. "I know this feels like the end of the world, and I've been there, believe me, I've been there. But you will be okay."

But in order to be okay, I need to be here. And I'm not. I'm floating away. The balloon inside my head is getting smaller and smaller until it disappears altogether into the blue sky.

I don't go to school for the next three days. I stay in my room and fill the time with my flapping and with pi. I sleep too. Long, dark sleep that is neither restorative nor dream-filled. It is as close to dead as I can get without dying.

Miney and my mom take turns checking on me, and sometimes they sit on my bed. A safe two and a half feet away so we don't touch. But they rock with me, their rhythm matching mine, and I like it. The almost-company. A tiny reminder that I am not alone. Not completely.

On what must be Tuesday afternoon, one day in, Trey knocks on the door. I do not stop rocking. I do not lift my head. There will be no guitar lesson today.

"I'm here for you, buddy. Whenever you're ready," Trey says, but I am not ready.

Later I hear Trey and Miney in the hall. I try to pay attention, as if listening to their words and translating them into sentences I understand will help bring me back.

"You've done good work with him," Miney says, and I get stuck on that word, *work*. "He'll be okay."

"You think?" Trey asks. "I don't know. That was . . . scary. Has this happened before? This bad?"

"Not really. Not like this."

"I thought we were making progress." I think about guitar riffs. Latch my brain onto the sequence of notes Trey taught me last week.

"You were. He's been doing great. He made a friend. He's been cracking jokes. He seemed to be really connecting . . . until now," Miney says, and then their words get softer. I can't tell if it's because they are moving farther down the hall or if it's my brain closing back in.

This will end soon, I realize much later. I feel the despair seeping away. That's not true. The despair—that horrifying realization that I am not just disliked but *hated,* and that I have managed to lose the only friend I've ever had—that feeling is not going anywhere. Still, I decide it's time to come back, and I feel my mind hardening around its edges, putting its tray tables and seats upright in preparation for landing.

I swing my legs over the side of the bed and stand. I'm dizzy with hunger and greedily suck up the smoothie my mom has left on my desk. I shower, and when I go to wash my hair I am shocked by how little there is. I had forgotten about my makeover. Afterward, when I open my closet and see that my mother must have gotten rid of my old shirts and khakis, I fight back the panic. I reach for my new clothes. If normal people can handle buttons and creases and hoods, so can I.

When I walk downstairs, Miney and my mom are chatting quietly in the kitchen. My mom offers to make me my favorite sandwich or heat up chicken soup, as if I've been laid up with the flu. Miney's hair is back to its normal color, and she is not wearing pajamas. It occurs to me that this is the first time I've seen her dressed since she's been home. Something deep inside of me sighs at this realization, loosens up an invisible knot.

"I'm going to school today," I announce, too loud, I think. This is the first time I have spoken in three days, and I'm out of practice. I am going to school and if anyone asks me to die, I will say, *No, thank you,* and keep walking. Or maybe I won't say anything at all. Either way, Gabriel and Justin are the ones who should be suffering, not me. I did nothing wrong.

"Not right now," my mom says, laying out an elaborate assortment of food in front of me, each item on a separate plate, just how I like it.

"I'm not scared," I say.

"It's not that, Little D. It's evening. School's closed," Miney says, and she reaches over and touches my shoulder. She might be testing me. I don't flinch.

I look out the window and see that the sky has turned dark and blue. A bruise. I want the world to be green again. Like Kit's eyes.

"Eat," my mother says. "And then we'll figure out what to do next."

Her *we* sounds nice—not like the *we* of *What are we going to do with you?* This *we* implies that I am not alone, that we are all on Team David. I imagine us as a ragtag group of do-gooders on the side of the underdog and the wronged. Team David, in my imagination, looks a lot like the Bad News Bears.

"Okay," I say, and then I dig in, making my way clockwise

from plate to plate. After a little while I look up, and my mother and sister are still here, sitting and watching me eat.

"Welcome home," my mother says, her voice thick with surprise, like I had gone away to a place she thought I might never come back from.

Later, Miney and I take a walk around the block. We bundle up in our winter coats and scarves and gloves, like we used to when we were little and my mother would send us out to play in the snow. I used to hate being forced outside and away from my books, into the wet and the cold. I remember the stinging flesh in the gap between my sleeve and my glove, how that one inch of exposed skin ruined everything. I never understood how Miney could keep on building snowmen and making snow angels with cold wrists.

Now I don't mind it so much. I like the bulk of my coat. The way I feel buttoned into it, like getting tucked into bed.

"Fresh air will do us good," Miney said. I agreed since I'm already off schedule—I have not practiced martial arts in three days, which is the longest break I've taken since I started training—and we are here, walking down the street. It looks like the rest of Mapleview has all gone in for the night. There are few cars. No one else is walking.

"I like your hair," I say, pointing to the spot that used to be purple.

"I thought I needed a change, and then realized that's not what I needed at all," she says. I think about her words, weigh each one, the same way my mom squeezes fruit in the supermarket, but I don't come out the other side. I don't know what she means. "I'm proud of you, you know. School hasn't been

173

great lately, and then something happened, nothing big or anything, but I know how you feel. I've been where you've been, sort of."

"You sat and rocked back and forth in your room reciting pi for almost seventy hours straight?" I ask.

"Okay, not *exactly* where you've been. But the public humiliation part, totally. And honestly, I realized that if you are brave enough to go back to school and face all those jerks, then I can too. So thank you for that. But that also means I'm leaving soon. Consider this your first warning," she says.

"Okay," I say. The old me would have cried or screamed or begged her to stay. But I'm not the old me anymore. Despite the events of the past seventy hours, I am growing up, getting stronger. I'm miles away from Normal—I will never live in the same state as Normal, nor do I necessarily want to—but I'm getting a little closer. I'm a refugee on Normal's border. It will be okay when she goes. I will be okay. And I assume she will be too, because she's Miney. "Just don't dye your hair again. I like to recognize you when you come home."

She smiles at this and nudges me with her elbow. Both of our hands are in our pockets, so it becomes a game, our nudging.

"I doubt you actually humiliated yourself," I say.

"I sort of did." I don't ask how, because I know from personal experience that it's not fun to talk about the ways we've embarrassed ourselves. Then you have to feel it all over again in the retelling. And if Miney wanted me to know more, she would have told me.

"How long till you leave?" I ask.

"A week, maybe? But I'll be back for spring break. And there's FaceTime." I nod. "So I saw some of those texts you got. I wish I could kick all those kids' asses."

"I actually could," I say, and for a moment I let myself picture it. A series of palm-heel strikes and the entire football team would be on their backs. "I could kill them if I wanted to."

"Please don't." I laugh, because we both know I never would. When I was little, I used to get upset if I accidentally stepped on a bug. I may have mastered the art of self-defense, but I don't like to hurt things. And anyhow, despite how they all feel about me, I don't wish anyone dead. Not even Justin or Gabriel. Even if I believe the quantum theory that consciousness survives death, I don't want their bodies to go still forever.

I wouldn't mind if they moved away, though. That would be nice.

"What are you going to do at school tomorrow?" Miney asks.

"Same as always. Put on my headphones. Ignore them all."

"And Kit?"

I think about Kit's eyelashes, how the snow gathered and nestled between them, like it was a good place to rest. I think about her fingers linked with mine.

I see her back as she ran away from me as fast as her legs would take her.

I think about the contours of the word *disgust*, its guttural *g*.

"I don't know," I say.

CHAPTER 22

KIT

After three days, David is back. He's sitting at our table, head-phones on, eyes trained downward. When he was gone, I re-joined Annie and Violet at lunch. I listened to them brainstorm a new short list of guys who would be acceptable prom dates. I told Violet I liked her high-waisted jeans. I went to all my classes and to the newspaper meeting and then went home afterward and watched Netflix with a bowl of popcorn bigger than my head. I've eaten turkey and hummus on rye two times a day. I should win an Academy Award for Best Actress in a movie called *Normal*. No doubt I'd be the first half-Indian girl to win.

In the evenings, when my mom gets home from work, I've blasted my music in my room, the acoustic equivalent of a DO NOT ENTER sign.

I realize how much I've missed talking to David.

I approach him slowly. I feel awkward, like we're strangers again. Like this is no longer *our* table. Could be I don't know how to act around the only person in the whole wide world who would describe me as the prettiest girl in school. Not even my own mother would be so charitable. *Pretty doesn't just happen, Kit*, my mother likes to say. *You have to try.*

"Hey," I say, and sit down across from David. "How're you holding up?"

He looks up, pops off his headphones. How did I forget about his great haircut and cool clothes? I may not be the prettiest girl in school, but there is no doubt he's a really cute guy. Of course, he's also the weirdest, which can make for some cognitive dissonance.

"Not great," he says.

"I have something for you." I slip the notebook out of my bag and slide it over. He makes no move to take it.

"Did you read it?" I notice that his eyes are on my clavicle, which is a part of my body I've never had occasion to think about until I met David. I resist the temptation to put my fingers on the freckles he drew. I considered ripping that page out—keeping it as a reminder that there was once someone who thought I was beautiful—but I realized it wasn't mine to take.

"Some. Not all. I know I shouldn't have, but I got curious and so I sort of flipped through. I'm sorry." I have caught David's honesty disease. I didn't need to tell him the truth. I should have just said *not really*. That would have been close enough.

Turns out, though definitely strange and random, there was nothing too disturbing. He didn't expose me. Instead, on a fresh sheet toward the back, there was a short list under the title Kit and D's Accident Project:

Never talk about the AP at school.

Library?

Research car specs.

Calc.

Bad idea to help? Definition of friend zone?

This last one made me laugh out loud.

"I figured." I wish he'd put the notebook away so we could pretend it never happened. I want us to go back to the way we used to be together. Comfortable. "I didn't know if you'd sit with me today. After everything."

"Well, you said only nice things about *me*." I mean it to sound like a joke, but it falls flat. There are, of course, a lot of people in this room he didn't say nice things about. I can't imagine what that must be like—knowing everyone in school has read exactly what you think of them. It's all very *Harriet the Spy*, except without the guaranteed children's book happy ending. Of course I've had a million mean thoughts about my classmates, but they've mostly stayed safely locked inside my head. I excel at keeping things to myself. Another post-accident-acquired skill. "So where have you been?"

"Home." David's eyes meet mine. "Did I make you run away the other day? I don't know what I said—"

"You? No, it wasn't you. It was . . . that . . . place," I say, and he nods like he understands, and maybe he does, but then again maybe he doesn't. It's hard to tell with him. Sometimes I think he is the only person who understands how to have an actual conversation with me these days, and then I think about his notebook, how different he is, and wonder if I've been imagining it all. If I've been so desperate for a real friend that I've created this other David in my mind who doesn't exist.

"You're fast, you know," he says, and for the first time since I sit down, he smiles. He looks even better this way: happy. I don't think I'm making him up. I really don't. "I mean, I've never seen anyone run that fast."

"Yeah, well."

"You talk to your mom?" he asks, and I shake my head. "You will eventually. When you're ready."

His voice is certain, and I hang on to that. Because whenever I think of talking to my mom, the tears bubble up fast and the words get clogged in my throat. I have been ignoring her knocks on my bedroom door, her text messages, her calls. I look up at David, trying not to cry. I've been holding everything back. Boxing these feelings up, throwing a label on the outside, organized and sorted, like I can convince myself that they take up barely any space at all. Just a corner of a closet shelf.

You know what actresses actually are? Really good liars.

Before I have a chance to say anything, the entire football team approaches our table. A block of biceps and thick thighs, standing shoulder to shoulder. And then, like we are in a bad teen movie, Joe Mangino, a beefy guy with buck teeth, steps forward. He flips David's lunch tray. An empty milk container goes flying onto the floor.

"Are you serious?" I ask, and stand up, though now that I'm on my feet I have no idea what I can do in the face of all these muscles. These guys are big and they are not my friends. I can't just ask them to stop, like I did with Justin and Gabriel. Well, I can ask, but they're not going to listen.

"Stay out of this, Kit. This little shit needs to die," Sammy Metz says, who looks like—is—a linebacker. A giant oak of a boy. He'd look good next to Willow.

"Don't you think that's extreme?" David asks the question

like he genuinely wants to know the answer. There isn't an ounce of fear in his voice. So calm and collected it's borderline creepy. Suddenly he seems less alien, more robot. "You want me to die? I've spent almost three days thinking about it, and I still can't figure it out."

"Not only do I want you to die," Joe says, "I want it to hurt. Badly. I'm just deciding: Should I shove my boot down your stupid throat or should I feed you your own nuts?"

"You know, if you shove your boot in my face it's unlikely to fit in my mouth. And I have no intention of eating my own testicles," David says, and then turns his head away, as if he is no longer interested in the conversation. Takes a bite of apple, then puts it back on its plate. We watch him, and when he looks up again, he seems surprised we are all still here. "What do you want? Everyone's watching. Obviously you can't touch me right now."

"We're going to get you, Drucker. When you least expect it. We're going to get you," Joe says, again with the horrible clichés. Is that what he does on weekends? Watches bad movies and practices the resident jock's lines in front of a mirror? *Step one: Flip lunch tray. Step two: Make scary but generic threats. Step three: Take more steroids and grow even bigger breasts.*

"Move it along, gentlemen," Mrs. Rabin says, approaching the table and ushering the football guys away. She doesn't ask David if he is okay, though. Instead she glares at him and shakes her head.

"What's up with Mrs. Rabin?" I ask.

"What?"

"That look. What'd you do to piss her off?" David motions to his notebook.

"Uh-oh." I wince. "Teachers too?"

"Yup." David shrugs, up and down, like he's being manipulated by an amateur puppeteer. His body language, I realize now, is as stilted as everything else about him. "Hope this doesn't hurt my college recommendations."

Later, in AP World History, Ms. Martel drones on about the impact of the Industrial Revolution: blah, blah manufacturing and steam engines and terrible factory conditions blah blah. I text David. We both have our laptops open so we can iMessage and look like we're just taking notes.

He's sitting three rows over and one ahead—I guess he's been sitting there since September—and I study his profile. I like his lush eyelashes, and the slope of his cheeks and the way he cocks his head to the side and stares out the window.

Me: Are you scared?

David: Of what?

Me: The whole frickin' football team!

David: No. Do you know what I am scared of, though? Sentient artificial intelligence. And global warming. In equal measure.

Me: They could kill you.

David: I know. If we create machines that can learn to feel the whole range of human emotions, we are all dead. And I think we've long passed the tipping point in global warming. I expect apocalyptic weather will soon become the norm.

Me: I meant the football team! Maybe you should tell someone. Like the principal.

David: Oh. On one hand they've made it clear they want me dead. On the other, I doubt they actually want to do the dirty work. Not to mention they'd have to dispose of my body.

And all their prior threatening texts could be used as evidence against them by the police. They're stupid, but not that stupid.

Me: ?

David: I think it highly unlikely that they'll kill me.

Me: I didn't mean it literally. I meant they could mess you up.

David: Again unlikely. Also, I know various forms of self-defense, including but not limited to kung fu and krav maga. They should be scared of me.

Me: Really?

David: Yup. But you know what I don't understand?

Me: EVERYTHING.

David: That's a joke, right?

Me: Yes, David, that was a joke.

David: Right. So what I don't get is why everyone is mad at me, instead of realizing I'm the one who has been wronged here. Not a single person has come up to me and said, "I'm really sorry this happened to you." Not one person.

Me: I'm really sorry this happened to you.

David: I'm being serious.

Me: So am I.

David: Thank you.

Me: You're welcome. You really know krav maga?

David: Would I joke about something like that?

CHAPTER 23

DAVID

"I thought college would be easier," Miney says on Tuesday morning. She is sitting in our breakfast nook, digging into a pile of pancakes. My dad is manning the stove with his headphones on, the same pair I have, though instead of listening to music, he prefers audiobooks. He claims it allows for efficient multitasking, but it has the unintended perk of allowing Miney and my mom to talk without him hearing. I'm just beyond the door, eavesdropping. I realize I don't actually have the power of invisibility, but I come pretty close. "Like it would just be an extension of high school. But then I got there, and I had to make all new friends. And no one seemed to like me."

"Laur, of course people like you." My mom leans forward and squeezes Miney's hand. Miney is being ridiculous. Everyone likes her. That is one of life's constants, like the chemical makeup of water.

"It's not just that. As you know, rush was a disaster. My classes are seriously hard. And there was this guy. . . ."

"And?" my mom asks.

"And nothing. Well, not quite nothing. I really liked him, Mom, and I thought he was interested too. And so I saw him out one night and I, like, basically threw myself at him in front of everyone and he made it superclear he wasn't at all into me. It was beyond embarrassing. Plus I don't really have any friends. Not real ones yet, anyway. It just feels like college is one rejection after another. Maybe I picked the wrong school. Or maybe I'm just a big loser."

"Who are you and what have you done with my daughter? One guy doesn't like you and you come running home?" my mom asks. "He's obviously an idiot."

"He's actually supersmart, Mom. He was my physics tutor. I was the idiot." Miney puts her head down on the table and my mother strokes her hair like she's a small child. I think she might be crying, but I can't tell from here.

"That's why you've been moping all this time?"

"Little D, you scared the crap out of me. Stop lurking!" Miney screams when she notices me. Darn new clothes and their crinkly sounds. My khakis were much more inconspicuous.

"I wasn't lurking. I was eavesdropping," I say, and step into the kitchen.

"Stop it," Miney and my mom say at the exact same time, so I have no choice but to say, "Jinx, a Coke," though I don't drink caffeine.

"Maybe we should talk about this later," my mom says, and Miney nods. I wonder what my dad will say when he finds out that Miney needed a physics tutor. Since last summer, he has been putting a lot of pressure on her about college. He's adamant

184

that she major in something useful, like math or biology. Before she left that's all he could talk about: how Miney needed to understand how much school was going to cost my parents, that she better finally figure out what she was good at, that she should stop wasting time putting on makeup and instead apply herself in the sciences, like I did.

"Anyone can be prom queen, but not everyone has the opportunity or the capability to learn from Nobel Prize–winning geophysicists," he would say, and Miney would look him straight in the eye and say: "I was homecoming queen, actually, and some parents would be proud of that." I stayed out of it, though it's not quite true that *anyone* can be homecoming queen or king. I certainly can't. Miney might not be the best person to talk to about quantum theory, but she's a genius in her own way.

"I just want to say I love you guys and I'm so lucky to have the two bravest kids in the world, and sure you both make mistakes, but please don't let anyone or anything ever make you feel small, okay? Either one of you," my mom says, and stands up and kisses both me and Miney on the tops of our heads as she makes her way to the sink. My mom likes pep talks. It's kind of her thing.

"Statistically speaking, it's unlikely we are the two bravest kids in the whole world," I say.

"Just say *I love you too, Mom*," my mom calls over her shoulder.

"And I have no idea how one can feel small. I assume I feel exactly proportional to my size." Miney kicks me under the breakfast table. I look up and she's glaring at me.

"I love you too, Mom," I say.

★   ★   ★

I pull my car into my parking space at exactly 7:57 a.m., which gives me one minute to gather my backpack and head toward the school entrance. I'm back on schedule, which I realize in the aftermath of slipping over the edge last week is even more important than usual. I need to stay focused, follow my routine, find my peace in its rhythms and repetition. My playlist is ready to go and so I slip on my headphones, as I always do when I exit the car. Which is why I don't see them at first. The football team lined up in the parking lot. A wall of solid meat.

Could be a coincidence, I tell myself. They might not be waiting for me. But I free-ear it just in case I need all my sensory abilities.

"Drucker!" Joe Mangino says. Or is it Sammy Metz? I can't tell them apart without my notebook. To me they both look like the hanging slabs of an unidentifiable animal you'd find in an old-school butcher shop. Cold and pasty white where the fat is. This guy is more rodentlike than porcine. "We wanted to chat with you. Say hi."

"Hi," I say, and then instantly regret it. A stupid reflex.

"So it's no secret that we want to beat the shit out of you," Meat Boy—that's the perfect name for him, Meat Boy—says, and I find myself nodding along, because he's right, it is no secret. Though I thought they wanted to do worse. I thought they wanted to kill me. "Don't worry. We're not going to do it here or right now. Just wanted to remind you. In case you had forgotten. Keep you on your toes."

"I haven't forgotten," I say, and look up and spy Kit coming out of her car one row over. I wish she had been a few minutes early or late, which is something I've never before wished, since I like watching her walk into school each morning. Not strictly a necessity for my routine, because she's only on time about three out of five days, but like the lunch lady remembering to wear her hairnet or when my phone switches to track two when I round the corner to my locker, it means good things.

I keep walking, but Meat Boy stops me with a bump to my shoulder. There's a crowd now. Justin and Gabriel are here too, just behind the throng of football players, all in the middle of the parking lot.

"Hold on a second," Meat Boy says, and the crowd moves around him to form a semicircle. I don't know how they do it. No one says, *Gather round* or *You stand here*. It just happens organically. Like they can smell something is about to happen and want front-row seats. "You haven't been excused."

"Do we really have to do this?" I ask, annoyed, because it is 7:59 and I haven't allotted for this pit stop. I will be late. I don't like being late. I will also have to find a way to walk through this crowd, and I hate crowds. They feel like putting on a turtleneck or a shirt with a collar, both of which are barbaric inventions.

"Say it. Say: 'May I be excused?' " I look up at him, confused. Why should I ask to be excused? I don't need a hall pass to go inside the school. He is not a teacher. We are of equal authority here.

Oh. The feeling comes before the understanding. Something sneaks its way into my body, weaves its way around my intestines. I recognize this cold ache. This is what all of middle school felt like.

I want nothing more than to put on my headphones, walk inside, and get back on track. Forget this delay. Wipe this encounter away with an eraser.

And then I see Kit and her two friends, whose names I always forget and who I think of as Cinched and Hippie. They join the crowd, curious to see what's going on.

"Hey, 'tard. Say, 'May I be excused?' Come on, now. You can do it."

"Leave him alone," Kit says, and my stomach clenches. A sharp cramp that feels like someone kicked me in the gut.

"Sweet. Sticking up for your boyfriend," Meat Boy says, which gives me a quick frisson of pleasure. He referred to me as Kit's boyfriend. Her boyfriend! But then I see Kit's face, which has closed, like that day I told her she was a good driver, and now I want to kill Meat Boy. Kit looks happier with her face open.

"Get out of my way," I say.

"Your girlfriend is a fine piece of ass, huh?" I know from Miney that calling a girl a fine piece of ass is not respectful, maybe because it falls under the subcategory of the no-talking-about-a-girl's-weight rule? I look over to Kit, but of course I can't read her expression. Is she telling me to fight for her? To run?

"Stop it now. This is your first warning," I say, just like I learned from the kung fu video. I am giving my opponent a fair chance to walk away. Peaceful resolution is always preferable to fighting.

My body is humming. I could hurt them if I wanted to.

And then, suddenly, I want to.

Meat Boy is laughing. The whole line of them are laughing. At me. I flash back to seventh grade, being stuck in a locker with my hair full of toilet water and feeling the cold drops slip down my back in slimy chunks. That smell. I think about all those texts. How I've been treated as *less than* for as long as I can remember. Why is being like them the baseline?

"Last chance," I warn, and take a step forward, hoping that they will break apart and make room for me to pass. They don't.

Today I will veer from my routine. Break out of my comfort zone, as Miney likes to say. I will do what needs to be done. Take one for the team, as the expression goes. There will be no getting back on track, though for just a second, before it all starts, I close my eyes and picture myself in school, rounding the corner of the hallway just as Mozart hits D minor.

And then, as I hear that perfect note in my mind, I open my eyes and step forward one more time.

I drop-kick Meat Boy.

I sit in the principal's office with a bag of ice on my face that smells like cafeteria food. Not one food in particular, but instead a sickening amalgamation of all the food that they serve in there: chicken nuggets and french fries and boiled broccoli. An undertone of meat loaf. My nose is bruised, but other than that I am fine. I can't say the same about the football team.

"What are we going to do with you?" Principal Hoch says. The dread that had lifted with that very first kick and with that very first crack, as if that single noise and that single motion themselves had caused all the heaviness to evaporate, now resettles on my shoulders. For about seven minutes, I was a warrior. A hero. A defender of girls. Or one girl. The only girl who matters.

I was not David Drucker. Class loser.

Both of my parents are here, which means this is serious. Usually it's just my mom who comes, who hears these *What are we going to do with you?* speeches. Usually they end with me promising to try harder, though I never really know what I'm promising to try harder to do.

Be normal, I think.

Be like the neurotypical, which is another way of saying "everyone else."

Be less like me.

I no longer want to be less like me.

"I don't think 'we' need to do anything," I say, and as I speak I realize my tongue is swollen. Someone must have snuck a punch to my mouth. I don't remember the specifics of the fight. It was all action and reaction, autopilot, no thinking. A clean, quiet brain. Later I will take the time to reenact it in my head, figure out all the sequencing. Savor it a little.

Immediately afterward, when my thoughts came rushing back, I smelled blood and heard shouting and all I wanted was to take a shower. To be free of other people's bodily fluids.

"I was merely acting in self-defense. I even gave Meat Boy a first warning, which I thought was incredibly generous."

"Meat Boy?" Principal Hoch asks. I shrug. I have a fifty-fifty chance of getting his name right. He's either Joe Mangino or Sammy Metz. Not that it matters. Both got hit eventually.

"The first guy I kicked," I say.

"We have a record of death threats," my mother says. "On David's cell phone. This was obviously self-defense."

"Three of our students had to go to the hospital," Principal Hoch says. "That sounds like more than self-defense."

"With minor fractures," my dad chimes in. *"Minor."*

"I can't condone this sort of violence," Principal Hoch says, and I don't know where to look. I hadn't expected my dad to speak up or to defend me. He usually lets my mom do the talking. But then again, he's the one who taught me self-defense.

"Tell me: What was my son supposed to do? The entire

football team was lined up waiting for him. They've previously accosted him in the cafeteria. Do you need me to read you the texts?" my mom asks, and grabs my phone from my backpack.

"I don't think that's necess—"

"'You little shithead. I'm gonna kill you,'" my mom reads in a flat tone. "'Die, retard. Do us all a favor and die.'"

"She can keep going. There are plenty more," my dad says, like my mother is reading a grocery list. *Eggs, bacon, strawberries. Die, die, die.* I need her to stop.

I want to slip on my headphones. I want to flap my hands. I do neither.

I try to appear as normal as I can while holding a bag of foul-smelling ice to a blue throbbing nose while I think about Kit, who smells nice and whose nose is perfect. Not too big and not too small, just right. She's a Goldilocks of a person.

I don't remember seeing her after that first kick. Did she like it? Me defending her?

"Please, Mrs. Drucker, we've discussed in the past the possibility that this school just might not be the right fit for David. That there may be somewhere else better suited to his needs." This is the first time I've heard this, and the insinuation that I might be transferred hurts even more than her use of the word *needs*. I don't look at Principal Hoch. I am folding in on myself, smaller and tighter and smaller and tighter still, until I disappear. I want to be something that can't be seen at the molecular level.

I cannot transfer schools. Not now. Not after Kit.

Since I can't put my headphones on, I force myself to imagine what they feel like. I play pretend. Feel the weight of them. The quick vacuum seal when they first envelop my ears. The rush of white noise on the "Relax, Little D" playlist that Miney made for me before she left for college. The slow filling up of my body by the neutral sounds.

"Principal Hoch, shall I start reading again? Because I think if you take a step back and look at the situation reasonably, my son is the target here. He's not the one who has acted inappropriately. Your beloved football team ganged up on him." My mom is practically spitting. She's angry. I know this because she has a vein three millimeters to the left of the middle of her forehead that throbs when she's mad. Miney taught me that trick, and it has proven a both helpful and reliable guide to my mother's moods.

"No doubt those texts are inappropriate, and we have a zero tolerance policy to bullying at this school. But we do need to put this all in a larger context. There was provocation—"

"Are you kidding me?" My mom explodes. Her entire body is shaking, and my dad puts an arm around her to keep her from spinning right out of the room. "That notebook was private. It was stolen, for God's sake! I don't understand what's going on here! It's your job to protect my son!"

"But don't you see? I *am* trying to protect him. It's not just the football team. Obviously a lot of the kids have trouble with David. I want to keep him safe." Principal Hoch's voice is mis-leadingly calm. I want to float away on it, but I know I can't. I need to be here. If I don't focus, I will find myself at that school for kids with special needs, where they don't know what to do with someone who takes a course load of five AP classes. How will I explain in my applications that I was forced to transfer mid–junior year? I will not get into college. I will never escape Mapleview. I will be the loser everyone here expects me to be. No. "Maybe he'd be better off—happier, even—in an environment where he'd make actual friends."

"Last time we spoke, just a month ago, you said he needed to get involved in the school community," my father interjects. "He's joined the Academic League. And he's doing a guitar showcase in a few weeks. He has a social skills tutor. His grades are stellar."

For a moment I almost object, since I have no intention of doing a guitar showcase and I'm not sure if I'm still part of the decathlon, since I missed the meeting last week due to my being incapacitated and therefore unable to attend, but then I get caught on the first part of what my father said. *Last time we spoke.* My parents talk to Principal Hoch on a semiregular basis? Also, what social skills tutor?

"I appreciate that, I do, and there is no doubt David is doing phenomenally well when it comes to academics. That doesn't change the fact that I now have three kids in the hospital."

"Who put themselves there," my mother replies. I keep my mouth shut. Use all my willpower not to say it out loud, to claim what is mine: *No, I put them there.*

"Kids who are socially isolated do scary things," Principal Hoch says, and for maybe the first time in my life I understand the implication. She is suggesting I'm one of those crazy people who could end up committing a mass shooting. I hate guns.

"You misunderstand me, Principal Hoch, and the very essence of my personhood. I don't believe in violence, unless it's for self-defense purposes. In this case, I was provoked. I gave a first warning. I followed all the rules of fair combat. I was left no choice but to protect myself. I could have died otherwise. And, I'd like you to know, I am not socially isolated, which is one of the indicators for that sort of antisocial, sociopathic behavior. I am now friends with Kit Lowell."

"Excuse me?"

"Kit Lowell is my friend. We sit together at lunch every day," I say, and maybe there is a little too much pride in my voice. I don't care. It feels as good to say this sentence out loud as it did to kick Meat Boy in the face. "If the concern is I don't have friends, well I do. Kit. And maybe José too, though I find the fluorescent rubber bands on his braces to be a confusing choice."

"You're friends with Kit Lowell?" Principal Hoch asks, and even I can detect the disbelief in her voice.

"Yes, I am," I say. "And she's friends with me too."

CHAPTER 24

KIT

For the past fifteen minutes, I've been debating whether to knock on the principal's door. The thing is, this is all my fault. If I hadn't sat at David's table, Gabriel and Justin would never have stolen his notebook, and if they hadn't stolen his notebook, the football team would not have decided he was Enemy Number One. And also it wasn't until they mentioned me (or my ass, to be specific) that David went ballistic. I'm sure David can work this into some complicated algorithm, but the fact is: This is on me. Let's be honest, other than my mother sleeping with Jack, pretty much everything else is.

But when I hear Principal Hoch ask, "You're friends with Kit Lowell?" all condescending and disbelieving like that, like she thinks that I'm some imaginary friend that David has made up, I decide I have no choice but to waltz right in.

"David and I *are* friends," I proclaim as I push open the door a tad more dramatically than I intend. "And this wasn't David's fault. It was mine."

Only after the words are out, when I see David and his parents and Principal Hoch look up at me in shock, do I realize that I'm being totally inappropriate. Then I think: Could this hurt my chance of getting into college? Never have I felt more desperate to leave Mapleview than I have in the past few weeks.

"I'm not sure this involves you," Principal Hoch says to me.

If I were smart I'd walk out. I'd go home and pack a bag and move to Alaska. Or Hawaii. Or Paris. So what if I don't speak French? There is nothing left for me here. I seem to be blazing all the freaking bridges at once. Even I'm getting sick of my morose teenage girl shtick. It's time to molt and shed this version of myself. Maybe I'll even get rid of the name Kit, which is too close to Kitty, my dad's name for me. Now Kit feels too loaded. I could go back to being Katherine. Or try out something altogether new. Kath or Katie. Just K. A mysterious initial.

"The thing is, it's my fault, not David's," I repeat. I'm doing this. Barging into the principal's office and making a case, which isn't my case at all. This isn't even about me. I'm a side note to this story. The part you skip over to get to the good bits.

"Kit, this isn't your fault. But see, we are friends. What Kit just did is the very definition of friendship," David says, and turns back to the principal. "'We' don't have to do anything with me." David puts the *we* in air quotes. "I'm doing just fine. I've made friends. Just like a normal person. And you should value me as a student here as much as you do the football team."

"We do value you, and no one said you aren't a 'normal person,'" Principal Hoch says, countering with her own air quotes around *normal person*. If David's entire life did not depend on this meeting, I'd laugh at their finger talking.

"Actually, that's exactly what you've been saying. You are implying he doesn't deserve the protections you give every other student and that he doesn't have the same right to be here," Mrs. Drucker says, and for the first time I take a good look at her. She looks just like Lauren but older. She's beautiful, and I wonder if that's hard for David to have such a beautiful mother, like it is sometimes for me. But then I remember he's like Lauren, stunning too, and anyway, I imagine it's different for a guy. Though my mother and Mrs. Drucker are equally attractive, what Justin would call MILFs, they have very different styles. My mom likes glamour and general badassery, tight clothes, and high heels. Mrs. Drucker sports a loose-fitting peasant top, faded cuffed jeans, and gray Converse sneakers. She looks like she could practically be a student. Her hair is even pulled back into a messy ponytail—all jaunty and exuberant. Unlike my mom, Mrs. Drucker doesn't seem to try; in fact, it's like she's actively not trying. "You've been suggesting that he go to a special school."

"David does not need a special school," I say. I keep my voice calm, but really I feel like screaming. I can't take it anymore. The whole world is upside down and no one else seems to notice.

The football team threatens to choke David with his own balls and he's the one who might have to transfer?

My dad is dead.

My mom is alive.

And so am I.

So am I.

Why can't I shut up?

"Kit, would you excuse us?" Principal Hoch asks. Maybe I should pack a bag and go to Mexico. Mexico is a more logical choice, since they speak Spanish, which I kind of know, though I suspect I might speak it with Señora Rubenstein's same New Jersey whine, and I could drink margaritas there on the regular. I've never actually had a margarita, but they definitely seem like something I would like. My dad spent six months living in Oaxaca after college and promised he'd take me there one day. Maybe I should just take myself.

Poof. Disappear. Just like he did. I wonder how long I could get away with using my mother's credit cards. Would it be long enough for the world to right itself again?

No. I've been wrong. Time isn't the issue. The world will never be right again.

"Can I just say that David is awesome and he shouldn't get in trouble for this?"

"Please get back to class. Again, no one asked for your opinion—"

"With all due respect, let the girl talk," David's dad says. He's wearing khaki pants and a blue polo shirt, echoes of David's old uniform. When David wore it he looked like an electronics store stock boy, the person to ask about the best TV. His dad looks like the manager.

Principal Hoch reflexively defends herself and says, "I'm just trying to keep this private," but then changes her mind. "Kit, go on."

"Think about it—it's not David's fault he got his notebook stolen. It's mine. I made him a target. And it's because of the notebook that the whole school hates him. Don't get me wrong. He is no way normal." I stop, look at David. Smile a little. "Sorry, it's true. But who is? And since when is normal a requirement for high school?"

"I like her," David's dad says to no one in particular.

"I know, right?" David's mom says.

"I hear you saved the day," Lauren—aka Miney—says to me as she slides into the booth at McCormick's. She doesn't introduce herself. She's Lauren Drucker. She doesn't have to. David's parents are taking us all out for burgers to celebrate, though David and I have to be back to school before the bell for physics.

"Not really," I say. Lauren looks me up and down. I'm wearing jeans and a flannel shirt and ankle boots, an outfit my mother bought for me, since she's better at getting dressed than I am. Lauren looks cool even with chipped sunglasses on her head, and messy hair and clothes. I'm too intimidated and embarrassed to ask her how she pulls it off.

"Mom said that because of you, David's not getting expelled from school."

"I don't know. I think David was the one who kicked ass today," I say.

"Literally and figuratively," David says.

"I've never seen anything like it. He was like a kung fu master."

"Krav maga, mostly. With a few traditional karate moves," David says.

"But you had his back. I dig that," Lauren says, and the part of me that still hasn't outgrown the insecurities of freshman year gets a thrill from her approval.

"To Kit!" David's mom says, and the entire Drucker family raises their milk shakes and toasts me.

Later, when we are leaving the restaurant and David's mom stops to say hello to some lady she knows and David and his dad are debating whether it was fair of astronomers to demote Pluto from the status of planet, Lauren pulls me out of earshot of the rest of her family.

"I owe you a big thanks," she says. "For getting the notebook back. For talking to the principal. Seriously. It's hard not being at school to help him—I really hate being so far away—so thank you for stepping in. I didn't realize how much I'd miss him. Or here, actually."

"You don't have to thank me for being David's friend," I say. "I like hanging out with him."

Lauren's eyes narrow and then widen again, and for a second I wonder if she's tearing up.

"You're right," she says. "He's good people. The best, actually. Just one more thing, though," Lauren says, putting her hand on my arm to stop me from walking away. I notice that her feet are encased in unfashionable men's furry snow boots, which somehow look fashionable on her. How does she do that? She's just made of magic. There's no other explanation.

"Yeah?"

"You're probably good people too, but just so you know, I love David more than life itself, so if you hurt my brother in any way, or if you even *think* about hurting him, I will ruin you. I may not still live here, but I can still do that," she says in the hurried whisper of a Mafia don, which come to think of it is not unlike a homecoming queen, even an ironic hipster version. Her eyes are dry now and cold. "Understood?"

"I think so."

"Good," Lauren says, and then she throws her arm around my shoulders in a weird, semi-friendly half hug. "I think we're going to get along just fine."

I am at the weekly newspaper meeting, but no actual newspaper business is getting done because all anyone can talk about is the Fight. People are gossiping about it so much it has earned capitalization.

"Did you see that headlock move? It was like something out of UFC," Annie says.

"I really thought he was going to kill Mangino. Like ten guys from the football team are in the hospital," Violet says, who despite being our chief news correspondent tends not to always hew to the facts.

"More like Man-gina," says a puny freshman boy I've never noticed before, making the kind of joke that would have been suicidal if Joe weren't a safe distance away in the ER.

"How'd he learn to do that, Kit?" Violet asks.

"I have no idea." I'm only half listening. Mostly I'm trying to come up with a way to ask Mr. Galto to add my name to nominees for editor in chief. Since I'm not skipping town to Mexico after all, I need to get into a good college, preferably one on the other side of the country. I bet I'd like California: sunny skies, boys in shorts year-round, reading my textbooks while lying out on a beach towel. When I imagine West Coast Kit, I am the kind of girl who can rock a bikini and sunglasses and whose entire existence can be described by the word *frolic*. In other words, the opposite of who I am now.

Mr. Galto, please consider me for EIC. I realize I haven't been as reliable lately, and I missed the meeting, but I've worked my butt off for the past two years, and if you give me this chance I'll do better. Yes, I'll ask him afterward, just like that. He's the type to respond to groveling.

"Unless we're doing a feature on the fighting prowess of one Mr. David Drucker, which we are decidedly not, I think we need to get this meeting back on track," Mr. Galto says, and I sit straight in my chair and have my laptop out as if I'm poised to take notes. Taking position as the model student I used to be. I can still fix this. "First order of business, the new EIC. Drumroll, please . . ."

My stomach drops. I'm too late. My three years of hard work and ass-kissing all down the drain because I couldn't keep it together and was too distracted to ask Mr. Galto to consider me. I had lost track of the timing.

"Congratulations to Violet and Annie, our new co–editors in chief!" The room explodes in applause and Violet and Annie squeal and hug, because the only thing better than being editor in chief is sharing the position with your best friend. I force myself to smile, to pretend I'm not about to cry, that I didn't completely and totally self-sabotage.

I'm happy for them. I really am. Still, I not only feel like I lost something, but even worse: I've accidentally solidified my position as the odd man out in our threesome. Made something I just couldn't deal with at the moment permanent.

Violet looks over at me, and though she doesn't say anything, I know she's asking me for permission to be excited about this. I make my smile brighter. Give her some teeth.

And when Annie gives me a tentative Brownie salute, I give it right back.

Only later, when I'm back home, locked in my room, hiding from my mother and the rest of the world and wondering what my dad would have thought about me screwing one more thing up, do I allow myself to cry. For the third time since he died. That seal is officially broken.

CHAPTER 25

DAVID

Suddenly people want to talk to me. I'm stopped so often on my way down the halls that I don't even bother with my headphones. I let them dangle around my neck in that casual way like a rock star necklace.

"Dude, you're a monster!"

"Yo, man, didn't know you had it in you!"

"Hi-yah!"

Enthusiastic sentences are shouted in my face, often with crazy hand gesticulations or faux karate kicks. I even get a few high fives, which I don't think allow for an alternative interpretation other than *good job*. I'm about ninety-seven percent sure that none of these people want me to die. At least not today.

"You're late," José says when I arrive at the decathlon meeting. I am not late. I am twenty-three seconds early. Instead of saying this, I show him my phone, which is synced to Greenwich mean time to the second. "Okay, fine. But traditionally we ask that members arrive by two-fifty-seven."

"Well, then you should have told me that," I say, looking around at the group. There are seven people here. Two girls. Five guys, including myself and José. I don't know their names and can't look them up because my notebook no longer accompanies me to school. "I appreciate specificity."

"Noted," José says. "What happened to your face?"

"How can you not already know this? He, like, demolished the entire football team. Joe Mangino, who is officially the worst person in the world, is in the hospital because of this guy!" a kid with a hairstyle I believe is called a mullet says, and then fist pumps the air. Miney does that sometimes, though she accompanies it with the words *Can I get a woot woot?* I never oblige. I have no idea what a *woot woot* is.

I consider correcting Mullet, since there are probably worse people in the world than Meat Boy—like, say, ISIS members, or even Justin—but I remember that it's rude to correct people. Then again, this is the Academic League, so you'd assume they'd want to get their facts straight.

"I cried every day of freshman year because of Joe Mangino," José says.

"Drucker, our freakin' hero," Mullet says, and stretches his arms out wide. "Meet the team."

A girl with yellow pigtails and glasses and an awesome T-shirt that says DON'T TRUST ATOMS; THEY MAKE UP EVERYTHING smiles at me and puts out her hand, which I assume means she wants me to shake it, and so I do. Her palms are cool and soft. I search my brain for her name, but all I can come up with is Wheelchair Girl. I consider that she may be the second-prettiest girl in school, though it's still too early to officialize it, especially because I haven't spoken to her yet. That T-shirt is too little to go on. She must be a senior, because we don't have any classes together.

"I'm Chloe. On behalf of all of us, who have endured much verbal abuse from those guys through the years, and also on behalf of José's copious tears, I salute and thank you," Chloe says, and does a little wheelie with her chair as punctuation.

"You are very welcome," I say, and wonder if I'm flirting. Does my ability to banter extend beyond Kit? Probably not, but can't hurt to try, as my mom likes to say.

"Okay, Drucker, we're expecting you to kick ass for us at next week's meet against Ridgefield Tech. The team is all Asian, so they're amazing," Mullet says.

"That's racist," I say.

"I'm Asian, though. I'm allowed to say it. My people slay at this shit." I don't say anything back because I don't know if being Asian allows you to say racist things about other Asians. I'm not aware of this carve-out.

"Tell us everything you know about quantum mechanics," José says, and then, just like when I drop-kicked Meat Boy, my whole body sighs with pleasure.

"Where have you been?" Trey asks with a big contradictory smile on his face when I come home to find him waiting on my front porch. He has his guitar in his lap, and his feet are, as usual, in flip-flops even though he has been presumably stuck outside for at least seventeen minutes. I do not like looking at his exposed toes and their spritely hair patches.

"Oh no, I forgot about our lesson!" I say, and my heart drops. I never forget prescheduled events, but the meeting devolved from Academic League prep to a debate about the existence of the multiverse and the mechanics of the time-space continuum, and I must have gotten lost in the conversation. Chloe is surprisingly well read in the quantum world and knows almost as much as I do. Mullet is an expert in the field of theoretical mathematics. José is a history whiz. The whole experience turned out to be stimulating in the good way, not in the Jessica's blond hair or Abby's perfume sort of way. "Sorry."

"Seriously? You forgot?" Trey asks as he follows me inside and upstairs to my room, where we practice. "That's awesome!"

"It's been a big day." I'm rattled. How could I have forgotten my lesson? And why would Trey think that's a good thing? Routine is important. That's why tonight, like every Tuesday night, is pasta night, and also why, contrary to my mother's insistence, risotto doesn't count. (If it was a designated *Italian* night, not a *pasta* night, she might have a point.)

"Your sister texted me about the fight. You okay?" he asks, and points to his nose, which is decidedly less blue and swollen than mine.

"Fine."

"I heard you joined the Academic League. That's rad."

"I assume we'll have to pay you for the full hour even though it's a short lesson, so let's get started." I play a few chords as a hint that I'd like our work to commence, just in case I am being too subtle.

"No rush. Let's talk a little first," Trey says, and puts his guitar on the floor, like we have no need for our instruments. "We can go over our time."

"Will my mom be charged extra?" I ask.

"Don't worry about it."

"I'm not worried. I'm clarifying."

"No, you won't be charged extra," Trey says, and then blows up his cheeks and lets out a deep breath exactly like Miney does. Trey swings to look at me—he's sitting on my rotating desk chair; I'm on the bed—and he does this weird thing where he forces me to make eye contact. This technique of his invariably precedes a question that will make me uncomfortable.

"David, why don't you ever ask how I am?"

Phew, I'm relieved. That's an easy one. I thought he was going to bring up his showcase again. Recent out-of-character events like hanging out with Kit and fighting the football team and joining Academic League notwithstanding, me getting up onstage with a guitar in front of *people* is just not going to happen. I have my limits.

"Why would I do that?"

"Because it's polite to ask someone questions about themselves from time to time," Trey says.

"We have only sixty minutes a week allotted to my learning how to play the guitar and I'd prefer not to waste them."

"Come on. We've been working together almost ten months, and you know almost nothing about me. Whether I have brothers or sisters. What my major is. Where I live. How old I am. Aren't you curious?"

"Not really." I assumed he was an only child, since all his insistent chattering suggests he is desperate for company. My mother told me he was a college senior, so that makes him about twenty-one. And as for major, he seems suited for the liberal arts. I'd guess comparative literature or art history.

"People like it when you make small talk. It makes them feel like you care," Trey says.

"What's your major?" I ask, because though I appreciate efficiency, I do not like hurting people's feelings. And now that he's brought it up, I am curious. Could be I have him pegged all wrong. It certainly wouldn't be the first time.

"Double major: math and psych." He says the last word firmly, like if I were transcribing the conversation I should put it in all caps. *Math and PSYCH*. But I'm distracted by his empty neck. For the first time, he's not wearing his conch shell necklace, and its absence and the consequent pale expanse of skin— one more break in our routine—bring on a sudden wave of depression and hopelessness. I feel like crying or lying down in a dark room, which is inconvenient given I'm about to start my weekly guitar lesson.

Maybe I'll buy him a scarf for Christmas. Cover up his neck, which given his toes is surprisingly hairless.

"I wouldn't have guessed math, and if you're a psychology major I bet you like reading the *DSM* too," I say as a thought forms in my brain the same way I burrow into complicated algorithms. Lego pieces stacking on top of each other until they manifest into something recognizable. Like pointillism.

The wave of depression rolls away and is replaced by a vivid certainty.

For once, I understand. Ten months too late, maybe. But I finally get it.

"You're not really a guitar teacher, are you?" I ask.

"What do you mean?"

"My dad told Principal Hoch today that I have a social skills tutor. That's you, right?"

"I like to think of our work together as multifaceted," Trey says. He picks his guitar up off the floor and fiddles with the strings. "I mean, I do teach you how to play, but I also hope I teach you other stuff as well."

"I didn't realize. I feel stupid." Why is it I have to go through life only seeing part of the picture when everyone else gets to see the whole thing? Like my magnification level is set at fifteen thousand percent. "I wish you had told me. Then I wouldn't have rushed us through all the talking."

"Really?"

"Well, yeah. I could probably learn guitar from YouTube, but there's nothing on there for how to talk to other kids in high school. Believe me, I've searched," I say.

"Okay then." Trey puts down his guitar, looks up at me.

"So do you have any brothers or sisters?" I ask.

CHAPTER 26

KIT

"Sweetheart, open up." I wake to my mom banging on the door, loud and intrusive. My cheek is wet with drool and tears. My eyes feel swollen and heavy to open. I must have fallen asleep mid–emotional breakdown. I'm embarrassed all over again by what seems to bring on the waterworks these days. Small things instead of the big ones.

It's not like this is some lifelong dream. This is the *Maple-view High Bugle* we're talking about. So I'm not editor in chief. Who cares? It's not like I was particularly passionate about the newspaper anyway. I'm not like David, who gets carried away with all the things he's interested in, reading college-level text-books late into the night. I still have no idea who or what I want to be when I grow up. This was simply a way to pad my college application. Nothing more.

"Leave me alone!" I yell. My voice is shaky and sad. It

gives me away. Now that my mom senses I'm vulnerable, she'll pounce. This is precisely when having brothers or sisters would come in handy. Someone to share my mom's focus.

"I'm coming in." She opens the door, using what is apparently a spare key to my bedroom that I did not know existed. Like my happy family, my privacy has been an illusion. I wonder what else is a lie.

I do not look up. Do not give her the satisfaction of seeing me like this. It would be better if she just thought I was angry. That I hate her now. This pathetic version of me makes it look like there's room for her to wiggle her way back into my life. I want to scream, *I'm not crying about you!* but I don't seem to have the energy.

"We need to talk," she says. She sits on my bed, and also my toes.

"Ow!" It doesn't hurt, but I don't feel like being mature about anything.

"I understand you're mad at me," my mom starts, readjusting so she's not squashing my feet. "And you have every right to be. Still, I think you need to hear me out."

"No."

"Kit."

"No."

"Stop being a baby," she says, which, for some reason makes me snap. I'm tired of playing adult. Of trying to be a good sport. I'm suddenly revved up and burning with rage. This must have been what David felt like earlier, when he started drop-kicking the football team. I need to learn krav maga.

"Are you serious right now? I'm the baby? I'm not the one who slept with my husband's best friend. You're a cheater and a liar."

"Please, honey," she says, all conciliatory, arms outstretched as if I am four years old and all I need is a hug from Mommy to make my boo-boo better. Like my words bounced right off her.

"Do you have any idea what you did to Dad? He was going to divorce you. He was going to break up our family. That's how much you must have hurt him!" I am screaming at the top of my lungs, so loud that our neighbors the Jacksons can probably hear me even with their windows closed. I don't care. I need this to stick. "All because you're a big slut."

"Kit!"

"Stop saying my name! You don't get to say my name! You don't get to do anything!"

"Kit!" she yells again, but I can't hear her. The anger is too loud and fuzzy, like radio static. White noise on white noise.

"I wish it was you who died. Not Dad. You. It's not fair," I say, and then I curl into a fetal position and cry, because though I have just said the most hurtful thing a daughter can say to a mother, and even though I saw the words land like a punch on my unflappable mother's face—she actually *flinched*—I feel no satisfaction. Even worse, as soon as the words are out I realize that they are not true. I loved my dad, maybe even more than I love my mother. But still, despite myself, I need her more. Always have.

My mom puts her hand to her mouth, as if she is trying to stifle a silent scream. She's more ashen than usual, pale enough that she's almost the same color as me. And just like that, her composure dissolves.

"Oh God," she says, and then starts sobbing into her palm in large gulps. "Oh God, you're right. It's not fair. He's really gone. And he died without knowing how much I still—have always— loved him."

"Mom," I whisper, but I make no move to comfort her. I just unfold my body, sit up, curl my knees back in. I'm still fetal, though at least I'm upright.

"I get why you're punishing me. I know I deserve all of it. But just know you can't hurt me any more than I'm already hurting. He was my husband, the father of my child, we were together my entire adult life. I don't even know who I am without him," she says, and clutches at her chest. "The love of my life died—he *died*, Kit—at pretty much the only moment in twenty-six years when he doubted me."

And there it is. For the first time, my mother says three simple words—*he died, Kit*—and at least that part, the *he died* part, is the truest thing she's ever said.

"Why'd you do it?" I ask, and the tables flip once more. I'm the one sounding like the grown-up again. "Don't tell me you were lonely. I want to know why you were willing to sacrifice everything."

She sighs, closes her eyes, and then opens them, as if gathering herself.

"I *was* lonely. That's not an excuse. It's just the truth. Part of it, anyway. Your dad had his books and his practice and you. He wasn't the type to say to me, *Hey, honey, you look beautiful*. He didn't often even say *I love you*. He just wasn't that kind of man. I knew that when I married him, and in the beginning I never really needed it. I felt good about myself. Not just about how I looked, but about everything—our marriage, you, my work. For years, it all hummed along nicely. It seemed, I don't know, so greedy and American to ask for more than that. Then one day I looked in the mirror and suddenly I was forty-five and I realized I couldn't remember the last time anyone, including Dad, had paid any real attention to me. I felt . . . taken for granted. Like I was invisible," my mom says. "You are too young to know what that feels like. At your age, every day is like being center stage."

Of course my mom would think that's what sixteen is like. In high school, she was a clear-skinned Indian goddess among pasty, pimpled white girls. She was like a Lauren Drucker, not a Kit Lowell.

"I talked to Dad about how I was feeling and he dismissed it and told me to get my nails done or go get highlights, which felt so condescending. He said I was making a big deal out of nothing. Things were fine. *We* were fine. All marriages go through shifts. I don't know. He wasn't hearing me. It felt like more than just a lull; I was scared things had permanently shifted. Middle-aged doesn't mean it's all over, right?"

I don't answer. Middle age seems an eternity away.

"Jack was feeling depressed about his divorce, and Dad thought it would be good if he spent more time with us, to cheer him up. Sometimes we'd talk, and he became my friend too. I really needed a friend then. This life can be so lonely. You have no idea."

I want to tell her she's being condescending, but I'm too tired to talk. My anger has curdled into something sour. Suddenly I don't know why I asked my mother to explain. I don't want to hear about her loneliness. About the truth of adult life. I don't want to know any of this. I want to ask her to stop, but she keeps going.

"One night while your dad was away at that dental convention in Pittsburgh and you were over at Annie's, Jack and I had dinner and got stupid drunk. I don't know, for a moment it's like I equated your father with my parents. I got that ridiculous adolescent feeling of needing to rebel, needing to shake things up, no matter the cost. I made a mistake. One time. Still, one of us should have stopped. I should have said stop."

"That's not a mistake. That's a betrayal," I say, finding my voice. "You didn't just betray Dad, you betrayed me too. Our three-person family. And your explanation doesn't undo that damage. Lots of people are lonely. Maybe everyone is. They don't go around—"

"I know. Again there's no excuse. We were drunk and stupid and thought—no, we didn't think. We just did. We immediately regretted it and, for better or worse, I told your dad. I had to tell him. I've never not told him anything. And that's when he filed. Before I even had a chance to explain."

I take a moment to rewrite the story I made up in my head. The old version had my dad coming home early from work one day and finding my mom and Jack in their bed. I imagined tears and punches, soap opera levels of drama. The old version had an ongoing affair, not a onetime drunken hookup. The old version did not leave room for remorse and confession. The old version involved that terrible, terrible word *love*.

"You're too young to understand any of this. Look at you. My baby. You are too young to have lost your father, and in such a cruel way. You shouldn't have to even know about my ridiculous midlife crisis. You are just too young for all of it. I want to throw myself in front of you, I want to stop all this life from happening to you. But I can't. I just can't." My mom wipes her eyes. "I know you will judge me and maybe hate me, and you have every right to. But I love you no matter what. I was stupid and selfish and one day when you're older you might understand—I think your dad was beginning to—but for now I can't ask you to understand. I can only ask you for your forgiveness."

She lifts my chin so I'm staring her straight in the eye. Both of our faces are wet, and our bodies are trembling with pent-up grief and rage and regret. She's not wrong. I do judge her, I do hate her for what she's done—but I also love her, and I don't know how to reconcile those things.

"You know the part that makes me saddest of all? I can't protect you anymore. I can't fix this for you. Any of it," she says.

"I don't need protecting," I say. I don't say *I forgive you*. I don't say *I love you*. Instead I repeat the words again: "I don't need protecting."

The trouble is we both know that's another lie, just like everything else.

Later I have a crying hangover. My head aches, my eyes are red and swollen, and my stomach feels hollowed out. With my door closed and my desk chair tucked behind the knob so my mom can't just waltz in even with her secret key, I take a deep breath and I decide that if I want to keep my friends—and I do—I better reach out. I dart off a quick text.

Me: Congrats on EIC, guys. Really. I should have said it earlier.

Violet: Whatevs re EIC. You totally deserved it too, but thanks.

Annie: TY, K.

Violet: You'll stay on the paper, right?

Me: Course.

Violet: Phew. Hey, party at Dylan's on Friday. You in?

Annie: Pls say Y. Pls. Pls. Pls. 🖤🖤🖤🖤🖤🖤

Me: 👦 Dylan or 👧 Dylan.

Annie: Duh, 👧

Me: K.

Annie: Bring your bf, DD.

Me: David's not my boyfriend.

Violet: Maybe he should be. That beat-down was hot. I'm totally #teamdavid.

Annie: TD! BRING HIM.

Me: I don't know if he'll want to come.

Annie: For the eleventy billionth time, BRING HIM.

CHAPTER 27

DAVID

At 7:57 a.m. on Wednesday morning, I cross paths with Kit just as we make our way into school. She smiles at me and makes the *take off your headphones* motion, which I do. If I leave my music on and we talk while walking, I'm pretty sure I can still round the corner to a track change.

"Your face looks better," she says, wincing. "Does it hurt?"

"Not too bad." My right eye is ringed in blue and my lips are swollen, but my nose has returned to roughly normal dimensions. In the shower I noticed seven small bruises along my torso, and I'm pretty sure I'll lose my left thumbnail. Meat Boy apparently has two casts. He will have to sit out the rest of the football season. I'm not complaining. I have not received a single threatening text since yesterday. For the time being, my peers are okay with me continuing to live.

"So there's this party on Friday night," Kit says.

"There are probably lots of parties on Friday night," I say, a line which sounded much smoother in my head than out loud.

"Well, this particular one is a Mapleview high school party at Dylan's."

"Boy Dylan or Girl Dylan?"

Kit smiles to herself, though I have no idea why she'd find that amusing. "Girl Dylan."

"Right." I believe Girl Dylan has red hair that starts out small and fans out across her back. It's spectacularly geometric. "The one with the orange triangular head?"

"I guess?" Kit asks. "So I'm wondering, do you want to go?"

"With you? To a Mapleview high school party?"

"Yes. With me. To the party. Though now I'm starting to regret asking, because you're making this so much harder and more awkward than I thought it would be."

"I'd love to go to Girl Dylan's party with you," I say, quickly accepting before Kit can rescind her invitation. If I didn't know it was inappropriate, I'd do a little dance right here. I suddenly understand the appropriate usage of Miney's *Can I get a woot woot?* because I want two of them—a *woot* and then another *woot*—whatever they may be. I'd maybe even add in some lasso arms.

"Okay," Kit says.

"Okay," I say, and try but fail to keep my face neutral. Nope, I smile so big it hurts my lips. I slip my headphones back on, round the corner at track change number three. A good start to the day.

I'm at the mall again, shopping for Friday night. Miney has declared this journey a necessity, though I don't understand why I can't just wear one of the outfits we bought last week. I've been rotating my new clothes on a mutually agreed-upon schedule with my mother that allows maximum repeatability by me but also makes time for biweekly washing. The thought of adjusting to more new clothes makes my body itch.

"Will it be noisy at the party?" I ask Miney, since she's a serious partygoer and is therefore an expert. I say this loudly, because it happens to be noisy here too, as we pass the food court, my least favorite part of the mall experience. Too many mixed culinary smells and crying children and people pushing past while carrying an unwieldy number of shopping bags.

"Yup."

"Distractingly so?" I ask.

"For you, yeah, probably. But you definitely can't bring your headphones."

"Will it be smelly? Will there be lots of people throwing up?" In almost every teen movie party scene, the heroine drinks too much and vomits on her potential love interest's lap. I like Kit a lot, but maybe not that much.

"Nah. I mean, it happens sometimes, usually later in the night, but you'll be fine."

"So put a number on it. What do you think is the likelihood of someone vomiting on or near me at Friday night's party?" I ask as we move into the atrium part of the mall, which has a high glass-domed ceiling and a grand piano. It's the opposite of the food court—empty and open and the only part of this whole place that I don't hate. The music isn't half bad—I mean, there's a reason the pianist is playing in front of Nordstrom and not at Carnegie Hall—but it's a tolerable sound track.

"Two point four percent," Miney answers with uncharacteristic precision. I do not ask her how she arrived at that number, but estimating that she's been to at least one party a weekend for half a decade, this means she's been proximate to throw-up about six times.

"Those are reasonable odds."

"Little D, you'll be fine."

"What if the football team is there?"

"They will likely hide from you, since you are, like, the Ultimate Fighting Champion now."

"In UFC they don't abide by rules. I abide by rules. I fight with honor."

"Right."

"Can you please also give me instructions for dancing?"

"Excuse me?"

"I need instructions for dancing. Like how do I move my body to music in front of other people? Break it down. Step by step."

"Seriously? Dancing isn't one of those things that come with instructions. It's not like putting together Ikea furniture."

"Please help me."

"Well, first of all, *this* is not the sort of music that will be playing." She motions to the pianist, who is bald and bearded, which I've always found to be a bizarre combination. You would think you would want cranial and mandibular hair consistency.

"No Ravel's *Bolero*. Got it."

"No classical music, period. They'll probably just play all the crap that's on the radio."

"I amend my original request. I need instructions for dancing to noise."

"You just move your body to the beat. Feel the music." Miney puts her arms up and sways to sounds I do not hear. She closes her eyes, leans on the tips of her toes, and jumps. After approximately ninety seconds, she stops and looks at me. "Your turn."

"I don't think so." Miney doesn't respond. She just waits.

"Fine." I copy her, jump up and down, though I don't actually jump down, which is a misnomer. I let gravity do its job. My sneakers make discordant squeaks along the marble floor.

"No. Stop. You look like you're having a seizure. Think of dancing like having a conversation but with the music instead of with another person. It's all intuition and instinct."

"Right. Because I'm good at all three of those things. Intuition, instinct, and having conversations with other people."

"Little D, sarcasm becomes you. Seriously, though, you got this. Just like when you're talking to Kit, follow her lead. Look for the cues. If the song is fast, you move faster. If it's slow, move slower, more intimately. Maybe for you it won't be about instinct."

"Then what will it be about?" I ask.

"Well, you're good at details, right? Noticing the small things? And you know how to listen. Like really listen in a way no one else can. So maybe use those skills? Do it your way."

"You're not making sense. Dance my way? I don't have a way."

"You do. Everyone does." We have reached the center of the atrium, and the sun is glaring down. It's too hot in here. Ravel suddenly seems like an aggressive choice for the mall. I think through the numbers, applying values to a cost-benefit analysis of the chances of my humiliating myself if I decide to dance at the party. The math feels uncomfortably random, like I've assigned numbers just to make myself feel better. "And this could be your chance. Say you're dancing with Kit, maybe you lean in a little and bam, you guys kiss."

"Do you think this is my once-in-a-lifetime opportunity to kiss Kit Lowell? And if so, what do you think are my chances in that regard?" I ask.

"Yes, and I think your odds are about two point four percent."

"So you're saying that on Friday night I have an equal chance of getting vomited on as I do of getting kissed?"

"Welcome to high school," Miney says.

CHAPTER 28

KIT

"You look beautiful," David says right into my ear, so close I shiver. My back presses against a speaker blasting crappy music, and I flip my hair in a way I've seen Jessica do, right then left then right again. I instantly regret it because I have the kind of hair that frizzes, not flips. I am wearing my mom's red bandage dress and her most expensive heels, and I'm carrying a full bottle of some fancy Scandinavian vodka, the total effect of which makes me feel like I'm in a Halloween costume. *Cocktail party grown-up.* I took—well, stole—all this without asking, of course, despite the fact that my mom would have happily lent me her clothes, if not handed over the alcohol. That would have meant having to talk to her, and I'm not ready for that. The silence between us has turned malleable and soft, though. I suspect we are now being quiet out of self-protection. We are both too raw for words.

I still eat dinner alone in my room.

I still hate-love my mother.

The party is too crowded—most of Mapleview High is here, even a few guys who graduated last year and go to the local community college—and people are dancing anywhere they can find space. On couches, side tables. They bounce around against each other as if this is a rave and not Dylan's parents' living room. Gabriel and Willow eat each other's faces right in the center of the makeshift dance floor, the sort of making out that gives kissing a bad name.

Abby and Jessica giggle from the sidelines. Based on their bloodshot eyes and the bag of Cheetos they are sharing, I'm pretty sure they're high. Neither of them would be caught dead eating something fluorescent, scratch that, *eating at all*, sober.

"Thanks," I say to David, and hope he doesn't notice that I'm blushing. My mother, when she feels like complimenting me, almost always suggests some adjustment (*Maybe try a different shirt, Kit? Yellow doesn't suit your skin tone.*), then only once I've taken her advice and changed does she say I look *lovely. Beautiful* feels like an upgrade.

"It's too loud," David says, again into my ear, and I want him to keep talking. Because it feels good, him leaning in like that, tickling my ear with his breath. He's right, of course. It is way too loud. I have no idea why I come to parties. It's not like I actually want to talk to any of the people here or, God forbid, dance. David and I would have been much better off heading to McCormick's alone to have burgers and milk shakes.

I lead David by the hand, past Justin, who is deejaying, away from the noise and throngs and into the kitchen. If the other room felt like mayhem, here it feels postapocalyptic. The overhead lights are on. Bottles, ketchup packets, and empty potato chip bags litter the countertops. There's a puddle of something yellow on the floor, and for Dylan's sake I really hope it's beer, not pee, though let's be honest, they taste and smell the same.

Violet and Annie lean against the counter and sip from red plastic cups and greet us with weary enthusiasm.

"Hello!" they say in unison, and give me a semi-drunken hug, then lean into David, who at first doesn't know what to do, but eventually leans in too.

"This is disgusting. Why don't people clean up after themselves?" David's wearing a fitted blue cashmere sweater and jeans that border surprisingly on skinny. He has a leather jacket crooked on his arm. He looks handsome. I have trouble looking away. He rolls up his sleeves and starts to gather up some trash.

"You can leave it," I say. His sister must have picked out his clothes. It has her stamp of effortless cool. I wonder if she could give me lessons. I'd pay. Seriously.

"Really? I don't really get what we're supposed to do here otherwise," David says.

"We're supposed to just have fun."

"Have fun. Sure. I can do that," he says, though he looks uncomfortable and has what I think of as his processing face. Like he's translating my words from English to whatever language it is he speaks in his head. "But it's loud. Like really, really loud. Even in here. And the lights are too bright."

"Have a drink. That should help." I pour out four clear shots from my mom's bottle.

"I'm driving," he says.

"Good answer. More for me, then, my DD," I say, a stupid play on the words *designated driver* and *David Drucker*. I'm glad he is responsible, but I don't want to think about driving.

I hand Violet and Annie their shots and swig mine and

David's fast, one after the other. They burn on the way down. Like David, I no longer have any idea about how to have fun, *how to just be,* and so I have decided if I am going to survive this party I need a little help. I don't really see any other way.

"Slow down," Violet says, looking at my now-empty glasses. I've drunk before, but not a lot and not often. "The night is young."

"So are we," I say, and take a third shot just as fast. Violet gives Annie a look, but it turns out Annie's on my side on this one.

"Touché," Annie says, and pours out more drinks and hands them around. She even pours David a cup of soda. "To hashtag Team David!"

"To David," I say.

"To me?" he asks, adorably confused.

A few minutes later, or maybe much later, I can't really tell, David takes my hand and leads me outside to the backyard, which is mercifully quiet. My head is humming and my edges are blurry and the world is rolling. I'm drunk. That much is obvious. How drunk I am and how much I will regret this tomorrow remain to be seen.

"Do you want my jacket?" David asks, and I shake my head, which is, of course, a mistake. A wave of nausea hits fast and hard.

"Let's sit down," I say, and we find our way to the back porch steps. I scoot up next to David, since it's cold out. We are the only people dumb enough to be outside. Even the smokers have abandoned their cigarettes for the warmth of the house.

"You okay? You're not going to throw up or anything, are you?" he asks, and I don't know why I find this hilarious, but I do. I laugh and then he does too, and the laughing and the cold somehow clear away the nausea.

"Nope. I pinky-swear I will not blow chunks." David winces, and then of course my face goes red. Why did I have to say *blow chunks*, which is by far the least romantic word combo in the English language? I could have just said no. "I mean, I'm fine."

"You match, you know? Your outsides *and* your insides are beautiful," David says, and he throws one arm stiffly over my shoulder. The movement is awkward and clumsy and because of this awkwardness and clumsiness—not despite it—I'm charmed. Or maybe it's the four vodka shots and whatever concoction Annie made for me. Either way, I like sitting here, with David's arm heavy around my shoulders; I like studying his profile, basking in the glow of his compliments. I want to reach up and feel the tiny bit of stubble along his jawline. Unlike the rest of the guys here, he is more man than boy.

"I like to match," I say, which I realize makes no sense but I think still comes off in a flirty way. It's so much easier to flirt drunk. How come I never realized this before? This is the sort of basic information I'm sure someone like Lauren Drucker already knows. David smells good, and the crook of his neck seems inviting. The sort of place where I should rest my dizzy head. And I do. Nuzzle right in there. Which is something I would never do without liquid courage.

"We match," I say, and as soon as the words are out I already know that tomorrow will come and I will remember this moment and wince. *We match??* And so, even through this drunken haze, I feel relief when he doesn't laugh at me. Instead he squeezes me a little tighter, brings me a tiny bit closer so my edges are against his edges, and it's all warm. Our bodies fit. I secretly sniff him, and get rewarded with his fresh lemony scent.

I want him to kiss me, I realize. There is nothing else really left for me to want. I can't undo the past two months. I can't make my dad be alive. Or my mother not be a cheater. I can't undo the accident, am no longer naive enough to think that figuring out the math could somehow make it better. I can't become editor in chief. I can't change or fix any of it. But kissing David would feel good, good enough for me not to think about Lauren's warning that I better not hurt her brother, good enough for me not to worry about whether David will understand the concept of a casual hookup, good enough for me not to think about why I ever started the Accident Project in the first place.

Good enough that I will not think about my dad or my mom or anything at all.

David has told me I am beautiful, not once but twice, and right now I really feel that he isn't lying, that I am, or maybe that one day I could be, beautiful, inside and out.

Kissing David would make me forget.

Is that so wrong? For me to want to forget for just a little while?

Kissing David would feel good.

Do I need a better reason than that?

Team David, I think. I'm totally on Team David.

CHAPTER 29

DAVID

Kit's head is resting on my shoulder. She is wearing a red dress that makes her look like a mummy. It's made of supertight blood-colored bandages, the kind of dress that should be illegal for a teenage girl because she looks about twenty-five, not sixteen. I want to touch her. I want to tell her that she is the first girl I have ever loved, since I think that must be what this feeling is. Love.

I have never felt this way before. I've never had someone loom so large in my brain that the rest of the stuff gets crowded out. Out here, in this quiet backyard, I can tune out the distant thump of the music. Out here, with her head on my shoulder and the smell of her shampoo—almond and honey—and the feel of her soft hair against my cheek, I can forget that I am David Drucker. I can forget everything. That I'm the kind of person whose mom has to hire a social skills tutor so I can learn how to have a basic human conversation. That I'm the kind of person who routinely receives texts that say things like *Die, loser.* That I'm the kind of person who would be stupid enough to go into a bathroom stall with Justin because he promised he "had something cool to show me."

How do I kiss her? Miney gave me a ton of advice, like not to jam my tongue down Kit's throat or to be too slobbery. She even made me watch YouTube tutorials on technique. But we never got around to how to actually do it. How do I move from us sitting next to each other, ostensibly observing the stars and listening to the eerie creak of the swing set, to putting our lips together?

"Kit?" I decide I will just ask her to kiss me. Or better yet, ask if I can kiss her. Best to be direct and clear. Leave no room for miscommunication, my specialty.

"Hmm," she says, which I assume means *yes.*

"How would you feel about me— I mean, what do you think about the idea—" I can't say it. *How would you feel about me kissing you? Can I kiss you?* would be better. Yes, that would be more accurate. I want permission, not a complicated discussion of her emotional state.

Can I kiss you? Four simple words. I can do this.

I turn my head again, and as I talk my lips brush her forehead. Almost a kiss. Just seven and a half inches off.

"Can I—?" But before I can ask the question, her head shifts and she leans in and wraps her hand around the back of my neck and closes the gap. Seven and a half inches erased just like that. Her lips are on mine, and we are kissing.

All I can think is *Kit kissed me,* over and over until I stop thinking altogether.

CHAPTER 30

KIT

I am kissing David Drucker. I am kissing David Drucker. I am kissing David Drucker.

I was wrong. I had assumed this would be his first kiss, that it would be fumbling and a bit messy but still fun. No way. Can't be. This guy knows exactly what he's doing. How to cradle the back of my head with his hands. How to move in soft and slow, and then pick up the pace, and then slow down again. How to brush my cheeks with even smaller kisses, how to work his way down my jaw, and to soften the worry spot in the center of my brow. How to pause and look into my eyes, really look, so tenderly I feel it all the way down in my stomach.

He even traces the small zigzag scar on my eyebrow with his fingertips, like it's something beautiful.

I could kiss him forever.

I'm going to kiss him forever.

I am kissing David Drucker, and yes, I've forgotten everything else.

Because his lips are back on mine.

Because this, right here, is the best kiss of my life.

We kiss and kiss and kiss and only stop when David pulls away, cups the sides of my face with his huge hands, and says: "There are cops here. We've got to go."

Even that sounds romantic. He has morphed from dorky classmate to partner in crime. We hold hands and run to his car and he opens the passenger-side door for me. Offers his jacket one last time.

"I'm okay," I say. "You kept me warm." He smiles at me, and even in the dark I can see that he's blushing. And now I am too. I'm hot all over.

"At least take my scarf." He pulls a scarf from his jacket pocket and winds it around my neck. Cashmere, as soft as his sweater. Everything he wears is soft. He takes both edges and then pulls me toward him again, a suave move, and we kiss one last time. My chest tightens, my body tingles, and I allow myself to dissolve into him. It seems wrong that we ever need to leave this moment. I want to stay right here.

"Get a room!" I hear Gabriel shout as he walks by, but I don't care. Team David, I think again. I'm definitely on Team David.

We don't talk on the ride home. We don't have to. I feel warm and giddy and like I have a secret that I want to keep all to myself. David Drucker, who is so many different people all at once: the guy who always sits alone, the guy who talked quantum physics even in my dad's dental chair, the guy who held my hand in the snow. I kissed David Drucker, the guy I most like to talk to, and it was perfect.

Four a.m. Alone in my bedroom. The butterflies I have savored all night suddenly turn to bats. My mouth is sour. Everything spins. David's scarf feels hot and itchy on my neck. Too tight. I feel the opposite of beautiful.

The regrets start singing their cruel song in my ear. Grating and on automatic repeat.

Then suddenly the accident starts playing on my ceiling. Headlights. Screeching tires. My foot twitches slowly. Always too slow.

I remember everything.

Make it stop.

I crawl to the bathroom with only a second to spare.

I blow chunks until dawn.

CHAPTER 31

DAVID

I spent ninety-six glorious minutes kissing Kit Lowell. Ninety-six minutes where her mouth was against my mouth, or my mouth was against her neck, or my mouth was against that amazing freckle cluster at her clavicle. I could spend the rest of my living days kissing Kit without getting bored, without stopping except for the physiological imperative of occasional sleep and food and to relieve myself.

Best. Night. Of. My. Life.

After I drive Kit home, I lie awake on my bed. My mind is spinning but, for once, in a good way. No need to talk myself out of or down from this sensation. Kissing Kit wasn't too tangy or too loud or too rough or too moist, like I had feared it might be. It wasn't too *anything*. It was perfect. Kissing Kit was a *privilege*.

I replay the evening over and over again in my head, especially that very first minute. How Kit pulled my face toward hers, that feeling of her hands clasping my neck, the lack of ambiguity about what she wanted.

Everything was clear.

She picked me.

She kissed *me*.

Me.

For just tonight, I can pretend that I am something approximating cool. I wore a leather jacket that purposely looks worn in. My jeans were fitted, like a boy-bander's. I looped my scarf around Kit's neck and left it there, so she'll have to see me again, if only to return it. I thought of that move all by myself. I didn't learn it from YouTube or Miney's instructions or a teen movie.

And now that I've been exposed to this feeling, perfect mouth against perfect mouth, the natural order of things, I wonder why people don't kiss all day, every day. How does anything ever get done?

I feel reborn. No longer Mapleview's resident hand-flapping weirdo. There is hope for me in the wider world, hope that I can leave this place one day and start over as someone else. Me version 2.0. Me smoothed out a little.

Love. I test the word in my head a few times. Let it bounce around my brain, the same way I tackle a formula, slowly at first, then accelerating exponentially, until it comes out the other end whole and solved.

Love.

Yes, it is clear what has happened here. What Kit has done to me.

She kissed me.

And then biology took over.

A dopamine rush. And maybe a hit of seratonin and adrenaline too.

A beautiful chemical reaction.

And just like that, I am madly in love with Kit Lowell.

Since love is new for me, I start as I would with any other intellectual exercise, and I Google: *What do you do when you love someone?* From there, I stumble upon the rules of courtship, which is a layman's way of saying "human mating ritual." Apparently, the surest indicator of a person's attractiveness is whether their face is symmetrical, and so I measure mine and am relieved to discover my halves are of roughly equal dimension. Good. Next, in order to prove their reliability to support future potential offspring, men need to spend money on the object of their affection. Though I bring no income to the table at present, I decide the best way to show Kit that I'm a suitable partner is to demonstrate my other genetic attributes. I may not be good at small talk or making friends or abiding by high school social etiquette, but it's incontrovertible that I'm exceptionally talented at science and math. I need to show off to her, just like a ribbon-tailed astrapia grows its tail feathers. I grab my notebook and write out my two-part plan.

First, I will stay up all night and finish the Accident Project. Show Kit the real-life applications of my skill set and the myriad and unexpected ways it can benefit her.

Second, I will invite Kit to the Academic League meet. It's a bit obvious to use the event as a courtship display, but as Miney likes to say, *if you got it, flaunt it.*

Instead of sleeping, I draw diagrams, calculate axes and velocity, research car models and their various braking systems. My scientific calculator goes warm from overuse. On the Internet, I find experts on car collisions and delve deep into forensic message boards. Learn about head injuries, broken chest cavities, punctured hearts. I pull up the pictures I took of the accident site and blow up on my thirty-inch monitor the one Kit sent me of her dad's car. A Volvo smooshed up like an accordion on the right side. I zoom in with my new camera software. Examine the blood on the passenger-side dashboard. Stencil the splatter pattern. I read the newspaper accounts of the crash, which has a photo of the other car, a navy-blue Ford Explorer with a shattered windshield, half-folded in on itself. A car reimagined as a paper airplane. In the background, there's a Mini pulled over to the side that has minimal damage: just two broken headlamps, a big dent in its hood. The article doesn't mention its involvement, but based on my own analysis, I assume it was behind the Volvo. Another car changes things. Adds a layer of complexity. I wish Kit had mentioned it before.

I line my three pictures up next to each other, as if they form a comic strip, though this is not at all funny.

No matter how many times I check my work—and I do, over and over again, maybe as many times as I have relived kissing Kit—the math does not make sense. By my calculations, the *only* calculations, Kit's dad shouldn't be dead.

"What's wrong?" Miney asks when she comes into my room on Saturday morning and finds me at my desk in the same clothes as last night. I'm flapping. "Didn't go well last night? I so thought that leather jacket would seal the deal."

"What deal?" I ask. My head feels heavy. It is nine a.m. and I haven't slept at all. I rub my face, attempt to wipe away the fatigue, which is a wasteful expenditure of energy at just the time I should be conserving. Fatigue is not something that can be wiped away like a smudge. I am not thinking clearly. "The party was great. Perfect, actually. Well, not the party part—parties are horrible, I don't know why people go to them—but the rest of it, the *Kit* of it was great. Amazing."

"Really? Then why do you look like someone ran over your dog?"

"We don't have a dog."

"Focus, Little D."

"What?"

"Tell me what's wrong." Miney's wearing pajamas, though it's a clean pair I don't recognize. Her eyes are less bloodshot. Whatever mysterious illness she was afflicted with seems to have resolved itself. "You do not look like someone who has had an 'amazing' night. Did you kiss her?"

"Yup. Well, actually she kissed me."

"She kissed *you*?"

"Yup."

"And?"

"And I'm in love."

"That's great. Though maybe you should slow down a bit. It's a little early to be throwing the L-word around." She plops down backward on my rotating chair, like she is a football coach in a movie about to deliver one of those *huddle up* speeches.

"It doesn't matter. None of it matters," I say, and shiver because I already feel the loss before it's even happened. I will never kiss Kit again. The whole thing is over no more than twelve hours after it began. Weirdly, this realization doesn't just reset me back to my pre-Kit life, Me 1.0, when kissing her had seemed as impossible as crossing the space-time continuum. When I was resigned to a lifetime of solitude. Now it is so much worse. I can't imagine going back to that empty lunch table on Monday morning. Being again that guy everyone used to call shithead. The longing for Kit feels physical. Like my heart is blinking.

Alfred Lord Tennyson was an idiot. He was wrong. It is not better to have loved and lost than to never have loved at all. If I had never loved at all, I wouldn't be here flapping. I'd be downstairs, after a restful night's sleep, reading the *DSM* and eating Saturday morning pancakes. I wouldn't know what it's like for everyone else. What it means to not be alone. Just how far and how long I've lived away from planet Normal.

"The Accident Project. I can't figure it out," I say.

"Please speak English," Miney says.

"Kit asked me to do one thing, to help her figure out how her dad died—well, not how, exactly, but the when, the moment of braking, so the larger 'how,' I guess, and the math doesn't work. The math always works. It's the only thing I know how to do, and I can't do it."

"Little D, calm down." She reaches to pat my back, but I jerk away from her hand. I don't want to be touched. My body is flaring. "You have so much more to offer than math. That's not why Kit kissed you. You realize that, right?"

"He's not supposed to be dead. Dentist is not supposed to be dead."

"Who's Dentist? Kit's dad? Of course he shouldn't be dead. It's a tragedy—"

"No, you don't understand. The math doesn't work."

"So?"

"It's not a tragedy. It's a lie."

CHAPTER 32

KIT

My first thought when I wake up on Saturday morning is I want to die. Because if I die, then the nausea will stop, the room will still, and I won't have to face the shitshow that has become my life. In bed I stare at the white ceiling and think about my mother's confession. She got drunk and made a mistake. Alcohol clouds your judgment, she said. Makes you listen to the wrong voice in your head.

Just because you are forty-five doesn't mean you don't sometimes feel and act sixteen, she claimed, which is probably the most depressing thing I've ever heard in my life, because you want to know my big secret plan right now? The only freaking thing I have in my back pocket? The idea that eventually I'll age out of this horrible life stage and never, ever look back.

I wonder what David is thinking about this morning. Based on his amazing kissing skills, it's entirely possible he has a secret life. After last night, I realize I know nothing about the real him. I realize how silly—how naive—it is to assume you know anyone at all. Look at my mother and me. We are made of smoke and mirrors.

I check my phone and find a bunch of texts.

Mom: You okay? Left a glass of water and two Advil by your bed. You looked rough last night.

Under other, more normal circumstances, I would expect a lecture, though somehow I doubt my mom has the nerve to criticize today. I am sixteen acting sixteen. She's in no position to judge.

But I don't remember seeing my mom last night, and that part, the not remembering—which was one of the reasons for drinking in the first place—makes me feel worst of all.

Me: Hanging in there.

Mom: I'll check on you in a little bit, okay?

I pause for a second before texting back. I am sick and tired and weak. As pathetic as it sounds, I want my mommy. I'm too hungover, too broken for anger. This feels like it must be the bottom.

Me: Okay.

I open a group message with Annie and Violet.

Annie: OMG. OMG. OMG. KL +DD! Wld b LMAO if I wasn't so hungs.

Violet: Annie, how much coffee have you already had this morning?

Annie: 4 cups. Y?

Violet: SO MANY ACRONYMS. WHO ARE YOU!?!

Annie: Stop shouting. My head hurts.

Violet: K, you okay? That was A LOT of vodka. SO WE NEED DETAILS. Go David!

Annie: Go David? No, go Kit! V, u see that leather jacket? Swoon.

Violet: I like his slightly stubbly jaw.

Me: Ugh, so sick. Vodka shots were a mistake. Kissing David . . . was not.

There. That sounds almost like the old Kit. Funny and light. The old Kit was happy or at least happy enough. The old Kit didn't understand depression.

Violet: It's like overnight he went from nothing to being superhot.

Me: D was always cute. It's just no one ever thought to look at him.

Annie: Except you. Who knew K had such good hot-guy-dar?

Me: I don't like him because he's hot.

Annie: Come on.

Me: Fine, I don't like him JUST because he's hot. He's also all kinds of awesome.

Annie: Whatever you say.

Violet: Call me shallow, but for me that stubble would be reason enough.

Annie: I wonder if when he talks dirty, he gets all science-y. Oooh, your matter makes my particles throb.

Me: Shut up.

Violet: When we get together it's like a chemical reaction.

Annie: I want to insert my proton into your neutron.

I read David's texts last. Maybe I should let myself enjoy this unexpected development. An amazing night of kissing. The delicious possibility that I might get to kiss David again. Even enjoy my friends' gentle teasing, because it reminds me of how we used to be. Maybe for right now, that should be enough to get me out of bed. Let David be the tide that moves my time forward.

David: Thank you for an amazing night! Damn cops.

David: Can't stop thinking about you.

David: Will you come to my Academic League event next week?

Then, about two hours, later:

David: Kit, are you there? WE NEED TO TALK.

David: Kit, call me immediately.

David: Seriously, call me the second you wake up. I need to talk to you.

David: Kit?

David: Kit, it's about the Accident Project.

The texts span the night. The first two are from sometime shortly after he dropped me off. But the last five came in early this morning in exactly fifteen-minute intervals. When I read the words *Accident Project*, they hit hard. A sucker punch. No, more like a pulverization of all my internal organs. The reminder I don't need.

The Accident Project.

Again I sprint for the bathroom.

This time I don't make it.

* * *

"Are you okay, Kit?" my mom asks again when she finds me slumped over in the hallway. Her tone isn't angry. It's scared. I have never been the sort of kid who breaks rules. Any rebelling I've done so far has been careful and deliberate and far away from adult eyes. But I am marinating in my own vomit, obviously hungover from a night out; my chin is red and raw from David's stubble. I want to tell her that I'm fine. Absolutely, perfectly, one hundred percent fine. That it's not really the drinking that made me throw up. At least not this last time, anyway. It's all bigger than one night out. I want to tell her I am broken, that I'm starting to suspect that not even time can fix me.

I want to tell her that I have, that we have, made a big mistake.

I want to tell her to leave me the hell alone. That I'm better off without her.

I want to tell her to stay and hold me and make it all better.

I want her to tell me that there are worse things than telling the truth.

When she sits next to me cross-legged on the floor, though, I say nothing at all. Instead I lie down on my side and put my head into her lap. Just hand over the burden that is my brain.

Instead of talking, I cry.

"It's going to be okay, sweetheart. I promise. It's all going to be okay," she says, and strokes my hair.

"How?" I ask. I can't get out more than that. And that's all I want to know: *How, how, how. How can it be okay?*

"I have no idea. All right, so maybe it won't be okay. Not really. Not the same, but we'll survive this. That's a start, right? Survival? We've still got each other."

"Right," I mumble into her thigh. I don't want to die. Not

246

really. I just suck at living. Is it true? That I still have my mother? It doesn't always feel that way.

"For starters, we can shoot for not sitting in puke." I start to get up—my mom is, after all, wearing a silk T-shirt that she sometimes lets me borrow—but she holds me in place. "Wait one more second. I need to tell you something while I have you captive. I know I screwed up, but I love you and your dad. When your father's parents died—your grandparents—your father, well, it broke him, and for a long time he was like someone without batteries. Kind of like how you are now. Pathetic and dangly. Empty and sad."

"Thanks."

"I mean how *we* are now. I'm just as pathetic and dangly, though let's be honest, I smell better." I give my mother a small smile. Despite everything, I can do that. "But over time, Dad started becoming himself again. Not the same person he was before. Not even close. He became a better, stronger, Humpty Dumpty–glued-back-together version, and that's when I really fell in love with him. Head over heels. I decided that, no matter what my parents had to say about it, he was going to be my person. The thing is, sometimes people grow from breaking. That's what I think was happening with your father and me before he died—I truly believe we were going to work things out—and it's what I think we both should aim for now. Not just survival. We need to become even better versions of ourselves. In honor of Dad. We owe him. That's the least we can do for the people we love."

I let her words roll over me. Soak in her blatant optimism. I can be better. *We* can be better. The new Kit could one day be somebody I'm proud of. Somebody my dad would be proud of.

It's okay I'm not the same person I used to be. I'm not supposed to be.

Maybe we can make meaning out of something that feels so completely devoid of sense, even if only to make ourselves feel better.

Or maybe this: I can be the old Kit *and* the new Kit. I can be *both*. I'm an *and*.

"You're such an overachiever, Mom," I say.

"Good thing so are you." I nod. Decided. Galvanized. Brave. "One of the few perks of the shit so monumentally hitting the fan is you discover who your real tribe is. It's the only way through. So make sure you find yours, Kit."

"Okay," I say, and start assembling my team in my head. I think back to middle school, when we'd have to pick players for dodgeball in gym. David was always chosen last. I imagine him standing there, looking two feet above everyone else's heads, his hands flapping at his sides—something he still does occasionally, though I'm not sure he realizes it—and I want to go back in time and hug him, whisper in his ear that he can come stand by me. Tell him if he gets tired of flapping, he can hold my hand instead.

"I very much hope you'll consider including me," my mom says in her quietest voice, and I realize this is the closest someone like my mother gets to begging. When I don't immediately respond, she says, "At the very least, hashtag squad goals."

I laugh. My mom loves to try to talk like a teenager. A few weeks ago, I overheard her on the phone complaining about how she was tired of *adulting* and the last time we watched a romantic comedy together, she wanted to *ship* all the secondary characters.

"Yeah, we can work on that," I say, and realize just how

much I've missed my mom recently. How I can't make it through without her. That there will always be room in my tribe.

I unwind the soiled scarf from my neck. Hold it out for my mom to take. A bizarre, vomit-soaked, cashmere peace offering.

"Do you think this is dry-cleanable?" I ask.

Me: Hey. Just woke up. We can talk. I'm just crazy hungover, so can you give me a few hours?

David: You were drunk last night?

Me: Um, yeah.

David: Like drunk enough to be hungover?

Did David not notice me drinking? At one point I think Annie and I started swigging straight from the bottle. He was standing right next to me.

Me: Apparently.

David: So. Does that mean—

There's a long pause, that terrible pulsating ellipsis, and I wonder what he's doing. Is he writing? Thinking of what to say next? What does he have to report about the Accident Project? What was I thinking, getting him involved with that? It seems so pointless now. An act of desperation. Or self-sabotage. There's no unwinding what happened. My father's death isn't some sort of logic problem. It's a tragedy.

David: Does that mean you didn't mean it? That you only kissed me because you were drunk?

Me: What? No. Yes. No.

David: Please explain.

Me: I mean, I wanted to kiss you and the drinking made me more comfortable.

David: You were uncomfortable kissing me?

Me: No! That's not what I meant. I was . . . shy. Are you serious right now with these questions?

David: Of course. I'm always serious.

Me: It's not a big deal.

David: What isn't? The kiss? You being drunk? Or the Accident Project? You are opening new loops, and it's confusing.

Me: I was talking about last night. LAST NIGHT was not a big deal.

David: It was a big deal for me.

Me: Oh. I didn't mean. I just. Never mind. Let's talk in person. Texting isn't working.

David: What service provider do you have?

Me: Why?

David: If your texting plan isn't working, could be your provider. I'll look up on Yelp who has the best coverage in Mapleview.

CHAPTER 33

DAVID

Miney wants to help but I don't let her. I need to figure out how to do this on my own; I'm ready. It's the least I can do for Kit. I'm pretty sure after today she will no longer want to kiss me, much less sit at our lunch table. I hold out hope for the slim possibility that this will be received as good news, that I will be hailed as a conquering hero for uncovering the truth. That's what she wanted, right? For me to figure this all out?

I can't trust my instincts. Trusting my instincts gets me stuck in a locker with someone else's shit in my hair.

I arrive at McCormick's fifteen minutes early and snag the same booth we ate in last time. I order two milk shakes, one for me and one for Kit, while I wait. If there is a multiverse, somewhere else, not here, instead of sitting and waiting for the horrible moment when I will tell Kit that the accident did not happen in the way she thinks it did—that it's all lies—we would be kissing. Yes, we would be kissing, maybe even on a bed.

And then she is here. Her face is free of makeup and she's wearing her K-charm necklace and that big man shirt she's taken to donning twice weekly, and this way, without any attempt to hide the blue circles under her eyes, she seems even more essentially herself.

I decide I like her even better with her natural face. The red mummy dress last night was a little intimidating. Now she just looks like a girl. My favorite girl, maybe. But still just a girl.

"Wow," I say, the words escaping before I have a chance to think them through.

"What?" she asks, and sits down across from me and reaches for her milk shake. Takes a sip from the outside of the glass and ends up with a white line above her lip that she wipes away with a napkin.

"You. I like you even with a milk mustache."

"Stop, you're going to make me blush," she says, and then, like magic, her brown cheeks get a pink glow. "Listen, your texts, I don't know, freaked me out."

"First, can I kiss you?" I ask, and she shrugs and I don't know if that means yes or no. I decide to be brave and go for it. I switch to her side of the booth, and I put my hands on both sides of her face and I lean in slowly and touch my lips against hers. It's different than last night. It's soft and sweet—in both senses of the word—and too short, and when Kit pulls away she looks at me with wet eyes. She shakes her head.

"You're the one who wanted to talk, remember?"

"Right," I say. "Right. So the thing is . . ."

"What?" The way she's sitting, it looks like Kit is bracing herself. Her hands are in front of her face, as if I'm going to sneak in an uppercut. Why would she think that? Or is she shielding herself from my lips? I have no read on the situation.

"I've done a lot of research, and I don't think your dad was driving that car," I say.

"What are you talking about?" Kit asks, and her voice is all growly and low.

"Well, I did the math and I studied the blood spatter and the photos and, well, everything, and given that his injuries were ultimately fatal, there's no way he was driving that car. The newspaper never actually specified he was alone, and I'm pretty sure he was in the front passenger seat. So someone's been lying to you and I'm sorry to be the one to tell you and please don't hate me. All I wanted was to solve the equation for you."

"Okay," she says, but she doesn't smile or say thank you or slap me, all of which seemed like equally reasonable possibilities when I played this out in my head.

"Maybe he was having an affair, like your mom, and his, um, mistress was driving and that's why no one told you?" I ask.

"What? My dad was not having an affair." Her voice goes even quieter. Almost a whisper. Like she is water evaporating.

"There could be lots of explanations. But the how—that's what you wanted to know, right? The how of it? It isn't what we thought. And I know you don't like open loops just like me and this is one hell of an open loop," I say. "I'm sorry."

"Actually, it's not an open loop." Still quiet. Too quiet.

"A woman was definitely driving. I can tell by the positioning of the seat that the driver couldn't have been more than sixty-five inches tall, most likely sixty-four. Unless he was having an affair with a very short man."

"My dad wasn't having an affair!" she shouts, and just like that, everything changes. Kit is so loud the other people in the restaurant look over. "And my dad wasn't gay, you dumbass!"

"I'm sorry," I say again, and hold up my hands much like she did earlier, when it looked like she thought I might hit her. I don't understand what's going on. We went from kissing to yelling in fewer than three minutes. I suspected she'd be mad, that I could be ruining things by telling the truth, because that seems to be my downfall—my genetic predilection toward honesty and disclosure. Still, I didn't think it would be like this. I thought Kit was different from the other kids. That she didn't hurl hurtful words—*dumbass, idiot, retard*—at me just because she could.

I was wrong, like usual.

But unlike usual, this feels devastating. Like recovering from this moment is impossible.

"I'm sorry," I say for a third time. I don't know what I'm apologizing for, other than being too much myself. Kit drops her head onto the table and starts to sob. Her crying is gulpy and wet and unpleasant. I go to pet her hair—because even after all this, even after the *dumbass,* I still can't help but want to touch her, but then I decide against it. She hates me, and maybe I hate her too.

My mind races. We will never eat sandwiches across a table from each other again. And when I think about that—the seventy-three school days left in which I will now be sitting by myself, how my world will now be Kit-less—my hands start to flap. I cover one with the other and feel relieved Kit's face is down. I can't let her see this version of me.

I recite pi silently so the balloon in my head doesn't go loose again. I stare at the back of Kit's neck. Study the curve of her hairline. Imagine drawing it in my mind. Imagine tracing it with my fingertip.

And I wait.

CHAPTER 34

KIT

This table smells like french fries and my cheek feels sticky with someone else's leftover ketchup or maybe jam. Better not to know. I lift my head, take a paper napkin from the dispenser, and dry my drenched face with the little dignity I can still muster. Who knew you could hit bottom twice in one day?

"I'm sorry," I whisper, because it's hard to find my voice. I don't want to be the girl who spent the morning sitting in her own vomit and the afternoon crying in public with recycled condiments on my cheek. I want to be better than this. "I shouldn't have yelled at you."

On the way over to McCormick's, I resolved to be brave and honest. I realize I can't keep going, not like this. My mom wanted us to build and then live in a glass house of lies. But it's time to start throwing rocks. Let it shatter and rain down and cut us all up.

I will say these words out loud, the truth: *I was driving the car. It was me.*

No. I cannot say anything. My mouth has gone dry.

David stares at my shoulder. His fists are clenched tightly in his lap. He probably wants to throttle my neck. I don't blame him. My mother was wrong to try to bury the truth like it was a physical thing. As if keeping my name out of the newspaper meant it never happened in the first place. My mom's job is to spin things, and so she did what she does best. Ten minutes after a doctor told us my dad had died, she was in action, like the covert superhero I always knew she could be—*Mandip Lowell to the rescue!*—spinning what had happened into something more easily digestible.

We all know this was an accident, she said to the reporter, a grizzly older man with an unruly white mustache who looked annoyed that our family tragedy had interrupted his dinner plans. *Why ruin a sixteen-year-old girl's life?* As if my life hadn't already been ruined, as if reality turned on what people read over breakfast the next morning with their coffee.

Let's just leave her out of this, she said, and I stood next to her, totally numb, it never once occurring to me to speak up and object. *I'm not asking you to lie,* she said. *I'd never to do that. Just keep it vague enough to let people come to their own conclusions.* The next morning, a picture of the accident scene graced the front page of the *Daily Courier,* and the reporter did exactly as my mother suggested. No mention was made of a second passenger; anyone who read the article came to the natural conclusion that my father was driving. My mother and I did nothing to correct this wrong impression. One more verbal sleight of hand.

Poof, just like that, I was never in the car, my involvement almost completely erased. There was no follow-up, no additional questioning, just my name on an accident report buried in the bowels of the police station. Apparently people die in car accidents all the time.

My mom said, *Dad would have wanted to protect you.* I believed her because I wanted to.

But we should have started clean. When the whole thing is not sugarcoated with euphemisms like *accident,* when my mom doesn't pat my back and say *It wasn't your fault,* when she doesn't spin the truth. There are words for what I did: vehicular manslaughter.

"I don't understand what's happening here," David says.

"I knew he wasn't driving." I stop, because the tears are getting in the way. I want to do this right, but I am not naive. Words are not things that can be handed over, simply passed from person to person and let go. They are a string. You're still left holding one end in your hands. "There's something I didn't tell you—"

David can be trusted. He can keep my secrets. He'll help make it better. Hold up the other end.

Maybe this is what I wanted all along when I started the Accident Project—for David to find out the truth, for me to finally be exposed and honest. For me to spectacularly self-sabotage and start over.

When I was little, my dad used to sing "You Are My Sunshine" to me before bed, even that sad second verse no one else seems to know or remember: *The other night, dear, while I lay sleeping, I dreamt I held you in my arms. When I awoke, dear, I was mistaken, so I held my head down and cried.*

The song echoes in my head, in his voice, and it makes me think about David's theory of consciousness. Maybe my dad lives on in something as intangible as song lyrics. Maybe my dad can be with me when I need him.

When I awoke, dear, I was mistaken, so I held my head down and cried. Can I sing that as my confession to David? Those are simpler words. Easier to say than: *I was driving. It was me.*

"I get it," David says, before I have a chance to explain myself. "Of course. How could I have missed it? I *am* a dumbass. *You* were driving." The words come out with enthusiasm, like he's just aced the SATs, emphasis cheerily on the *you*. He is smiling and his volume is too loud.

This is nothing like those other times, when David's honesty felt good and refreshing: air, underwater. This time, it's sharp and cold and precise, like being stabbed, and he whips my dad's singing right out of my ears.

People at the other tables can hear us. I'm sure of it. I need him to stop talking; I need to undo whatever it is I've started. The world begins to spin, and his face morphs from handsome to cruel. I fold over myself. "You were driving, right? Your dad was the passenger. It all makes sense! You're exactly sixty-four inches tall. I can't believe I didn't think of it until now!"

He sounds perversely excited. Like this is one for the win column. Like I should high-five him in celebration: *Yay, David! You figured it out—I killed my dad!*

"Please, stop. Let's not . . ." I am begging. I can't do this. I can't. Not here. Not like this, with his maniacal grin and booming, self-congratulatory voice. I understand my mother's lies. The truth is too ugly. I want to put our string back in my pocket. What was I thinking?

Help me, Dad.

I was mistaken.

I was mistaken.

I wanted David to tell me that nothing could have been done to stop the car in time.

I wanted David to exonerate me.

I did not want this.

"I don't understand why you lied to me, Kit," David says, and then his face morphs again, and now he sounds accusatory. There is no warmth to be found. Not even a sliver of compassion or humanity. He's Hannibal Lecter sitting down to an ice cream bowl full of my insides.

"Please . . . Please stop." But my words are lost to the Formica table. I cannot lift my head. The tears flood my face, but I am not crying anymore. I am what happens after crying.

So I held my head down and cried.

Where are you, Dad? Where did you go? I can't hear his voice. It is gone.

"How could you, Kit?" David demands, as if this has anything to do with him.

"David—"

"You're like everyone else. A liar. You were driving that night. It was you. You lied!" David shouts, and then, like in a horror movie, because that's what this has become, my very worst nightmare, everything goes quiet.

Someone drops their fork. I hear an audible gasp.

I had stupidly expected a soft landing. Not free fall.

I was wrong yet again, because of course I haven't yet hit bottom. Here it is. Even colder, darker, lonelier than you'd expect.

I was mistaken.

I turn my head and that's when I notice: Gabriel and Willow in a booth right next to us, eating pancakes covered in whipped cream. The kind of food happy, simple people get to eat.

They've heard every single word.

CHAPTER 35

DAVID

I figured the puzzle out. I did exactly what Kit asked. But it was a setup. A wild goose chase. A lie. *Her* lie.

McCormick's goes quiet and then there's a collective gasp. A man I've never seen before unfolds his long legs from a nearby booth, comes over to our table. I am supposed to get up and move out of the way, though I don't know why. Kit is leaving open too many questions: Why didn't she trust me with the truth? And doesn't she want to know the math? I have hard numbers for her. Comforting facts and calculations. I stayed up all night for this.

The man puts his arms around Kit and starts to walk her out of the restaurant. The whole thing happens so quickly, I almost miss it. Kit doesn't look at me. She doesn't say anything except "Jack?" like it's a question, even though it's clearly not, because that must be the man's name. He looks like a Jack.

I hate him.

"I got you, Kitty Cat," he says. Kitty Cat is the perfect nickname for her because cats are confusing and creepily smart and can contort themselves. I can see a cat using the sleeves of a sweater like gloves.

"Wait!" I say, but they don't stop. Kit looks back at me, one last shocked look, and I see that her face is wet and pale, and for the first time I can read her eyes, even though I don't want to.

And then, only then, when I force myself to make eye contact, do I finally understand what has happened. How and how much I have broken.

"Oh crap," Miney says when I tell her the whole story. I ran home from McCormick's, so discombobulated I left my car parked in the lot. I am cold and wet from rain and my body is shaking. I'm trying not to lose it, because losing it won't help.

I don't let myself think about pi. I do not deserve its numbing relief. I also don't allow myself to think about Kit's face, because it hurts too much. Like being irradiated.

"I mean, I was so nervous, I forgot rule number four. *Think about the situation from the other person's perspective.* Everyone there heard, Miney. Everyone. What am I going to do?"

"I don't know," Miney says in a quiet voice.

"What do you mean, you don't know? You have to know. You have to help me," I say, my voice thick with panic.

"I'm not sure I can. Let me get this straight. First, you smiled like you did something good? And then you started yelling at her and accused her of killing her father and other people heard you?"

I nod, too ashamed to explain the sequencing of events. I

was happy to solve the puzzle and then heartbroken to learn about the lie and then, too late, always too late, I realized I was seeing everything upside down.

"I screwed up," I say. I notice that Miney's suitcase, which has been open and throwing up clothes all over her floor for the past two weeks, is zipped closed and next to the door. She is fully dressed. Her hair is combed, and she smells fresh. "Wait? You're leaving? Like right now?"

"In a couple of hours. I told you I was going. I've been giving you warnings in daily intervals just like you asked."

"But, Miney, you can't go. I need you to fix this."

"I can't always fix things for you. Honestly, I have to get back to school. I have my own things to fix, David—"

"Please don't call me that."

"Okay, sorry, Little D. I don't know if she'll forgive you, but I think you know what you need to do. You don't need my help the same way you used to."

"Of course I do. Today demonstrates that I absolutely, unequivocally need your help."

"No. Today demonstrates that you are still you and you'll occasionally make Aspie mistakes." She takes a quick breath—we've never used the term *Aspie* between us. And yet of course the word fits so much better than *David*. I'm not sure why I've resisted it for so long. So Asperger's is no longer in the *DSM*. It doesn't mean it's not at least somewhat descriptive of me. "But look how quickly you figured out what you did wrong. The old you might have not even noticed Kit was upset. Or might have insisted that she was being overly sensitive. You're getting better at this empathy thing. Like anything else, it requires practice."

"Not for you."

"Well, don't tell Dad, but I'm basically flunking physics, so you know, we all have things to work on. Apparently, though, you can learn anything in ten thousand hours."

"So in one point one four years I might be normal?"

"Nah. Probably not." She smiles at me, squeezes my arm. "But normal is way overrated. Believe me."

"I need to apologize to Kit."

"Yes. Yes, you do. Even though she lied to you."

"And maybe buy her a present? Like an Edible Arrangement. Or a pair of those odd-duck pajamas that you like so much." I stare at Miney's desk. I don't want to look at her suitcase. Or at her. She already looks gone.

"Maybe skip the gift."

"Everyone likes fruit dipped in chocolate."

"Trust me on this one."

"What if she doesn't forgive me?" I picture my empty lunch table again. If Kit doesn't forgive me, maybe I could join José and Mullet and Chloe's table, which is only three over from mine. The new acoustics and perspective would take some getting used to, but I could do it. Although they are not as fun to look at and be with as Kit.

Miney shrugs.

"Kit's loss. There are other girls in the world."

"Don't go," I say, though I don't really mean it. I am just putting into words the urge I have to throw myself at her legs to keep her from leaving, like I used to do to my mom when I was a little kid. I realize she needs to return to school, that my own feelings on the matter should be irrelevant. "By the way, your physics tutor can't be that smart if he doesn't realize how great you are."

Miney smiles the old Miney smile, the kind she used to wear all the time, and then she envelops me in a huge hug. Though

I don't feel like being hugged, I let her, because she's my sister and my favorite person in the world and in a few hours she'll be far, far away.

"I love you, Little D. Just the way you are. So yeah, you can change, but don't ever really change, okay?"

"Okay," I agree, though I have no idea what that means at all. "I'm scared, Miney."

"All the best people are," she says.

CHAPTER 36

KIT

"People are surprisingly nice to you when they discover you killed your father," I announce at lunch, toying with a new persona now that my secret is out. Jokey, as if I'm not drowning in shame, as if treating this as something light can make it bounce right off me. I'm, of course, back at my old table. I haven't seen David since McCormick's. Jack, who always seems to appear just when I do and do not need him the most, was somehow miraculously at the restaurant with Evan. He drove me home. I was too shaken to register that it was my first time seeing him since my mother's confession. For that five-minute ride, he was Uncle Jack, and he delivered me to my mother, who took one look at my face and went straight to the bathroom cabinet to get me a Valium.

What happened in McCormick's went viral, just like David's

notebook, though in my case through texts and whispered conversations. You can still Google my name without finding a thing.

"Stop saying that," Violet says, though she doesn't flinch. Both she and Annie spent all of Sunday on my couch, after showing up at my house armed with pizza and a jumbo-size bag of M&M's. At first, I didn't say a word, and they didn't ask. We just sat and ate and watched television, and instead of resenting them, I appreciated that they were being delicate with me. Remembered that they had always been my tribe. Only later did the words start to form, and once I started talking I found I couldn't stop.

"My dad and I both wanted a Snickers bar," I said, staring straight ahead. I couldn't bring myself to look at them. "That's why we went out that night. But we told my mom we were just going to get milk. And my dad made me drive because he wanted me to get extra practice. You want to hear the strangest thing? The accident happened on the way home, and the milk carton was still sitting in the backseat. Not crushed, not even, like, a little bit dented. So weird. I still have half of the Snickers bar. I keep it on my desk, like some sick souvenir."

"It would be totally inappropriate of me to make a 'no use crying over spilt milk' joke, right?" Annie asked, and for reasons I can't explain, both Violet and I thought that was hilarious, and we laughed until we all had tears running down our faces. I realized then that maybe humor could help me through. Another way to bend time.

"It was an *accident*. It really wasn't your fault," Annie says. This is their new favorite mantra. Again with the words *accident* and *fault*, as if they are made of magic. I am absolved. Poof. It's all better. I don't mind hearing it, because I need everything I can get. I shouldn't have waited so long to talk to my friends. They've been so supportive. The opposite of David.

"I don't get why your mom wanted you to keep it a secret in the first place," Violet says.

"She was just trying to protect me," I say, and then I can't help it, I reflexively look over to David's table. But he's not there. He's a few rows over with the kids from Academic League. He catches me looking, and I quickly turn my attention back to the girls. "If no one knew, then maybe it wouldn't define me. And you know my mom. She's totally hard-core about everything. She makes me drive to school every day and run all sorts of errands, because she's worried that driving will become a thing for me. Like a phobia."

"Is it working?" Annie asks.

"Sort of," I say. "I still get a little shaky in the car, but it gets a tiny bit easier each time."

I have already warned my friends that the girl they used to know and love is gone. That they should give up trying to revive the old me. I'm not braver or stronger, as my mom hoped. I'm a new version. Possibly someone they could one day like better. Who knows? Maybe I'll turn out funnier.

My mom has found me a therapist who specializes in grief counseling, and she got herself one too. She's even talking about us seeing a third psychologist we can talk to together. We are mobilizing.

"Vi and I have decided to go stag to prom, and we'll be taking Uber. No driving needed. So will you come with us? Just us girls?" Annie asks. "Please, please, please!"

"Sorry, I can't," I say.

"Why not? If I can go and watch Gabriel and Willow make

out all night, you can at least come and pretend to have fun." I shrug. My dad would have been excited about prom. He would have taken a thousand pictures of me and posted them on Facebook without my permission and begged me to text him the DJ's playlist.

"Come on!" Violet whines.

"Sorry, guys."

"It's David, isn't it? Forget about him. He's a weirdo," Annie says. "Obvi we're no longer Team David."

"This is not about David," I say, though maybe it is, just a little bit. Because perhaps for a second there, before David was the enemy, I *had* pictured both of us dressed up and slow-dancing to some cheesy song. I *had* pictured another night just like at Dylan's party, when he looked at me like I was something worth looking at, when I allowed myself to forget.

After what happened at McCormick's, he sent me only one text. It was composed of two words: *I'm sorry.*

I might have killed my father, but I think even I deserve better than that.

CHAPTER 37

DAVID

I spend the first week after screwing everything up with Kit too ashamed to do anything except write her a stupid text. I keep it short, limit it to the words I know can't be the wrong ones: *I'm sorry.* I don't trust myself not to make a bigger mess of things by saying more. Whenever I pick up the phone to text again, I freeze up with anxiety. I don't feel like I deserve the chance to explain. I don't even deserve to share the same air molecules as Kit.

I have spent all my waking hours following rule number four by trying to imagine what she must be thinking. My guess is she assumes I am a sociopath. I smiled. At McCormick's, while we were talking about the accident, one in which she was driving and her father was a passenger, one that resulted in her father's death. *I smiled.*

And then, then I had the nerve to *yell.*

Since I am in my own brain, I understand why I did all that—the sequencing makes perfect sense to me—but to her, a person on the outside of my mind, a person who knows nothing about my synaptic responses, I must seem like a monster.

Here's what happened in that booth, with Kit sitting across from me and the cold milk shake in my stomach and the strange dimensions of my new clothes: My brain got narrow. It did what it's best at. It tunneled in. If that moment was a Russian nesting doll, I was paying attention to the smallest figurine. Pawing my way through the details of blood spatter and brake data and an algorithm I had elegantly designed. I found an answer, right there, at the very center. A tiny nugget. That's all I could see. The solution to a mathematical equation that had been troubling me for weeks. The missing data point.

I did not see all the other metaphorical dolls. The one wrapped around the smallest one, and the one wrapped around the next-smallest one and the next and the next after that.

What neurotypical people call the *context*.

I did not see Kit or the people nearby or the delicate nature of what we were discussing. Honestly, I did not see anything else at all.

"David, if I gave up every time I pissed someone off, I wouldn't have any friends either," Trey says a week later, after I've told him the whole sad story, even the parts that are hard for me to admit in the retelling. Our lesson today will be one hundred percent about social skills, since I am so shaken up about Kit I don't even bother to take out my guitar.

"She probably won't forgive me," I say.

"Maybe not. But you have to at least try. And if you really

271

do your best to apologize and she doesn't forgive you, then you move on. You messed up. It happens. There will be other girls, man."

"Not really. I mean, of course there are other girls in the world, but by definition there's no one else exactly like Kit, with her precise genetic and environmental makeup." I regret that I left my guitar in the closet. My hands want to move. The strings would come in handy.

"What's the worst thing that can happen if you try?" Trey asks.

"I make her hate me even more. I humiliate myself again. I spin out and crawl into the fetal position and start rocking in front of the entire school."

"I see you've given this a lot of thought."

"You're not helping," I say.

"How about this: You can't control how she reacts, but you can control what you do. So you do you. Be your best and hope for the best."

"I am paying you forty dollars an hour, and all you can come up with is *you do you*?" I ask.

"Your parents are paying me, smart-ass."

"Fair enough," I say, because it's true. They are.

And so five full days after my conversation with Trey, five days in which I apply my Russian-nesting-doll focus to winning Kit's friendship back, five days in which I think hard about what it means for me to do me—though I'm not sure the expression can be converted from second to first person—I am ready to put my plan into action.

I start with food. After all, we met at my lunch table.

CHAPTER 38

KIT

The following Monday I come home to find an insulated cooler on my doorstep with my name scrawled across the top. Inside is a huge container of homemade chicken tikka masala and white rice. The note attached has no words. Just three seemingly identical sketches of me in which I look sadder and prettier than I do in real life. Of course, I know immediately they are David's, but it takes me a minute to notice the differences between them.

In the first, the freckles on my chest are their normal shape. Almost but not quite a circle.

In the second, David has rearranged them into the shape of pi.

In the third, they form the infinity symbol.

I tack the three me's up on the back of my closet door, in a line, my sketched faces turned toward my hanging clothes. A place where only I will see them. Me transformed into art.

That night my mother and I eat David's food at the counter in the kitchen. We sit on our neighboring stools, the weight of truth nestled in the space between us. We are slowly growing used to honesty in this house, accepting the million different ways it unzips your skin and leaves you vulnerable. We are trying to be open to the terrifying possibility of being understood. And the opposite too, which is so much scarier. Opening ourselves to the terrifying possibility of not being understood at all.

The chicken is delicious. Almost as good as my grandmother's and way better than Curryland's.

On Tuesday, I open my locker to find a fat, dusty book, an old edition of the *DSM*. There's a big Post-it note and an arrow pointing to the section titled "Asperger's Syndrome."

I'm pretty sure I have Asperger's. This is an old DSM (the new one folds my diagnosis under autism spectrum disorders). I think this will tell you a lot about why I am the way I am (and why I acted the way I acted), though I can't use the Aspie thing as an excuse. It's more an explanation than an excuse.

There's a famous expression that if you've met one person with autism, then . . . you've met one person with autism.

So you met me.

Just me.

Not a diagnosis.

I realize I hurt you. I forgot to think about you first.

I did not put myself in your shoes, as the expression goes.

(Though as a sidebar, I think wearing other people's shoes is kind of disgusting; I'm only okay with the concept metaphorically.)

So you know, you are all I think about.

P.S. I recommend you change your locker combination for security purposes, but not till next week. I guessed your code on only my fifth try.

On Wednesday, in class, three tickets to a Princeton basketball game fall out of my laptop, with yet another note and another drawing. This time I am sitting in the bleachers of a crowded game next to Annie and Violet. I don't look sad. Instead I'm grinning, and there's something about my hair—it's loose around my shoulders and falling in a perfect pattern—that makes me look liberated somehow.

Because you said you loved spectator sports. You think I'm the weird one. (That was a joke, by the way, even though I'm not sure if I'm allowed to joke with you yet. Probably not, since we haven't spoken out loud to each other since the McCormick's Incident. This is my new life goal, by the way. To one day have permission to make you laugh again.)

On Thursday, in my mailbox, a bonsai tree.

You said your dad loved this kind of tree. I thought/hoped maybe you did too?

On Friday, I open my locker to find a new sketch taped to the inside. The picture is of two numbers, 137 and 139, but they are drawn to look human. 139 has a backpack like David's and his new short hair. 137 carries a shoulder bag like mine, and it wears a big man's shirt just like my dad's. The numbers walk down Clancy Street holding hands.

> *I just wanted you to know these are my favorite*
> *numbers and my favorite twin primes: 137 and 139. And*
> *since they are my favorite, I wanted to give them to*
> *you.*
>   *137 and 139.*
>   *They're yours now.*
>   *Please take good care of them.*

On Saturday, when I check my inbox, I have an email from David with the subject "This Gives Me Hope . . ." It links to an article about a Russian scientist who has, under lab conditions, created two identical snowflakes. I smile goofily at the screen.

On Sunday, David leaves an old-fashioned emergency crank radio on my front porch.

> *So we can always hear each other's waves. Clearly I*
> *need one of these more than you, but buying myself a gift*
> *did not seem in the spirit of this multistep apology.*

On Monday, after last period, Annie stops me from getting into my car. My hands are trembling a little, like they always do before I get into the driver's seat, but this time I don't try to hide them.

"David asked me to give this to you," she says, and hands over a piece of paper that looks ripped from his notebook. I look at her, a question in my eyes: What should I do? She shrugs.

"It never mattered before what I thought of David. It shouldn't now," she says, and gives me a *go get 'em* shoulder punch.

I unfold the paper.

~~KIT LOWELL: Height: 5' 4". Weight: Approximately 125 lbs. Wavy brown hair, pulled into a ponytail on test days, rainy days, and most Mondays. Skin is brownish, because her dad—a dentist—is white and her mom is Indian (Southeast Asian, not Native American). Class ranking: 14. Activities: school newspaper, Spanish Club, Pep Club~~

I've read all of it before, when his words first found their way onto the Internet from his stolen notebook, but now there is a big X through the entire entry, and written over it, in all caps:

FAVORITE GIRL IN THE WORLD. STILL MY FRIEND?
Please meet me on the bleachers after school. Please.
And I'm sorry. Sorrier than any person has ever been
sorry in the history of sorry people. I'll put in one last
please for good luck, even though I don't believe in luck.
I believe in science. Sorry. Again.

CHAPTER 39

DAVID

I wait in the bleachers, in the exact same spot we sat on that first day when Kit was just Kit Lowell to me, an entry in a notebook and someone I cautiously put on the Trust List. A few Notable Encounters. Nothing more. Now it occurs to me that outside of Miney, she's the first friend I've ever made. If she doesn't come, I will be heartbroken. Not literally, of course. My heart will continue to beat. I think. But there will be a literal and figurative ache.

I close my eyes and remember our first kiss. How she reached up and cupped the back of my neck. That feels like much longer than fourteen days ago. Time has changed shape since I met Kit. Can love be so powerful a force that it can skew the space-time continuum? Does it have the particle and wave heft of something like consciousness? I make a mental note to later think through the implications of applying quantum theory to love, or at least its chemical and hormonal approximations. That could make for a satisfying thesis for my future PhD.

She's not coming. It's obvious to me that this past week will turn out to have been just a fruitless series of desperate acts. I watch my classmates spilling out of school, in groups of two or three, their formations intimidatingly organic. Atoms into molecules.

Like usual, I am alone.

My headphones sound a siren call from my bag. I force myself to leave them in there. I will wade through all the noise around me, let it saturate my brain. The distant bell. Car engines revving. The anxiety humming through my body.

It was a long shot and I lost. Kit doesn't need more friends. Certainly not ones like me.

I direct my attention to the remote possibility that Trey is right. That one day I won't need Kit. That I will find a way to fill up my life with other people. That there are other girls in the world, and that maybe one of them will also feel like my Goldilocks of a person. Of course, all statistics point to Kit being an outlier. To this never happening again.

I close my eyes and I can't resist any longer.

I slip on my headphones and start the gentle recitation of pi.

"David?" One hundred and thirty-four digits in, I look up, and there Kit is, standing in front of me, looking exactly the same as she always does. There is no readjustment to a new iteration. That, at least, is a relief. She's not smiling.

The sky is low and gray and bloated. If this were a novel, it would be described as foreboding.

"Hi," I say, and take off my headphones. I realize I am

woefully underprepared for this moment. I should have written a speech. Or drawn a picture. At least figured out what I wanted to say. It occurs to me now that I never thought Kit might actually show up. "Do you want to sit?"

She nods and plops down next to me on the bench. She shields her eyes from the nonexistent sun with a cupped hand. We sit quietly like that for a few minutes.

"So?" she asks. "You asked me to come here."

"Do you ever think about how your name doesn't fit you? I mean, you're usually Kit in my head, but really I think your name should have a Z in it, because you're confusing and zigzagged and pop up in surprising places—like my lunch table and these bleachers. I really didn't think you'd come—and maybe also the number eight, because . . . never mind, and the letter *S* too. It's my favorite. *S*. So yeah, Z8S-139. Or 139-Z8S. That's how I think of you sometimes. In my head," I say, glad that words are at least coming out of my mouth. I'm too nervous to evaluate whether they are the right ones.

"I don't know if I can do this," Kit says.

I keep going.

"And my name doesn't fit either. I mean, really: David? Did you know there are approximately 3,786,417 Davids in the United States? My parents couldn't have gotten me more wrong. I should be a . . . a . . . I don't know what. Something with a *Y* in it."

"I literally have no idea what you're talking about right now."

"What I'm trying to say—badly, I guess—is that we each have the way the world sees us, and you were the very first person at this school, maybe the first person pretty much anywhere besides my immediate family, who looked at me and saw more than the weirdo flapping kid that everyone here has known as David, or I guess *shithead*. You listened to me talk. And I can't tell you how much I appreciate that. It was like the equivalent of being given a better name." She nods, and I wonder if she will get up and leave and we are done. Not friends. Not enemies. I tell myself I can count that as a win.

"I still . . . I mean, are we just not going to talk about what happened? Your kind of weird wasn't good or charming the other day. It was cruel. You hurt me," Kit says. "And I don't really care what your name is. Stop changing the subject."

"We never started on the subject—" Kit sighs, so I clear my throat. Begin again. "You're right. I'm so, so sorry. I can try to explain what happened, I mean, with my brain, because I hope you know I would never, ever, ever be intentionally cruel, especially to you. You're my favorite person. The thing is, I get hyperfocused, and that's what I was thinking about, the nugget inside, the answer, not what it all meant, actually. Does that make sense?"

Kit shrugs, a gesture that is in my mental *Pictorial Dictionary of Ambiguous Gestures*, and I don't know what to do. If I should keep talking or stop.

"I'm sorry. And I hope you can forgive me," I say, and I turn to look at her. Not her clavicle or her jaw or her left arm. But right in the eyes, where it's hardest.

"I dunno, I guess," Kit says, but she's the one to look away first. "That doesn't mean, though, that, like, we are suddenly besties again or something."

"We were best friends?" I ask. Of course she's mine, excepting Miney, who is family and therefore doesn't count. Never thought I would count as hers, though.

"I just mean I know I was the one who asked you to start the

Accident Project in the first place. I know that. The whole thing was super messed up. I know I didn't tell you the truth, or at least not the whole truth, but you shouted out my biggest secret—the worst thing that has ever happened to me, the worst thing that will hopefully ever happen to me—to the whole world. Like it was nothing. Like you didn't give a crap about my feelings."

"I'm sorry. Not just for the shouting. Or how inappropriate I was. I do stupid things like that sometimes. I am sorry for all that, of course, but what I'm most sorry for is that any of it happened to you in the first place, and that I haven't said that out loud to you. It's not fair. The fact that you were driving that car—the inexplicable cruelness of that bad luck—is the only thing in the world that I can think of that can't be explained by math or quantum theory. See, I don't usually use words like *bad luck*, and yet there are some things so totally out of our control that science hasn't even come up with a label for them. And they suck. And you don't deserve any of it. The accident wasn't your fault. Even the math says—"

"Okay," she says, cutting me off, like it's some sort of decision, like she's uninterested in my fault algorithm. Of course, I have no idea what that decision is or if it has anything to do with me at all.

"You couldn't have braked. There was nothing you could have done," I say, thinking this is the one last gift I can hand over, even if she's not sure she wants to hear it. After this, I'm all out. No more food or drawings. It's me.

"Of course I could have braked. I could have been faster with my foot. There must have been a moment—that's all I wanted to know. The when. So I could see it differently. Even if it was just in my mind," she says, looking out into the distance. I follow her gaze but don't know what she's staring at. All of Mapleview, I guess.

"No, you really couldn't have. If you'd braked, then everything would have been worse. Someone else would have died too, Kit. There was a Mini behind you, so if you stopped short, that car would have been crushed from two different sides. Both cars would have been hit. I can show you the model and the simulation I made, if you want."

"I don't think so," Kit says. "I mean, thank you, but there are some things . . . I just . . . can't."

"This wasn't your fault. Mathematically or legally. There is nothing you could have done. So instead of trying to watch it happen differently, why don't you try to not watch it at all?"

She looks up at me, her face full, but I don't know of what.

"I didn't meet her. The woman driving the Mini. I don't even know her name."

"You saved her life," I say.

"Maybe," she says, and nods, but she's again like water. Her smile is slippery and starts to fall off her face. "Thank you. Again. This was really nice of you."

"You saved her life," I repeat, because I don't think she's hearing my certainty. That this is a fact.

"You really think so?" she asks.

"I don't think so. I know so. Math doesn't lie."

"People do, though," Kit says. "All the time."

"Not me."

"No, not you," she says, and her smile firms up a little.

"So we're friends again?"

"Sure."

"I mean, we don't have to sit at the same lunch table—you

looked happy back with Annie and Violet—but it would be cool if we still talked sometimes. Like at school during other periods."

"Of course we can talk," she says, and I feel my stomach fill with relief. I have not lost everything.

"Just to be clear, I assume that there will be no more kissing?" I ask. She laughs, loud and hard, and it feels as good as it did the very first time I made her laugh. When it comes to Kit's laughter, I don't care much about my intentionality.

"We'll see about that."

"So . . . so . . . there might be?"

She elbows me, a friendly nudge, I think, and I nudge back. I take this to mean a warm *no, thank you.*

"Right. How about hand-holding? Can we do that?" I ask.

"David?"

"Right. I'll stop talking. We can just sit here quietly together."

"That would be a good idea."

"Okay," I say.

"Thank you," she says.

CHAPTER 40

KIT

David and I are sitting in the bleachers and all of Mapleview is spread out before us like a restaurant menu, and it's that hour in a late winter day when everything turns the same color of washed-out gray. The air is so thick, I feel like I could slice it and serve it like pie. Our small town looks even smaller from up here.

I let his words settle over me. The idea that I couldn't have changed a thing. There is math to point to, a model on his computer, apparently. I don't know yet how I feel about any of this, whether this changes things. Maybe it doesn't. Maybe there is no such thing as relief for me, only time.

I'm sure David has quantum theories to point to—the unraveling of our future selves, the existence of alternate universes, how healing can occur on a molecular level. I don't, though. I think it's all so much simpler than that. My dad was right: Unimaginably bad shit happens. We are left to choose whether to grow or to wither. To forgive or to fester. I'm going to choose to grow and forgive, for both myself and my mom. She deserves the same grace.

I look over at David and he looks over at me and he smiles and then so do I. We turn around again and face outward. I think, for some reason, of those three portraits now hanging in my closet. My chest tattooed with freckled possibility. Pi. Infinity. One open, one closed. Both forever. The thought makes me feel lighter, closer to whole. Bigger somehow.

"139-Z8S?" I ask. "Really?"

"Or if you prefer, I can call you: Z8S-139. Or Z8 for short."

"I'll think about it," I say. Looking at him now, I realize he's right. He's not a David. Not even a little bit. "What should I call you, then?"

He shrugs, that unnatural shrug he does, and today I find it adorable.

"I'll think of something," I say.

"Will you think more about the kissing?" he asks, and I laugh again and mimic his shrug. If he only knew how much I've thought about the kissing.

"Will you reconsider hand-holding?" he asks.

Instead of answering, I move my arm so it's next to his, so we are lined up, seam to seam. He reaches out his pinky finger and links it around mine and a warm, delicious chill makes its way up my arm.

We stay that way for a minute, in a pinky swear, which feels like the smallest of promises.

And then I grab his whole hand and link all his fingers in mine.

A slightly bigger promise. Or maybe a demand: *Please be part of my tribe.*

It's pretty simple, really. For once, things are not complicated. Right now, right here, it's just us, together, like this. Palm to palm.

The most honest of gestures.

One of the ways through.

Maybe the best one.

AUTHOR'S NOTE

I realize I'm breaking one of the novelist's cardinal rules by admitting that *What to Say Next* is my favorite of the four books I've written (five, if you count the one that will forever stay in a drawer). It's pretty much like a mom picking her favorite kid. But before this book, meeting my main characters has always felt a lot like looking at myself in a fun-house mirror—they're all alterna-mes.

With *What to Say Next*, though, instead of having to stare down my demons in a mirror, the experience felt much more like the best parts of giving birth. I love these characters (and writing about them) in that wholehearted, inexplicable way that I love my own children, which is to say, so much more than I love myself.

One of the many things I love about Kit is that she comes from a family that looks not so different from mine. Her mother is first-generation Indian American (her grandparents hail from Delhi) and her dad is American. My husband's grandparents are from that same region of India, but he's British and I'm American. When my real-life children are old enough to read this book and meet their fictional siblings, they'll get to see someone who looks like them represented in a novel.

And of course, this book also belongs to David, whose

voice I will miss in my head most of all. There is a famous expression that when you meet one person with autism, you meet one person with autism. Labels can be liberating, but they can also be limiting. In *What to Say Next* we meet David. Just David. And what a joy he is.

I wanted to write a story about unexpected connections and finding your tribe. About the wonder of finding an honest and true friend when you feel at your most alone. About the miracle of discovering that special someone who can see you clearly when you feel at your most misunderstood.

I hope you care about Kit and David as much as I do.

ACKNOWLEDGMENTS

Although my name gets to be on the cover of this book, the truth is that writing a novel takes a village. So if you didn't like this one, here are all the other people you can blame. Just kidding. All mistakes are mine. All credit is theirs.

First off, thank you to Beverly Horowitz, my editor, who pushed me to keep working and editing and tinkering and to ultimately just do better; I've met my perfectionist match and I'm so grateful. I owe an enormous debt of gratitude to my agent, Jenn Joel, one of the smartest and sharpest people I know; I feel so lucky to have you on my team. A forever thank-you to Elaine Koster, who is deeply missed.

A big thank you and huge hug to all the amazing people at Random House Children's Books: Jillian Vandall (the best publicist a girl could ask for), Kim Lauber, Hannah Black, Dominique Cimina, Casey Ward, Alissa Nigro, John Adamo, Nicole Morano, Rebecca Gudelis, Colleen Fellingham, and the awesomesauce Laura Antonacci. Deeply appreciative to the international rights team at ICM, to Sharon Green, and to my Internet water cooler, the Fiction Writers Co-op. A monster hug to Julia Johnson. And a shout out to Kathleen Caldwell and A Great Good Place for Books, which is indisputably the best indie bookstore in the world.

I did an enormous amount of research for this book. If

you're interested in learning more about the autism spectrum or how to be an ally, please email me through my website and I'd be happy to share my reading list as a starting place. I'm still learning. I hope you'll join me.

To the readers out there who make this writing books thing possible, you are my favorite tribe. I can't thank you enough for letting me do every day what I only used to daydream about. Thank you for your emails, for your letters, for your tweets, for your blog posts, for your photos, for coming out to say hi on tour, for all your support. You guys rock. I owe you my eternal gratitude.

And lastly, thank you to my kick-ass friends and family. To my dad and Lena for making everyone you've met since birth come to my events. To my brother for cheering me on. To Mammaji for all the child care and for making sure I nailed the details of Kit's family. To the rest of the Flore clan for letting me join the family. To my mother and grandmother, who, if the quantum physicists are right, I like to think live somehow in the souls of these pages. And lastly, to Indy, Elili, and Luca, who breathe meaning and love into my every day. I am the luckiest girl in the multiverse.

TURN THE PAGE TO START READING THE *NEW YORK TIMES* BESTSELLER READERS CAN'T PUT DOWN. . . .

A *NEW YORK TIMES* BESTSELLER

What if the person you need the most is someone you've never met?

TELL ME

THREE THINGS

JULIE BUXBAUM

"You'll eat up this book about a new girl at a prep school." —*Seventeen*

"Buxbaum's book . . . soars." —JODI PICOULT, *New York Times* bestselling author of *Leaving Time* and *Off the Page*

"Here are three things about this book: (1) It's sweet and funny and romantic; (2) the mystery at the heart of the story will keep you turning the pages; (3) I have a feeling you'll be very happy you read it." —JENNIFER E. SMITH, author of *The Statistical Probability of Love at First Sight* and *Windfall*

CHAPTER 1

Seven hundred and thirty-three days after my mom died, forty-five days after my dad eloped with a stranger he met on the Internet, thirty days after we then up and moved to California, and only seven days after starting as a junior at a brand-new school where I know approximately no one, an email arrives. Which would be weird, an anonymous letter just popping up like that in my in-box, signed with the bizarre alias Somebody Nobody, no less, except my life has become so unrecognizable lately that nothing feels shocking anymore. It took until now—seven hundred and thirty-three whole days in which I've felt the opposite of normal—for me to discover this one important life lesson: turns out you can grow immune to weird.

To: Jessie A. Holmes (jesster567@gmail.com)
From: Somebody Nobody (somebodynobo@gmail.com)
Subject: your Wood Valley H.S. spirit guide

hey there, Ms. Holmes. we haven't met irl, and I'm not sure we ever will. I mean, we probably will at some point— maybe I'll ask you the time or something equally mundane and beneath both of us—but we'll never actually get to know each other, at least not in any sort of real way that matters . . . which is why I figured I'd email you under the cloak of anonymity.

and yes, I realize I'm a sixteen-year-old guy who just used the words "cloak of anonymity." and so there it is already: reason #1 why you'll never get to know my real name. I could never live the shame of that pretentious- ness down.

"cloak of anonymity"? seriously?

and yes, I also realize that most people would have just texted, but couldn't figure out how to do that without tell- ing you who I am.

I have been watching you at school. not in a creepy way. though I wonder if even using the word "creepy" by definition makes me creepy? anyhow, it's just . . . you intrigue me. you must have noticed already that our school is a wasteland of mostly blond, vacant-eyed Barbies and Kens, and something about you—not just your newness, because sure, the rest of us have all been going to school together since the age of five—but something about the way you move and talk and actually don't talk but watch all of us like we are part of some bizarre National Geographic documentary makes me think that you might be different from all the other idiots at school.

you make me want to know what goes on in that head of yours. I'll be honest: I'm not usually interested in the contents of other people's heads. my own is work enough.

the whole point of this email is to offer my expertise. sorry to be the bearer of bad news: navigating the wilds of Wood Valley High School ain't easy. this place may look all warm and welcoming, with our yoga and meditation and reading corners and coffee cart (excuse me: Koffee Kart), but like every other high school in America (or maybe even worse), this place is a freaking war zone.

and so I hereby offer up myself as your virtual spirit guide. feel free to ask any question (except of course my identity), and I'll do my best to answer: who to befriend (short list), who to stay away from (longer list), why you shouldn't eat the veggie burgers from the cafeteria (long story that you don't want to know involving jock jizz), how to get an A in Mrs. Stewart's class, and why you should never sit near Ken Abernathy (flatulence issue). Oh, and be careful in gym. Mr. Shackleman makes all the pretty girls run extra laps so he can look at their asses.

that feels like enough information for now.

and fwiw, welcome to the jungle.

yours truly, Somebody Nobody

....

To: Somebody Nobody (somebodynobo@gmail.com)
From: Jessie A. Holmes (jesster567@gmail.com)
Subject: Elaborate hoax?

SN: Is this for real? Or is this some sort of initiation prank, à la a dumb rom-com? You're going to coax me into sharing my deepest, darkest thoughts/fears, and then, BAM, when I least expect it, you'll post them on Tumblr and I'll be the laughing-stock of WVHS? If so, you're messing with the wrong girl. I have a black belt in karate. I can take care of myself.

If not a joke, thanks for your offer, but no thanks. I want to be an embedded journalist one day. Might as well get used to war zones now. And anyhow, I'm from Chicago. I think I can handle the Valley.

....

To: Jessie A. Holmes (jesster567@gmail.com)
From: Somebody Nobody (somebodynobo@gmail.com)
Subject: not a hoax, elaborate or otherwise

promise this isn't a prank. and I don't think I've ever even seen a rom-com. shocking, I know. hope this doesn't re-veal some great deficiency in my character.

you do know journalism is a dying field, right? maybe you should aspire to be a war blogger.

....

To: Somebody Nobody (somebodynobo@gmail.com)
From: Jessie A. Holmes (jesster567@gmail.com)
Subject: Specifically targeted spam?

Very funny. Wait, is there really sperm in the veggie burgers?

....

To: Jessie A. Holmes (jesster567@gmail.com)
From: Somebody Nobody (somebodynobo@gmail.com)
Subject: you, Jessie Holmes, have won $100,000,000 from a Nigerian prince.

not just sperm but sweaty lacrosse sperm.

I'd avoid the meat loaf too, just to be on the safe side. in fact, stay out of the cafeteria altogether. that shit will give you salmonella.

....

To: Somebody Nobody (somebodynobo@gmail.com)
From: Jessie A. Holmes (jesster567@gmail.com)
Subject: Will send my bank account details ASAP.

who are you?

....

To: Jessie A. Holmes (jesster567@gmail.com)
From: Somebody Nobody (somebodynobo@gmail.com)
Subject: and copy of birth certificate & driver's license, please.

nope. not going to happen.

....

To: Somebody Nobody (somebodynobo@gmail.com)
From: Jessie A. Holmes (jesster567@gmail.com)
Subject: And, of course, you need my social security number too, right?

Fine. But tell me this at least: what's up with the lack of capital letters? Your shift key broken?

....

To: Jessie A. Holmes (jesster567@gmail.com)
From: Somebody Nobody (somebodynobo@gmail.com)
Subject: and height and weight, please

terminally lazy.

....

To: Somebody Nobody (somebodynobo@gmail.com)
From: Jessie A. Holmes (jesster567@gmail.com)
Subject: NOW you're getting personal.

Lazy and verbose. Interesting combo. And yet you do take the time to capitalize proper nouns?

....

To: Jessie A. Holmes (jesster567@gmail.com)
From: Somebody Nobody (somebodynobo@gmail.com)
Subject: and mother's maiden name

I'm not a complete philistine.

....

To: Somebody Nobody (somebodynobo@gmail.com)
From: Jessie A. Holmes (jesster567@gmail.com)
Subject: Lazy, verbose, AND nosy

"Philistine" is a big word for a teenage guy.

....

To: Jessie A. Holmes (jesster567@gmail.com)
From: Somebody Nobody (somebodynobo@gmail.com)
Subject: lazy, verbose, nosy, and . . . handsome

that's not the only thing that's . . . whew. caught myself from making the obvious joke just in time. you totally set me up, and I almost blew it.

....

To: Somebody Nobody (somebodynobo@gmail.com)
From: Jessie A. Holmes (jesster567@gmail.com)
Subject: Lazy, verbose, nosy, handsome, and . . . modest

That's what she said.

....

See, that's the thing with email. I'd never say something like that in person. Crude. Suggestive. Like I am the kind of girl who could pull off that kind of joke. Who, face to face with an actual member of the male species, would know how to flirt, and flip my hair, and, if it came to it, know how to do much more than kiss. (For the record, I do know how to kiss. I'm not saying I'd ace an AP exam on the subject or, you know, win Olympic gold, but I'm pretty sure I'm not awful. I know this purely by way of comparison. Adam Kravitz. Ninth grade. Him: all slobber and angry, rhythmic tongue, like a zombie trying to eat my head. Me: all-too-willing participant, with three days of face chafing.)

Email is much like an ADD diagnosis. Guaranteed extra time on the test. In real life, I constantly rework conversations after the fact in my head, edit them until I've perfected my witty, lighthearted, effortless banter—all the stuff that seems to come naturally to other girls. A waste of time, of course, because by then I'm way too late. In the Venn diagram of my life, my imagined personality and my real personality have never converged. Over email and text, though, I am given those few additional beats I need to be the better, edited version of myself. To be that girl in the glorious intersection.

I should be more careful. I realize that now. *That's what she said.* Really? Can't decide if I sound like a frat boy or a slut; either way, I don't sound like me. More importantly, I have no idea who I am writing to. Unlikely that SN truly is some do-gooder who feels sorry for the new girl. Or better yet, a secret admirer. Because of course that's straight where my brain went, the result of a lifetime of devouring too many romantic comedies and reading too many improbable books. Why do you think I kissed Adam Kravitz? He was my neighbor back in Chicago. What better story is there than the girl who discovers that true love has been waiting right next door all along? Of course, my neighbor turned out to be a zombie with carbonated saliva, but no matter. Live and learn.

Surely SN is a cruel joke. He's probably not even a he. Just a mean girl preying on the weak. Because let's face it: I am weak. Possibly even pathetic. I lied. I don't have a black belt in karate. I am not tough. Until last month, I thought I was. I really did. Life threw its punches, I got shat on, but I took it in the mouth, to mix my metaphors. Or not. Sometimes it felt just like getting shat on in the mouth. My only point of pride: no one saw me cry. And then I became the new girl at WVHS, in this weird area called the Valley, which is in Los Angeles but not in Los Angeles or something like that, and I ended up here because my dad married this rich lady who smells like fancy almonds, and juice costs twelve dollars here, and I don't know. I don't know anything anymore.

I am as lost and confused and alone as I have ever been. No, high school will never be a time I look back on fondly. My mom once told me that the world is divided into two kinds of people: the ones who love their high school years and the ones who spend the next decade recovering from them. What doesn't kill you makes you stronger, she said.

But something did kill her, and I'm not stronger. So go figure; maybe there's a third kind of person: the ones who never recover from high school at all.

CHAPTER 2

I have somehow stumbled upon the Only Thing That Cannot Be Googled: *Who is SN?* One week after receiving the mysterious emails, I still have no idea. The problem is that I like to know things. Preferably in advance, with sufficient lead time to prepare.

Clearly, the only viable option is to Sherlock the shit out of this.

Let's start at Day 1, that awful first day of school, which sucked, but to be fair probably sucked no more than every other day has sucked since my mom died. Because the truth is that every day since my mom died, she's still been dead. Over and out. They've all sucked. Time does not heal all wounds, no matter how many drugstore sympathy cards hastily scrawled by distant relatives promise this to be true. But I figure on that first day there must have been some moment when I gave off enough pitiful *help me* vibes that SN actually took notice of me. Some moment when the whole *my life sucks* thing was worn visibly on the outside.

But figuring that out is not so simple, because that day turned out to be chock-full of embarrassment, a plethora of moments to choose from. First of all, I was late, which was Theo's fault. Theo is my new stepbrother—my dad's new wife's son, who, *yippee,* is also a junior here, and has approached this whole blended-family dynamic by pretending I don't exist. For some reason, I was stupid enough to assume that because we lived in the same house and we were going to the same school, we would drive in together. Nope. Turns out, Theo's GO GREEN T-shirt is purely for show, and of course, he doesn't have to worry his pretty little head about such petty things as, you know, gas money. His mom runs some big film marketing business, and their house (I may live there now, but it is in no way *my house*) has its own library. Except, of course, it's filled with movies, not books, because: LA. And so I ended up taking my own car to school and getting stuck in crazy traffic.

When I finally got to Wood Valley High School—drove through its intimidating front gates and found a parking spot in its vast luxury car–filled lot and hiked up the long driveway—the secretary in the front office directed me to a group of kids who were sitting cross-legged in a circle in the grass, with a couple of guitar cases spread around. Like this was church camp or something. All *kumbaya, my Lord.* Apparently, that can happen in LA: class outside on an impossibly green lawn in September, backs leaned up against blooming trees. Already I was uncomfortable and sweating in my dark jeans, trying to shake off both my nerves and my road rage. All of the other girls had gotten the first-day-of-school memo; they were wearing light-colored, wispy summer dresses that hung off their tiny shoulders from even tinier straps.

So far, that's the number one difference between LA and Chicago: all the girls here are thin and half naked.

Class was already in full swing, and I felt awkward standing there, trying to figure out how to enter the circle. Apparently, they were going around clockwise and telling the group what they did with their summer vacation. I finally plopped down behind two tall guys with the hopes they had already spoken and that I might be able to take cover.

Of course, I picked wrong.

"Hey, all. Caleb," the guy right in front of me said, in an authoritative way that made it sound like he assumed everyone already knew that. I liked his voice: confident, as sure of his place as I was unsure of mine. "I went to Tanzania this summer, which was totally cool. First my family and I climbed Kilimanjaro, and my quads were sore for like weeks. And then I volunteered with a group building a school in a rural village. So, you know, I gave back a little. All in all, a great summer, but I'm happy to be home. I really missed Mexican food." I started to clap after he was done—he climbed *Kilimanjaro* and *built a school,* for God's sake, of course we were supposed to clap—but stopped as soon as I realized I was the only one. Caleb was wearing a plain gray T-shirt and designer jeans and was good-looking in a not-intimidating sort of way, his features just bland enough that he could be the kind of guy who I could possibly, one day, *maybe,* okay, probably not, date. Not really attainable, no, not at all, too hot for me, but the fantasy wasn't so outrageous that I couldn't revel in it for just a moment.

The shaggy guy sitting right in front of me was up next, and he too was cute, almost an equal to his friend.

Hmm. Maybe I'd surprise myself and end up liking it here after all. I'd have a great fantasy life, if not a real one.

"As you guys know, I'm Liam. I spent the first month interning at Google up in the Bay Area, which was great. Their cafeteria alone was worth the trip. And then I backpacked in India for most of August." A good voice too. Melodic.

"Backpacked, my ass," Caleb—Kilimanjaro-gray-T-shirt-guy—said, and the rest of the class laughed, including the teacher. I didn't, because as usual I was a moment too late. I was too busy wondering how a high school kid gets an internship at Google and realizing that if this is my competition, I'm never getting into college. And okay, I was also checking out those two guys, wondering what their deal was. Caleb, his climb up Kilimanjaro notwithstanding, had a clean-cut frat-boy vibe, while Liam was more hipster cool. An interesting yin and yang.

"Whatever. Fine, I didn't backpack. My parents wouldn't let me go unless I promised to stay in nice hotels, because, you know, Delhi belly and all. But still, I feel like I got a real sense of the culture and a great application essay out of the deal, which was the point," Liam said, and of course by then, I had caught on and knew not to clap.

"And you? What's your name?" said the teacher, who I later found out was Mr. Shackleman, the gym teacher SN warned me likes to stare at girls' asses. "I don't recognize you from last year." Not sure why he had to point so the whole class looked at me, but no big deal, I told myself. This was a first grader's assignment: what did I do with my summer vacation? No reason for my hands to be shaking and my pulse to be racing; no reason for me to feel like I was in the early stages of congestive heart failure. I knew the signs. I had seen the commercials. All eyes were on me, including those of Caleb and Liam, both of whom were looking with amusement and suspicion. Or maybe it was curiosity. I couldn't tell.

"Um, hi, I'm Jessie. I'm new here. I didn't do anything exciting this summer. I mean, I . . . I moved here from Chicago, but until then, I worked, um, at, you know, the Smoothie King at the mall." No one was rude enough to laugh outright, but this time I could easily read their looks. Straight-up pity. They had built schools and traveled to foreign locales, interned at billion-dollar corporations.

I had spent my two months off blending high-fructose corn syrup.

In retrospect, I realize I should have lied and said I helped paraplegic orphans in Madagascar. No one would have batted an eye.

Or clapped, for that matter.

"Wait. I don't have you on my list," Mr. Shackleman said. "Are you a senior?"

"Um, no," I said, feeling a bead of sweat release and streak the side of my face. Quick calculation: would wiping it bring more or less attention to the fact that I was excreting a massive quantity of water from my pores? I wiped.

"Wrong class," he said. "I don't look like Mrs. Murray, do I?" There were outright laughs now at a joke that was marginally funny, at best. And twenty-five faces turned toward me again, sizing me up. I mean that literally: some of them seemed to be evaluating my size. "You're inside."

Mr. Shackleman pointed to the main building, so I had to get up and walk away while the entire class, including the teacher, including fantasy-worthy Caleb and Liam, watched me and my behind go. And only later, when I got to my actual homeroom and had to stand up and do the whole summer vacation thing all over again in front of another twenty-five kids—and utter the words "Smoothie King" for the second time to an equally appalled audience—did I realize I had a large clump of grass stuck to my ass.

On reflection, the number of people who may have sensed my desperation? At least fifty, and I'm estimating on the low side just to make myself feel better.

The truth is SN could be anyone.

Now, a whole fourteen days later, I stand here in the cafeteria with my stupid brown sandwich bag and look around at this new terrain—where everything is all shiny and *expensive* (the kids here drive actual BMWs, not old Ford Focuses with eBay-purchased BMW symbols glued on)—and I still don't know where to go. I'm facing the problem encountered by every new kid ever: I have no one to sit with.

No chance of my joining Theo, my new stepbrother, who, the one time I said "hey" in the hall, blanked me with such intensity that I've given up even looking in his direction. He always seems to hang around with a girl named Ashby (yep, that's really her name), who looks like a supermodel mid-runway—all dramatic gothy makeup, uncomfortable-looking designer clothes, blank wide features, pink spiked hair. I'm getting the sense that Theo is one of the more popular kids at this school—he fist-bumps his way down the hall—which is weird, because he's the type of guy people would have teased in Chicago. Not because he's gay—my classmates at FDR were not homophobic, at least not overtly—but because he's flamboyant. A little much about muchness. Everything Theo does is theatrical, except when it comes to me, of course.

Last night, I ran into him before bed and he was actually wearing a silk smoking jacket, like a model in a cologne ad. True, my cheeks were smeared with zit cream and I reeked of tea tree oil, looking like my own ridiculous parody of a pimply teenager. Still, I had the decency to pretend that it wasn't strange that our lives had suddenly, and without our consent, become commingled. I said my friendliest goodnight, since I can't see the point of being rude. It's not like that's going to unmarry our parents. But Theo just gave me an elaborate and elegant grunt, one with remarkable subtext: *You and your gold-digger dad should get the hell out of my house.*

He's not wrong. I mean, my dad's not interested in his mom's money. But we *should* leave. We should get on a plane this afternoon and move back to Chicago, even though that's an impossibility. Our house is sold. The bedroom I slept in for the entirety of my life now cradles a seven-year-old and her extensive American Girl doll collection. It's lost, along with everything else I recognize.

As for today's lunch, I considered taking my sad PB&J to the library, a plan that was foiled by a very stern NO EATING sign. Too bad, because the library here is amazing, so far the only thing I would admit is an improvement over FDR. (At FDR, we didn't really have a library. We had a book closet, which was mostly used as a place to make out. Then again, FDR was, you know, public school. This place costs a bajillion dollars a year, a bill footed for me by Dad's new wife.) The school brochure said the library was donated by some studio bigwig with a recognizable last name—and the chairs are all fancy, the sort of thing you'd see in one of those high-end design magazines Dad's new wife keeps strategically placed around the house. "Design porn," she calls them, with that nervous laugh that makes it clear that she only talks to me because she has to.

I refuse to eat in the restroom, because that's what pathetic kids do in books and movies, and also because it's gross. The burnouts have colonized the back lawn, and anyway, I don't want to sacrifice my lungs at the altar of fake friendship. There's that weird Koffee Kart thing, which would normally be right up my alley, despite its stupid name: Why "Ks"? Why? But no matter how fast I get there after calculus, the two big comfy chairs are always taken. In one is the weird guy who wears the same vintage Batman T-shirt and black skinny jeans every day and reads books even fatter than the ones I tend to like. (Is he actually reading? Or are the books props? Come on, who reads Sartre for fun?) The other is taken by a revolving group of too-loud giggling girls who flirt with the Batman, whose real name is Ethan, which I know only because we have homeroom and English together. (On that first day, I learned he spent the summer volunteering at a music camp for autistic kids. He did not, in any way, operate a blender. Plus side: he did not give me one of those pitying looks I got from the rest of the class when I told them about my super-cool smoothie gig, but then again, that's because he couldn't be bothered to look at me at all.)

Despite the girls' best efforts, the Batman doesn't seem interested in them. He does the bare minimum—a half-hug, no-eye-contact brush-off—and he seems to shrink after each one, the effort costing him in some invisible way. (Apparently, there's a lot of hugging and double kisses at this school, one on each cheek, as if we are Parisian and twenty-two and not American and sixteen and still awkward in every way that matters.) Can't figure out why they keep coming back to him, each time in that bubble of hilarity, as if being in high school *is so much fun!* Seriously, does it need to be repeated? For the vast majority of us, *high school is not fun; high school is the opposite of fun.*

I wonder what it's like to talk in superlatives like these girls do: *Ethan, you are just the funniest! For reals. Like, the funniest!*

"You need some fresh air. Come walk with us, Eth," a blond girl says, and ruffles his hair, like he is a small, disobedient child. Sixteen-year-old flirting looks the same in Los Angeles and Chicago, though I would argue that the girls here are even louder, as if they think there's a direct correlation between volume and male attention.

"Nah, not today," the Batman says, polite but cold. He has dark hair and blue eyes. Cute if you're into that *I don't give a crap* look. I get why that girl ruffled his hair. It's thick and tempting.

But he seems mean. Or sad. Or both. Like he too is counting the days until he graduates from this place and in the meantime can't be bothered to fake it.

For what it's worth: 639 days, including weekends. Even I manage to fake it. Most of the time.

I haven't had a chance to really look without getting caught, but I'm pretty sure the Batman has a cleft in his chin, and there's a distinct possibility that he wears eyeliner, which, *meh*. Or maybe it's just the dark circles that make his eyes pop, because he looks chronically exhausted, like sleep is just not a luxury afforded to him.

"No worries," the girl says, and pretends not to be stung by his rejection, though it's clear she is. In response, she sits on another girl's lap in the opposite chair, another blond, who looks so much like her that I think they might be twins, and faux-cuddles her. I know how this show goes.

I walk by, eager to get to the bench just outside the door. A lonely place to eat lunch, maybe, but also an anxiety-free zone. No way to screw it up.

"What are you staring at?" the first blonde barks at me.

And there they are, the first words another student has voluntarily said to me since I started at Wood Valley two weeks ago: *What are you staring at?*

Welcome to the jungle, I think. *Welcome. To. The. Jungle.*